THE MILL FOR GRINDING OLD PEOPLE YOUNG

The Mill for Grinding Old People Young

GLENN PATTERSON

ff

faber and faber

First published in this edition in 2012
by Faber and Faber Limited
Bloomsbury House,
74–77 Great Russell Street,
London, WC1B 3DA

Typeset by Faber and Faber Ltd.
Printed and bound by CPI Group (UK) Ltd, Croydon, CRO 4YY

The right of Glenn Patterson to be identified as author
of this work has been asserted in accordance with Section 77
of the Copyright, Designs and Patents Act 1988

A CIP record for this book
is available from the British Library

ISBN 978-0-571-28183-1

FSC
www.fsc.org
MIX
Paper from
responsible sources
FSC® C101712

2 4 6 8 10 9 7 5 3 1

For Miranda
Who made sure I was awake

"To the old, the new world of Belfast around them is generally too great for their grasp or comprehension."

"The fleeting show moves on without intermission."

George Benn, *A History of the Town of Belfast*,
Vol. II, 1880

A Short Note on Some Long Names

George Augustus Chichester, 2nd Marquis of Donegall, Knight of St Patrick, was more often referred to as Lord Donegall.

George Hamilton Chichester, 1st Baron of Ennishowen and Carrickfergus, the Marquis's first-born son, was known by the honorary title of Lord, or the Earl of, Belfast.

I

The telephone rang this morning.

Despite having rehearsed with me how to behave in such an eventuality, Mrs Mawhinney ran through the house, banging doors and calling my name, as though pursued by the hounds of Hell. In truth I was alarmed enough by it myself – I had been leaning forward straining to catch the final bars of "L'île inconnue" from a cylinder worn almost smooth from playing – that I dropped my spectacles on to the carpet as I started from my chair. In another instant I had trodden on them.

Mrs Mawhinney all but collapsed through the library door, collected herself, backed half out, and was making to knock as the ringing at last stopped.

I told her, please, to come in, take a seat, calm down.

The suddenness of the thing . . . she was saying between breaths . . . it had "put the heart sideways" in her.

I showed her my glasses. The bridge was bent and when I tried to straighten it I heard the faintest of creaks. Mrs Mawhinney would have had me let her go at once to Lizars, but with Christmas Day upon us there seemed little chance that her haste would be rewarded. Besides, I remembered some years ago having consigned a second pair to the back of a bureau drawer. They would tide me over to Monday.

We waited together another half an hour, going through the drill several more times, before resuming our occupations.

I was right about the bureau, but not about the drawer: the

spectacles were in the fourth one I opened. The lenses were a little dulled, my eyes more than a little weaker than when last I put them on, but so long as I held my book to catch the light coming in at the window – I had given up on the musical accompaniment – I could see well enough to read. (I have left them aside as I write this: the hand, I trust, after all these years, does not require such close scrutiny.) I held the book for two pages then lowered it and allowed my eyelids to close.

Towards luncheon the telephone rang again. I had managed half of the stairs, without the aid of my stick, before Mrs Mawhinney appeared in the hallway from the kitchen. She looked up at me. I nodded and her hand went out decisively towards the box bracketed to the oak panelling. She dropped a curtsy (unrehearsed) as she spoke my name then dropped another as she turned to me and said, "Mr Erskine, sir."

I negotiated the remainder of the stairs and took the earpiece.

"Well, well, well, what do you make of this?" said Erskine, with the pride of an inventor, or at least of a privileged custodian, reprising the role he had last performed when he presented me, on my birthday, with the gramophone, and the Berlioz cylinders that I now have to accept have been played out.

"Remarkable," I said, as I had said then, and meant it every bit as much. His voice this morning might have been coming from the next room and not the far side of the river.

Mrs Mawhinney was still in attendance. I signalled to her that I was quite all right.

Erskine, meanwhile, was inviting me to dinner at the Reform Club this evening – "unless you have already made another arrangement?" It was kind of him to allow me the possibility of refusal, even though he knows as well as any man living that I

4

would not otherwise have crossed the doorstep from now until New Year, nor been troubled by anyone approaching it, save possibly Erskine himself.

He was getting up a little party for his nephew, who was recently returned from a visit to London, in the course of which he had made photographs of the places alluded to in Mr Wells's "scientific romance" *The Time Machine*, which caused such a sensation when it was first published – what, a year, two years ago, now? These photographs the nephew had had turned into slides, which he intended to project by means of a magic lantern. It was all very short notice, Erskine realised (again the opportunity to refuse if I wished), but he had only heard late last evening that the room had become free at the club. He could send a carriage if I wished it . . .

Mrs Mawhinncy was none too pleased when I told her I had accepted. (Mrs Mawhinney, as I have noted, I am sure, many times previously in these pages, is not endowed with a face for dissembling.) She had a pair of sole fresh delivered.

I told her they would keep to breakfast.

She had a haddock for breakfast.

"It is Christmas, we will have both," I said.

I will be sorry in the morning that I did. They do not stint on their courses, or their portions, at the Reform Club. The smelts, with which we began, would alone have made a decent dinner for Mrs Mawhinney and me.

An audience of nine, not counting Erskine and his nephew, gathered in the Antrim Room afterwards with their port and cigars. I knew them all. In the case of most of them I had known their fathers (Erskine's being a notable exception), in the case of some their grandfathers.

A large board with a tablecloth tacked to it had been mounted on two chairs against the back wall. There was some business with the electric lights, which even two years after they were installed are the cause of some confusion and, on occasion, misgiving among staff and members alike; that switching off the lights, for instance, might cause a permanent disruption to the supply, or, worse, electrocution. Off, though, eventually, they went. (Switch-throwers happily unharmed.) The nephew himself oversaw the drawing of the curtains – they had to be "just so" – before declaring that we were ready to proceed with the slides.

We saw the park in Battersea, we saw Lavender Hill; we saw, as an aside, the new Battersea Bridge, the last of Sir Joseph Bazalgette's grand designs. (I knew Bazalgette, too; visited him once in Morden. He talked for two solid hours about sewerage.) We saw the wrought-iron entrances to several of the underground railway stations and listened to Erskine's nephew's ingenious equation of these with the burrows wherein the Morlocks dwelt; we saw the South Kensington Museum, the Alexandra Palace at Muswell Hill – Wells's "Palace of Green Porcelain".

The final photograph accompanied the passage in which the Time Traveller and his companion Weena proceed over a hill crest towards Wimbledon as the "hush of evening" creeps over the world. There was an answering silence in the Antrim Room as Erskine's nephew read of that great pause that comes upon things before dusk, when even the breeze stops in the trees. So vivid were the trees in the photograph – they had been tinted by hand – that I fancied our breath would have set their leaves moving, had any of us been breathing out at that moment. Erskine's nephew continued to read. His voice had a grating quality, but Wells's words got the better of it, impressing themselves on my memory: "To me there is always an air of expectation about that evening stillness. The sky was clear, remote, and empty, save for a few horizontal bars far down in the sunset." (These too with a tint applied to them.) "Well, that night the expectation took on the colour of my fears."

For nine people we gave a rousing round of applause. For *eight* people *they* did, I should say, at least to begin with. I remained staring at the blank tablecloth for some moments after the lights had been switched on in the room, remembering how the story ran on: the loss of Weena, the Time Traveller's desolation on his return, alone, to his workshop in Richmond.

When all the congratulations had been extended, all the questions asked about the equipment the nephew had used and the chemical processes he had employed – an inquisitiveness in matters of equipment and processes of one form or another being what had brought most of those present into membership of the Reform Club: them and their fathers and grandfathers – the discussion moved on to the future of our own city. (Thompson: "Perhaps at the end of eight hundred thousand years we will at last have our new City Hall.") Erskine, whose own career, and fortune, has been founded on the knack of never missing anything, tried to draw me into the conversation. Given the changes I had witnessed in my own lifetime, did I not think it foolish in the extreme to speculate on even eighty years hence? I replied that I sometimes felt as though it would be presumptuous of me to speculate on even eight weeks hence. "Nonsense, you will outlive us all," he said. In which case, I said, it would be our mutual misfortune. Rev. Dr Cathcart said, as he was after all bound to say, that we none of us knew the day or the hour – "no, not the angels of heaven," as the Apostle would have it

– and reminded us that there was still a large body of opinion that would robustly contend with Mr Darwin that the world had seen, or would ever in the future see, the multiple thousands of years that had so fired the imagination of this Wells.

I opened my mouth to respond, but the nephew cut across me. We were, with the greatest respect, rather straying from the point. He was of the firm opinion that the city was on the brink of a new Golden Age. The genius of our manufacturers, the skill of our workforce, had made Belfast a byword for quality and innovation. He spoke of the *Cymric* and her sister, the second *Oceanic*, construction of which, we would be aware, had already begun on the Queen's Island, not a mile from where we were talking, and which, when completed, would exceed in length Brunel's *Great Eastern*. (Exceed it too, it was to be hoped – between the maiden-voyage explosions and run-ins with rocks – in good fortune.) The one-thousand-foot liner was no longer a possibility, it was an inevitability for the Belfast shipyards, and let the competition try and catch them.

Never mind one thousand feet, Thompson said, if the rumour was to be believed the one-million-pound liner was already with us. Rodgers, at the rear of the room, said through that wheeze that has become habitual with him that if ships continued to grow at the rate they had grown in the last fifty years then by the next century's end we would be crossing the Atlantic on vessels a mile long...

My dinner was sitting heavily in my stomach – I really do, as a rule, eat so little these days – and now that the conversation had become general I thought that Erskine would not take it amiss if I asked to have the carriage brought round for me. It was not quite half past nine o'clock. Erskine himself saw me down the stairs (watched me, I should say, his eyes never once leaving my shoes) and out on to the kerb. It was all I could do, after he had handed me up into the carriage – it was a new-model brougham – to stop him tucking the blanket around my legs. He thanked me for coming; told me that he hoped his nephew's manner had not been too irksome. It was a common failing in the young, imagining they were the first ever to think or feel these things.

I thought to tell him that it was considered a failing when I was young not to have built a church or written a history by the time you were twenty-one; then thought better of it. "There are far worse failings," I said instead.

He put his hand on the door as the driver gathered the reins for departure.

"You know you would be more than welcome, tomorrow ..."

I stopped him. He makes the same offer every year, and every year, I am sure, I make the same reply: "It is terribly kind of you, Erskine, but Mrs Mawhinney has all the preparations made."

Mrs Mawhinney, in fact, is under strict instructions – this year, every year – to take herself off to her cousin's as soon as we have finished breakfast (haddock *and* sole!), and not to return until Boxing Day.

Erskine lifted his hand from the door in a gesture of surrender, or farewell, and the driver snapped the reins.

"If you change your mind you can always *telephone*," he called after me, down Donegall Place.

The street, despite the hour and the locked metal gates across the doorways, was as thronged as on a summer Saturday afternoon, the shop windows almost as bright. (I glanced higher up, would have sworn I caught sight at a top-floor sash window of a ghostly face, looking out.) Before the builder's hoardings where a year ago the White Linen Hall stood and where eight, or eight hundred thousand, years from now will stand the City Hall, fir trees and mistletoe were still being sold, and as the carriage turned down towards the Academical Institution I witnessed a group of boys – perhaps from the "Inst" itself – trying to hoop-la with a holly wreath the statue of the Rev. Henry Cooke. That gentleman, of course, had been no friend to the school in life, which is why it is supposed his statue stands with its back to it. A stream of pedestrians was coming towards this group, loosed on the night by the Grand Opera House, where the pantomime had just ended: *Dick Whittington*, if memory served. On an im-pulse I leaned forward in my seat and asked the driver, worthy citizen, to turn about and take me back the way we had come. He thought by this I meant that I had forgotten something at the club, but as we came again into Castle Place from Donegall Place I told him to carry on, up Royal Avenue, on, at length, to York Street, thence – turning right at Ship Street, right again – into the narrower confines of Sailortown.

The driver slowed the horse to a walk. Some of the rooftops here reached to not much higher than the crown of his hat; hardly a one of them had its full complement of slates, a chimney not in need of repair. He cast a look back over his shoulder at me. I urged him on – please – a little further and then a little further again until we had come out at last at a patch of waste ground be-low Garmoyle Street, looking across the Victoria Channel to the Queen's Island and the Harland and Wolff yard. "Here," I said.

The driver helped me alight. "You don't mind if I stay by the carriage?" he asked. The sound of its wheels had drawn several patrons out of the public house on the corner of the street. They gathered beneath the solitary functioning street lamp, watching with the driver as I made my hesitant way to the water's edge. Weeds had pushed up between the cobbles, mingling with the coal dross and the rusting iron and the remains of a thousand crates that had somehow fallen, just here, from ships coming in to dock.

"Sir?" said the driver, a caution dressed up as a question.

He may have had in mind the story, in the papers of late, of the woman who ran the length of the Newtownards Road to throw herself off the Queen's Bridge, a little upriver of us, her body, despite much searching of the shoreline, yet to be found.

"I can manage, thank you," I said, gratitude wrapped around rebuke. I steadied myself with both hands on the head of my stick. The fog that has been wreaking such havoc this past week along the coast of Scotland had been halted somewhere out in the North Channel by winds blowing across Belfast from the south-west. My view, notwithstanding the paucity of street lighting, the dulling of my lenses, was tolerably clear.

A voice called out from beneath the lamp, "You down to see the big boat, Mister?"

I waved a hand – "yes" – and peered out as though searching among the masts and the gantries for the *Oceanic*'s slipway, but hoping instead for a glimpse of something that predated the first ship to bear the *Oceanic* name, the whole White Star line, Harland's yard, the Queen's Island itself.

Behind me, the driver cleared his throat; asked if he might smoke a cigarette, "for warmth, like." I realised that in the time I had been standing there a fine rain had begun to fall.

I told him I had no objection whatever, then, seeing the flare of the match, catching the scent of tobacco on the air, asked if I might have one, too. For companionship, like. He offered me the package – Gallaher's Green – and I hesitated on seeing there were only two cigarettes left in it, but he shook his head to say I was not to let it concern me. I pinched the end of the cigarette between my forefinger and thumb while he struck the match, so that when I inhaled the shaft was drawn back to rest against the tip of my nose. It had indeed been a very long time since I had done this. The smoke was as sharp as grief, as searing as desire. My thoughts turned liquid and I felt for a moment that I had actually begun to fall. I leaned more heavily on my stick; inhaled again, deeper; inhaled again, deeper still.

When there was nothing left to inhale I let the ember fall, to fade between my feet.

"*The world is too good*," I murmured and touched my fingers to my lips. The driver was watching still. I plucked at a phantom shred of tobacco. He turned away. I allowed myself a few seconds more then picked my way back to the carriage.

"Thank you for the cigarette," I said as he helped me into my seat.

Our audience beneath the street lamp had dwindled to two women in shawls. One of them asked me was I some sort of Yankee.

"He's as Belfast as you or me," the driver surprised me by saying before I had a chance to speak. I pulled the blanket around my chest. The reins snapped, the hooves rang, the wheels rattled, and soon we had joined again the general stir.

The boys were gone from in front of the Academical Institution, but, however they had managed it, they had succeeded before they left in crowning Cooke with their holly wreath. He looked as ridiculous as they could have wished, as impotent.

Mrs Mawhinney must have been waiting in the hallway, so quickly did she appear at the door. She came right out to the carriage step. "Look at you, you are chilled to the bone," she said and asked the driver, as his master's representative there in her world, what Mr Erskine could have been thinking, calling on that telephone contraption, keeping me out till all hours in the depths of winter. (That was the order of her complaint, telephone before weather.) The driver, to his great credit, held his peace. I gave him ten shillings of a tip, which he was kind enough to say would keep him in "smokes" for some considerable time.

"Smokes!" said Mrs Mawhinney and took hold of my arm, as much to save me from corrupting influence as assist me to the door.

Inside, she warmed a pair of water bottles while I undressed for bed then left me here, propped against the bolster with my writing board and my journal. She paused in the doorway to wish me a happy Christmas.

"A happy Christmas to you, too, Mrs Mawhinney," I said.

I listened to her footsteps receding down the landing, as I have listened to them time without number in the years that we have spent alone here together, and for a moment – just for a moment – I imagined getting out of bed (imagined myself a man for whom the act of getting out of bed was as fleet as the thought), going to the door and calling after her . . . But what, and to what end?

On down the landing she plodded, and – a creak as the door opened, a click as it shut – into her apartments, so that now there is only the hiss of the lamp for company, the scratch of my nib, and, somewhere across this great, perplexing city, bells chiming the midnight hour.

II

Oh, G—!

Water . . .

Mrs Mawhinney may have been right. I awoke a quarter of an hour past, at ten after two, drenched in sweat, yet shivering. The bottles were cold against my feet; my head throbbed to bursting. I thought to ring the bell, but having untangled the bedclothes and sipped from the glass at my bedside I began to feel a little better (till that stab of pain just now). And it is – for all that it appears to be the dead of night – Christmas morning. Mrs Mawhinney's sixty-sixth. My eighty-fifth.

I rested the nib of my pen on the paper, looking at those last two words – *eighty-fifth* – breathing hard, until the full stop became a blot, spreading.

Water.

Where did I read of it: the young woman with an aversion amounting almost to the hydrophobic? A journal in the library at the Reform Club, maybe: an account of a book by a Viennese doctor – Bauer, or Breuer? Yes, Breuer and a colleague, whose name escapes me. The young woman was suffering from a form of hysteria, existing only on fruit, until with Dr Breuer's encouragement she was able to "wind off backwards" the thread of memory and arrive at the day when she walked into a room and saw, to her horror, her governess's little dog, lapping out of a glass on the table. And, like that, the symptom disappeared.

The "talking cure", the young woman called it. Perhaps one day the experiment will be extended, to men as well as women, old as well as young, and all will be enabled to understand the inner logic of the stimuli that caused them to act as they did at any given moment of their lives. It will come too late for me. I must in the time that is left to me be my own physician.

※.♡.※

My mother, "a slip of a girl", died on the evening of the day that I was born. My father remarried her sister, and his cousin, within the year, but within another year this wife too had died, trying to bring forth a child, my brother that would have been, had he not died with her. Fortunately, it might be thought, there were no more sisters, or eligible cousins, after that. In the spring of 1817 my father himself succumbed to the typhus that had followed the failure of crops in the previous "year without a summer". I was not quite four years old. For many years after I carried a memory of watching the gravediggers lower my father's casket into its shaft in the New Burying Ground and calling down cheerfully that I would join him, and all the others, soon, although my grandfather, which is to say my great-uncle, with whom I was sent to live, did his best to disabuse me of this notion. I never did see the open grave, for I never did attend the funeral. The rain that day was torrential. I was a croupy child, who had only just pulled through the winter. My grandfather had no desire to pay the undertakers to open the grave a fourth time in as many years.

Whatever the truth of it – and I have, as I say, no Dr Breuer to assist me – the dead, at that early age, held no terrors for me. Not so the living. My grandfather was a severe man (did it occur to me to reflect that he had lost two children of his own before unexpectedly acquiring me? It did not) whose idea of society was the Society for Discountenancing Vice and Promoting the Knowledge of the Christian Religion, of which he was a founding member, or, for a little light relief, the Religious Tract and Book Society for Ulster. Of that other Society for which the town had once been so renowned, however, he almost never spoke. It was but a short walk from his house at the northern end of Donegall Place, or the "Flags", as all who lived there then called it, to the corner of High Street and the Corn Market, where Henry Joy McCracken, leader of the Society of United Irishmen in the town, was hanged fewer than fifteen years before I was born (although as with everything before one's birth it might as well have been a thousand), and where the first Union flag was hoisted on the opening day proper of this fast-fading century of ours.

McCracken's sister, Miss Mary, who had received his body down from the scaffold, was still much abroad in my childhood days: a small woman in her middle years – old, I would have said then, not knowing how much older she would become, or that I would one day look back over a distance of some four and a half decades to my own middle age. It was said of her that she could not stand still for more than two minutes in the one place without a committee forming around her. My grandfather was a governor of the Belfast Charitable Society – the "Poorhouse"

– when Miss Mary stood still there for two minutes, allowing a Ladies' Committee to form and urge the Gentlemen to introduce a less punitive regime for the younger inmates: candles "sufficient for the hours of darkness", warm water for the washing of clothes; toys; blackboards; counting frames; a pole in the yard to play around . . . He remembered her as a child herself, walking through the town from the Manson School on Donegall Street (for that was the sort of the family: even in those far-off days, before legislation, they submitted their daughters to be educated), and later at entertainments in the Exchange. "As marriageable a girl as was to be found in the town," he pronounced, with unusual warmth and candour, on the one occasion when I pressed him on the subject; then almost at once he cooled, closed up. "But too devoted to the brother, finally."

My own education was, for the most part, conducted within the doors of my grandfather's house. Once in a while he would take a notion to send me out – to Mrs Davis's Classical School on Castle Street, to Messrs Acheson and Lyons in Castle Lane – but always within a matter of weeks, on occasion days, something would occur to prejudice him against the establishment in question, or its proprietor (my grandfather's schoolmaster, a Mr Eccles, had once composed an opera of such ambition he called it simply *The World*; anyone else was always likely to be a disappointment to him), and I would find myself once more in the schoolroom under our own eaves, working my way through whichever book my grandfather had seen fit to leave out for me that morning: *Philosophiae Naturalis Principia Mathematica*, *The Pilgrim's Progress*, or, not infrequently, the Bible itself.

As for the Academical Institution, which had opened its

doors not long after I was born, it was less a school than a theological battleground and my grandfather did not then or afterwards want for battlegrounds.

The house on Donegall Place had gardens at the rear running down to Fountain Street, a gate there that as a matter of principle my grandfather refused to have barred. ("Blessed is the man that endureth temptation," the Scriptures said, not "blessed is the man that hath temptation withheld from him.") The house, too, had anyone but thought to try the door, was almost always unlocked. It was tall, elegant, and as sparsely populated as the High Alps. My grandfather kept few servants – a housekeeper, who would have nothing but "Molly", a maid of all work, or rather a succession of maids (they could have little of Molly), and a man, Nisbet, who was closer to a secretary than a butler and closer to a companion than either – and with my grandfather either confined to his study, or out on what he called simply his "visits", it was possible for me to go from the day's beginning to its end without seeing a living soul indoors. Fortunately, my grandfather also encouraged exercise – the only carriage I ever saw him in was the one that bore his coffin – and had more fear of my health shut up in the house all day than my safety out walking alone. (Dr Trotter's *View of the Nervous Temperament* had attained with him the status of fifth Gospel: a healthful body houses a healthful mind etc.) In all but the foulest of weather, therefore, I would strike out each day the moment my reading was done, often along the Mall Ditch, which ran for the best part of a mile from the White Linen Hall to the Saltwater Bridge, and which had the advantage of being raised ("ditch" was a frank misnomer) above the quagmire that the land round about became after even a little rain; and we had, even then, more than a little rain. Along here passed the bulk of the traffic from the south, and I grew to anticipate the farmers and traders whom I would encounter according to the market being held that day, the pig men and the butter men, although most often by the time I was finished with Newton or Bunyan or the Minor Prophets, they would be making their way home again, their goods sold, their profits, or a large portion of them, evidently drunk.

The Falls Road was another favourite walk, as was, in a more northerly direction, the Shankhill Road as far as the old cemetery, the foothills practically of Black Mountain, where the names had already faded from the more ancient headstones centuries before anyone dreamed of a town called Belfast with a Mall Ditch, a Saltwater Bridge and an Academical Institution. In warmer weather I might cut across the meadows at the rear of the White Linen Hall to the Mill Dam at Cromac, and on the very hottest days might even strip to my undergarments and join with the other children kicking up water in the shallows, with never a thought for which of us came from a townhouse and which from a cottage on Sandy Row.

Often I went no further than the market at Smithfield Square, some two hundred yards from my grandfather's door, but so well screened by Castle Street and Hercules Street (for there was no Royal Avenue yet) as to seem five times more distant. I would wander among the stalls, persuading myself I was in as open a space as the town had to offer, and, now and then, if I was feeling especially emboldened, or derelict in self-persuasion, would venture into the narrower streets opening off the market square.

Smithfield then, three score years before the Corporation

was provoked, or shamed, into improvements, had the air of a gold-rush camp, with this obvious exception: there was no gold, nor much likelihood of it, only prospecting without cease for a claim on tomorrow. Whatever could be traded legitimately was traded; whatever could not be was traded anyway in the entries and laneways. My shoes were enough to attract the attention of the boys of that district, so that I was at every moment prepared to run, and was occasionally obliged to, although the chase itself, the calling of names, seemed, thankfully, to content them. A point was being made: I was there under sufferance.

On one such occasion – I was by then eleven – blown off course by a particularly persistent pursuit, I came upon a girl, three or four years older, to look at her, squatting in a court at the rear of a public house in the full flow of passing water. So astonished was I that I was unable to turn my head, or even avert my eyes. The girl's own eyes never left my face. There was a challenge in them, a challenge that, at eleven, I did not fully comprehend, although that it was sterner than any the boys had offered I was in no doubt. And still her water flowed. When at last it stopped the girl stood straight and wiped herself with some stuff, which she afterwards tossed on the ground at her feet. She remained longer than she need have with her skirts raised, or perhaps it was only my fascination that prolonged the moment of their fall. The courtyard was so dark that I could see nothing beyond the white of her thighs, but even that was almost too much for me. I staggered back, recoiling from the reaction of my own body, and in that instant the girl was gone, whether into the public house or into another doorway I could not have said, any more than I could have said where, in my agitated state, I myself went next, or how long I walked before I was sufficiently composed to return home, although I do remember that my grandfather had got in a little before me. I see him turning on the stairs as I walk along the hallway. I hear him asking what way I went and whom I met on my travels. (I do not hear my lie in reply.) I feel his finger beneath my chin as he turns my face towards the fanlight, peering.

"It has put a bit of colour in your cheeks," he says.

The following day I returned to walking the Mall Ditch, and the day after that, and the day after that. I walked along the Falls, I walked to the cemetery at Shankhill. (It still had its "h" when I was a boy, and even now that I know the name to be a derivation from the Irish *sean cill*, "old church", I still feel that absent spirant in my calves.) I pushed myself further and faster each day, but by the end of a fortnight I had given up the pretence and was back among the market stalls, trying to lose myself sufficiently that I might find my girl again. Because at night that was how I thought of her, on all those walks to places that were definitely not Smithfield that was how I thought of her. My girl. Would that all my obsessions had been so innocuous.

I had been poking about for some time, making essays into this entry and then that, retreating again, trying to reorient myself, or disorient myself anew, when I became aware of a boy on my tail. Beyond the fact that he was wearing a sort of military cap, I could get no accurate impression of him without stopping and turning about – an unwise course of action on past experience – but I had a sense of a height and build similar to my own. I gave him a minute or two more in which to overtake me, then I made a sharp turn to the left and another almost at once to the right that brought me face to face with a red hen perched on a butt before the half door of a cottage, from within which came the sound of a pestle being pounded against a stone mortar. The hen raised itself to its full height, showed me its tongue, the underside of its wings. I held up a finger – somewhere between "shush" and "stay" – and the hen jabbed out its head and bit me. I jumped, wheeling about, and there was the boy. I wedged the injured hand under my arm.

"Who are you?" he asked me outright.

He was, I judged, now that we were almost toe to toe, a good half a head taller than me. More importantly, unless his companions were a deal less agile in wit or limb, he was also on his own. I had nothing to lose.

"Who wants to know?" I said and stuck my chin out. He brought a fist up to rest against the point of it. Behind me the red hen settled itself discontentedly. The fist rose by degrees from my chin to the tip of my nose then, all unexpectedly, blossomed into an open hand with which its owner mussed the front of my hair.

"John Millar," he said.

"In which case" – I tugged the cap down over his eyes – "Gilbert Rice."

I ran past him, jinked left then right, slowing only when I had regained the market square. He caught up with me fifty yards further along, in the direction of the Flags, by a stall selling patched-up kettles and pans. He had taken the hat off and was making a great show of inspecting the peak, scowling the while.

"You needn't have been so rough with it, I was only having a bit of sport," he said. To which I might have retorted, "It is sport when you dole it out, but not when you receive it back," had not the black look already begun to lift from his face. Impetuousness ranked – ranks still – below surliness in my hierarchy of character flaws.

He had without further invitation or acknowledgement fallen into step beside me, hands clasped behind his back. We might have been two old acquaintances meeting of a Sunday evening for a promenade around the grounds of the White Linen Hall, with a military band for accompaniment and not the cries of the Smithfield hawkers.

"So, Gilbert Rice . . ."

"So, John Millar . . ."

"*Where have you been hiding all this time?*"

He told me he had lately come to stay with his grandfather (my ears, needless to say, pricked up at this), who kept the marble yard on nearby Berry Street. The yard's existence was news to me, although I knew the street well enough, for my own grandfather would take me there twice in the year to be measured by Mr Dalton, his tailor, for a suit of clothes, and twice in the year would ask the same question as he pored over the bill: "How much more growth can there be left in the boy?"

I adopted my gravest expression. "Are your parents then . . . ?"

"In Newtownards," Millar said.

"Ah."

"My father has the quarry there."

Despite his use of the definite article, the quarry at Newtownards had hitherto as much substance for me as the marble yard on Berry Street. We all make the mistake when children, of course, of fancying that we are at the very centre of the universe, that other people's lives take their coordinates from our own, but even as a full-grown man John Millar never quite understood how the rest of the world could fail to share his family's passion for stone. If anything his bafflement grew more pronounced with age. Every building we erected, he once said to me, contained the whole of history, because every piece of rock we cut was as old as the First Day of Creation. We could not bake a brick but we gave form to the very earth our earliest ancestors had trod. "Only imagine."

That, however, lay far in the future. (Mr Darwin farther still.) Back on that First Day of Our Acquaintance we had completed a lap of the square together. We stopped, facing one another.

"Will I see you here at the same time tomorrow?" Millar asked.

Something told me it would not do to be too quick to assent. I furrowed my brow; I scratched my ear. I almost, in the end, overdid it.

"Of course, if you would rather not . . ." He started to turn away.

"All right, three o'clock by the bedpans," I said, and like the old fellows who walked around the grounds of the White Linen Hall we solemnly shook on it, or as solemnly, on my part, as a person can whose forefinger feels as though it has in it suddenly a whole hand's worth of blood. As soon as I was alone again I inspected it properly. The skin was not broken, but the knuckle, where the hen had caught it, was as swollen as a worm's saddle. I hunted on the ground as I walked, kicking over paper and straw and cabbage leaves, until I spied a wizened green potato, which I instantly scooped up. Perfect! I hurried back to the entry where John Millar had cornered me. I barely broke stride before pitching the potato side-arm at the hen, fully expecting the thing to take flight in fright. It did not. One moment there was a living creature on the butt by the half door, the next there were feathers in the air. I stared in astonishment. A cry went up within. I ran.

It was not until I was getting undressed for bed that I remembered why I had gone to Smithfield in the first place that day. I decided once and for all to unburden myself of that particular obsession. Which is where I had rather leave the subject.

Millar's other passion, I discovered at our very next meeting, was handball. His grandfather's yard was just along Berry Street from a ball-alley run by a man called Billy Pollard, with whom Millar had in the short time since his arrival from Newtownards reached an understanding. In return for Millar's sweeping the half-moon of street before the front door, morning and night, Billy Pollard waived the sixpence a game he normally charged, providing, of course, that there were no paying customers wanting to play. I could not count the hours I spent in the months that followed sitting on a bench at the back of the court beside my new friend, shoes off, awaiting our chance, because nothing would do Millar but that I would love the sport as much as he, although to begin with, such was my bewilderment at the speed of the ball, the height and angle of the bounce, I offered as much challenge as one of his grandfather's slabs of marble.

I got better, though, much, much better. It was the one sport at which I think I might truly have excelled had not fate, in the shape of my grandfather's man Nisbet, intervened.

There were also in Berry Street, or in Charlemont Street, which opened off it, a number of fishmongers – "clan" would not be too strong a word, since they all seemed to hail from the same part of the world, that is to say below Newry, the

28

townland of Omeath. They were, as Billy Pollard himself said, "the very divil for handball", and for the related activity of betting on the outcome of handball matches, although Billy did his level best to keep gambling from encroaching on that half moon my friend Millar swept so assiduously; or at least from being seen to encroach.

One afternoon while Millar and I were sat on our bench an Omeath man approached and asked us, in that curious accent that they had (for amongst themselves they spoke only Gaelic), if we would mind his handkerchief while he played his friend. Millar, who had put out his hand to accept, nearly dropped the handkerchief in his surprise: it was tied in a knot around a pound's weight of coins. The two were at it for more than an hour, so evenly matched were they, with four or five changes of serve between each point scored. When the game had finished the friend came and demanded the handkerchief of us. Millar and I refused, but the man who had given us the thing to mind nodded (when he could raise his head from between his knees, he nodded) that we were to hand it over, whereupon his friend gave us each a penny. "*Maith na buachaillí*," he said: "Good lads."

Handkerchief minding thereafter became a regular occupation for Millar and me. Sometimes we would have several handkerchiefs to mind in the one game. Sometimes the person who had given us the handkerchief would take it back at the end, sometimes not. We asked no questions. A penny apiece was our usual reward, practically the first money I had ever handled: whatever I needed, in so far as I had any conception then of need beyond food and clothing, my grandfather bought for me, as he bought everything, on account, settling the bills on a grand tour of the town on the last day of every quarter.

The coins, as a result, presented me with something of a dilemma. One or two I could spend (half a minute took us – frequently – from Billy Pollard's to Gribben the confectioner's on Hercules Street), but only on what could be consumed before I returned home, where I could equally not display my earnings openly. After long deliberation I chose to hide the surplus in my room, next to the schoolroom at the very top of the house, in the space between the chest of drawers and the wall, where, the evidence of my eye suggested, no human hand, or its duster extension, had ever reached.

Millar had no such difficulties. He was saving to buy a book on Tuscan marbles, which he had seen on display in Hodgson's the bookseller, another of our afternoon destinations. For myself, I would have bought there *The World Turned Upside Down; or, No News, And Strange News*, with its cover of a dog seated at a table, playing the flute: "Here you may see what's very rare, the world turned upside down, a tree and a castle in the air, a man walk on his crown . . ." Except, as I have said, I could not buy anything for myself.

From time to time the Charlemont clan paid us in honeycomb, another of the specialities of that unusual street. (To this day I am unable to make a connection, beyond the phonic, between bee and sea.) It was on one of these occasions, an afternoon in early spring, when Millar and I were sitting against the outer wall of the alley, barefoot, honey dripping from our chins, that Nisbet chanced by on some errand. I scrambled to my feet, which was a mistake, because the sudden movement not only alerted him to my presence, but also advertised my guilty conscience. Nisbet's face registered first alarm (had someone *drugged* me and carried me here against my will?) then, as an Omeath man came out from Billy Pollard's and asked us for his friend's handkerchief, "minus the tax", a sorrowful determination.

He continued on his way towards Hercules Street, pausing just once to look over his shoulder as if to confirm that his eyes had not deceived him. I finished my honeycomb and licked each finger in turn before pulling on my boots. Already I had the feeling that it would be a long time before I had another.

The house when I returned was silent, as it often was, although now the silence seemed to have a greater intensity, not the mere absence of noise, but the deliberate withholding of it. I went to my room, three flights up, and sat down at the table before the window to wait. Far below, the town went about its affairs without me, a pantomime of productivity and politeness, hats doffed, hands offered, horses urged on, on, *on*. Inside, the bell for dinner did not ring. The lamps were not lit. I had begun to wonder if there was anyone at home after all when my grandfather called my name from the foot of the next stairs down but one.

Nisbet was leaving the study as I descended. He glanced up at me without expression then carried on down towards the hallway.

My grandfather closed the door behind us.

I was rarely admitted to this room and the novelty of it at any other time would have been enough to hold my fear in check. On one wall hung a view of a windmill on a hill, a cart passing beneath it, trying to reach the shelter of a village before the thunderclouds massing on the right closed in; on another, in a plain oak frame, the only painting anywhere in the house of my mother and stepmother, or so, by virtue of their proximity to his desk, I assumed them to be: two near-waifs with their arms clasped around one another's necks, as though for protection from the calamity that, their wide eyes had just foreseen, the future held in store for them. The globe on the desk itself called to mind the opera my grandfather's old teacher had composed, so that I would not have been surprised if it had by some mechanical means cleft open and a miniature player emerged, as I had once heard people sometimes appeared from cakes and all manner of unlikely things in the entertainments at royal courts.

My grandfather did not invite me to sit. He did not at first look at me directly.

Whatever of resolve that I had when I left my bedroom shrivelled to nothing the moment he shook his head, a single, sorrow-laden sweep. I had fallen short of his expectations, that shake informed me, far, far short.

"My first concern," he said at length, "from the day and hour I took you under this roof, was for your health and well-being. You were, as I have often told you, a sickly infant. That you survived those first years at all was a constant source of wonder to me, except that the Almighty had clearly ordained it."

A clock was ticking on the mantelpiece, disproportionately loud. Judgement Day, I thought, would be like this, the torment all within.

My grandfather told me that he had had an earlier report of my being seen running from an entry near the Market, which he had chosen to believe at the time was a case of mistaken identity. This new sighting, however, at the *ball alley*, could not be gainsaid.

He looked me square in the eye. "Without shoes?"

The idea clearly baffled him. I opened my mouth, but my tongue failed me. He shook his head again.

How I elected to use the precious gifts Providence had bestowed on me was, finally, between me and my Maker, although I should not be in any doubt that I would have to account for it. (The clock ticked. The accounting had already begun.) What was of more concern to my grandfather – for he had to accept now that the boy seen previously hurtling about Smithfield was indeed me – was that I appeared to have been treating that part of the town as an exotic playground. I had chosen to be there, unlike the unfortunates who inhabited the meanest of its hovels.

"It is not your disrespect for me that distresses me so much as your disrespect for them," he said, at which point I could restrain myself no longer, but began to cry, out of self-pity, no doubt, although there was something else in there too. It was, I thought long afterwards, perhaps the first time that I had truly grieved for my father and my brother, for the two girls clinging to one another on the study wall.

My grandfather watched me, unmoved. Tears in themselves were no atonement; they merely washed away the debris of the original fault.

I asked, when I had recovered myself a little, if I might be excused. I went then to my room where even without the aid of a lamp I was able to locate the columns of pennies behind my chest of drawers. It required two trips to carry them, their accumulated fluff and mouse droppings, down to the study. There were two hundred and nine of them in total: seventeen shillings and five pence. They might as well have been gold sovereigns, from the astonishment on my grandfather's face.

I spared him no detail in the story of their provenance and asked him if he thought, tainted though they were by gambling, God might nevertheless see fit to use them.

My grandfather laid his hand on mine. It felt like the hand of God Himself. "You will make a good boy yet," he said, and I cried twice as hard as before.

Some days later, Agnes, the maid, brought a letter to me in the schoolroom, the first I had received in all my eleven years. I do not know why it did not occur to me until I had unfolded it that it would be from Millar. He was back with his parents at the quarry in Newtownards. Our grandfathers, it seemed, had spoken together. He was sorry that he had not seen me before he left. He was sorry that he would not have the opportunity to show me the sandstone slab that had been cut there earlier in the week with the trail of a scorpion clearly visible, although how that might be no one was able to say, unless, as one of the quarrymen suggested, the scorpions had clung to the backs of the snakes when St Patrick drove those creatures from the island. He added a P.S.: "I got the book from Hodgson's!"

I wrote back that I was sorry too that events had taken the course that they had. I added a P.S. of my own: "I will remember you in my prayers," and many times I did. The way that my life went on over the next few years I had a lot of prayers to fill.

There was a saying in our town – bruited to the world at large by the Rev. Henry Cooke, in his address to a Parliamentary Committee on the state of Ireland – that when a man first arrived in Belfast he walked to an "Old Light" House; a few years later when he could afford a gig he rode in it to one of the

"New Light" Houses, which were more fashionable; and when at last he had a carriage he permitted himself to be driven to *Church*.

The Rev. Cooke attributed all the ills of this world – or at least of this town, where he was just then beginning to make a name, loudly – to the spiritual softening to which gigs and carriages and fashionable ideas gave rise.

My grandfather, as I have said, was a stranger to all things horse-drawn. In the years that followed I walked with him to Sunday-morning worship in a House whose light, strained through windows set high in the walls, failed even in summer to banish the gloom below. I walked with him there in the evening; I walked with him in between to the House of Correction on Howard Street, where the small number of women prisoners could be heard singing behind a screen, above the distracted mumbles of the men. Every visit to there, to the House of Industry, the Fever Hospital, and later – dreadfully – to the Lunatic Asylum, every second of every sermon through which I struggled to remain alert, brought me, I felt, a second closer to the boy my grandfather had it in mind for me to be.

And then in the blink of an eye, as it seems to me now, I was a boy no longer.

Shortly after I turned sixteen my grandfather secured for me an introduction to the Ballast Board, or, as it was known in the statute books, the Corporation for Preserving and Improving the Port and Harbour of Belfast. The Board itself, of which my grandfather had for several of his less senior years been a member, met once a fortnight to formulate the policies that were executed from a modest building (the "Ballast Office") on the spit of land separating the Town Dock and the Lime Kiln

Dock, at the eastern end of High Street and close to the town's very origins, the ford between the County Antrim and County Down sides of the River Lagan. One of the Board's first tasks, indeed, in the latter years of the previous century, had been to remove the remains of this ford, in the shadow of the Long Bridge, as an obstruction to river traffic. Commerce did not then – any more than it does now, when the Long Bridge itself is a fading memory – admit of sentimentality in Belfast.

A wooden observatory, accessed by means of a ladder in the attic of the building, afforded the Ballast Master – "Sir Clueless", as I was soon taught to call him – an uninterrupted view downriver and out into Belfast Lough; and, I was assured by two of the younger fellows, Ferris and Bright, effectively blinded him to whatever was occurring on the three storeys beneath his feet. "Which is not always very much," Bright informed me, and proceeded to cross his legs on a table strewn with tide charts, greatly pleased with himself.

Ferris for his part, besides furnishing me with the Ballast Master's sobriquet, ran through the names of the various other higher-ups – the Dock Master and Harbour Masters, north-side and south-side, the Pilot Master, the Constable, the Superintendent of Quarantine and their respective deputies – dismissing this one as a drunkard, that one as a glutton, the whole lot as nincompoops, and emphasising how rarely any of them were in the office to disturb his leisure and Bright's. Ferris's father had lost a small fortune in the Panic of 1825, but since he had only got his wealth in the speculations that preceded the Panic it had barely had time to distort the family's expectations. It had been like an uncommonly rich meal, Ferris would tell me: in one end and all too quickly out the other.

He crossed his legs on the opposite side of the table to Bright, fingers laced behind his head.

"So, young Rice, any questions?"

I understood that it was all a show, but it was a very entertaining one.

"Is there room on that table, do you think, for another pair of boots?" I asked, entering into the spirit, and Bright, in his delight (my grandfather's reputation, I rather suspect, had preceded me), almost fell backwards off his seat.

At some point in the forty years between the Board's constitution and my arrival there, one ingenious person had proposed that the improvement of the port and the provision of ballast to merchant ships putting back out to sea could be simultaneously effected. In those days the water before the town retreated to a depth of two or three feet at the lowest spring tides, at which point the docks on either side of our office were revealed for what they were, which was nothing more nor less than open sewers. The ballast sand and stone, sold at two shillings the ton, was therefore dredged from the riverbed, and month by month, year on year, the docks and the Board's coffers deepened, the atmosphere in the town grew a little less offensive.

Even then, however, the course from the Lough up the Lagan was too circuitous, the mudflats bordering it too extensive, for any but the lightest vessels to berth the greater part of the time. Larger ships were more often than not obliged to anchor at the Pool of Garmoyle, a full three miles from the town, there to await a favourable tide, or to offload their cargo into lighters (we called them "gabbards"), whose pilots, and the rowboat "cab-drivers", were possibly the only people to profit from the whole rigmarole. "A sixpence to take you up the river. Last one:

a sixpence to take you up the river . . . All right, room for three more standing at thruppence . . ."

Greater ingenuity still was required. Not a year went by but a new, foolproof scheme was heralded – ship canals, floating docks, enclosed basins, lock gates – and then six months later abandoned for want of government support or, which amounted to the same thing, finance. The town's merchants and mill owners were becoming restless. Belfast had through their industry and application turned itself into one of the foremost towns in the kingdom, rivalling even Cork and Dublin, Liverpool and Manchester, with upwards of two thousand ships annually, and against all odds, entering the harbour; but there was a limit to how far its trade could grow while the port remained in its present primitive state.

I had not been many months in my position – below Ferris and Bright and a little above the office cat – when the Board engaged Mr James Walker, heralded as "the second greatest engineer in the Empire" (Telford then being still alive, Telford himself having surveyed us in 1814), to devise another scheme. Although he had long been resident in London, Walker was by birth a Scot, like so many of those who were prominent in the commerce of our own town, and our port in particular. Some of them, indeed, he already numbered among his friends and acquaintances. For the evening of his arrival in Belfast the Board had organised a dinner in the Commercial Buildings on Waring Street, to which, it need hardly be said, I was not invited, although my grandfather by virtue of his past service was. His first instinct was to decline, being of the firm opinion that the majority of such occasions were excuses for excessive drinking, dressed up as "toasting". When they had run out of worthies to toast at the last dinner he had attended, the guests fell to toasting the proposer of the previous toast and then the proposer of that toast, and the proposer of that, and so on till there was not a drop left to be drunk, or a proposer capable of getting to his feet. My grandfather was a teetotaller *avant la lettre*. The Rev. Dr John Edgar, who stirred the Temperance Movement into life in the town when he emptied the remains of a gallon of whiskey out his manse window, frequently acknowledged my grandfather's example; as frequently as those who eschewed it lamented that the Reverend Doctor had not given prior notice of his intention to waste good whiskey like that, else they would have been standing beneath the window with their tumblers at the ready.

That my grandfather accepted the Board's invitation in the end was, I have no doubt, more for my benefit than Walker's. The dinner had been the talk of the office for weeks – Ferris and I had been tasked with copying the letters of invitation, all one hundred and eight of them – and had therefore occupied my thoughts and conversation in that small portion of the day that I spent in my grandfather's company, much to his, and Nisbet's, evident exasperation.

Nisbet it was who walked with him to Waring Street on the evening in question and who waited in the news-room of the Commercial Buildings until after the toasts had been made to the King (God grant him a speedy recovery from his most recent illness), the Duke of Clarence (God keep *him* in good health, just in case) and the Marquis of Donegall . . . and my grandfather felt able to make his exit.

I had been listening at the door of my room for their return and flew down the stairs to the hallway, but my grandfather was too tired to talk. "It will keep," he said, and I had no option but to let it.

I was waiting in the morning when he came into the dining room for his breakfast and waited patiently for several more minutes while he picked every last fragment of shell from the pair of boiled eggs that Agnes set before him. Then and only then did he tell me – pausing to dip the first egg in a little salt – that the Marquis himself had not been present to hear his health being drunk the night before, having had some urgent business in Doagh to attend to, although Lord Belfast – "the older son", as my grandfather referred to him – did put in an appearance, in the course of which he managed repeatedly to be discourteous to the guest of honour, several times addressing him as "Walters" until Walker offered to write the name down "that he might have less trouble remembering it in future".

"Anyone would think Mr Walker meant the town harm," my grandfather said, and bit the top off his egg.

Lord Belfast had for the previous ten years been the town's one and only Member of Parliament, having before that been the Member for the neighbouring borough of Carrickfergus, where he was succeeded, as he would in a short time be succeeded in Belfast (for the King, and the Parliament, did not long survive the toast in the Commercial Buildings), by his father's cousin, Sir Arthur Chichester, who would in turn be succeeded by Lord Belfast's own younger brother, *Lord* Arthur. There was a crude joke, indeed, with which I doubted my grandfather was familiar (I had got it from Ferris), that a visitor to the Donegalls was told that the Marquis was unable to see him at present "being upstairs with the Marchioness making a Member of Parliament".

"Of course," my grandfather went on, "if ever the port is improved the town will quickly outgrow the Chichester family. The Earl might yet have an inheritance, but he will have scant influence."

So great had the influence of the Chichester family been historically that its name in the person of the first Sir Arthur (the "Donegall", like the "Marquis", was a later addition) was written into Belfast's very charter. For close on one hundred years their castle had stood at the foot of High Street until, the story went, a servant too enthusiastic in the airing of a room she had been washing started a blaze that killed three of the sisters of the latest Arthur Chichester to reside there, after which he and his heirs preferred to live in London, leaving the day-to-day running of the place to their appointees, the Sovereign and the Seneschal. A portion of the castle's outer wall stood yet. I only had to look past my grandfather that morning to see it and, beyond, the overgrown gardens, known as Montgomery's market, currently lashed with rain, where fruit and vegetables were now sold three days in the week.

The family's return to the town, in the year after the Act of Union, had been wholly unexpected. The present Marquis had spent his youth amassing debts, many of which were "post-obit", that is to say repayable when he came into his title, and none of which he had the slightest intention of repaying if he could avoid it. Coming again to live in Belfast in modest circumstances (for a Marquis) on the Flags, nearest the White Linen Hall, was one tactic in the avoidance. It had not worked. Within a matter of years he had been forced to auction the entire contents of the house and flee again to Scotland. In a short while, however, he was back, having sold off the majority of his other holdings in Ireland, at which point, to the amazement, frustration, and finally outrage of his creditors, he diverted the funds into a country estate at Ormeau, scarcely a mile and a half from his town house. (He held on, too, to Fisherwick Lodge at Doagh, some ten miles to the north; it was always advisable to keep a second bolthole from bailiffs, and tiresome dinners.) When his grand plans for rebuilding Ormeau outstripped even these new revenues, "Lord Done'em all", as he had come to be known, began selling leases all over the town at rock-bottom prices. "The older son" was powerless to stop him, but he appeared to be drawing the line at the port. This was one asset that he would be sure his father did not give up cheaply, if indeed he gave it up at all.

What my grandfather neglected to tell me at breakfast, or, more likely, did not know – what, then, would have been of much greater interest to me – was that the boy serving Mr Walker as apprentice had been taken ill on the voyage across the Irish Sea, and at the time of the dinner the night before was being visited in his lodgings by Dr Murray, who gave him some of the same fluid of Magnesia solution he had recently given, with marvellous results (marvellous enough that he was being urged to patent it), to the Lord Lieutenant of Ireland himself.

A letter explaining the boy's continued indisposition was delivered to the Ballast Office a few minutes after I arrived at work, along with a request that some suitable lad substitute on the engineer's initial tour of the waterways. Sir Clueless descended from his eyrie with the letter in his hand to the room where Ferris, Bright and I were working, although Ferris, who had earlier carried the letter up, and who in the matter of eliciting information at least was resourcefulness personified, had already shared with us its contents. Shared and embellished somewhat: in Ferris's version the boy was already boxed up for dispatch back to London.

Had the weather not been so dismal that morning it might never have fallen out that I was chosen to accompany Mr Walker. Ferris, inevitably, was first with his excuse. He had a bundle of ships' licences that were to be completed by the end of the day. (The licences, in fact, were to have been completed by the end of the day before and would still be unfinished at the end of the day after.) Bright reminded Sir Clueless that he had already asked him, Bright, to reorganise the Board-meeting minutes, which had had to be moved to a tea chest after silverfish got into the cabinet. My own excuse – that I had never in my short time there, in all my years indeed of living in Belfast, set foot in a boat – was thus trumped before it was played, and out, a quarter of an hour later, I duly went, in borrowed rain cape and muffler, to attend on the latest Pretender to the title of Saviour of the Port of Belfast.

The rain, mercifully, had stopped, but the wind that had whipped it in off the hills continued to menace. The porters and dockhands I passed were practically bent double at their tasks. Bales of cowhides were being landed, the topmost skins as symmetrical as butterfly wings. A child's bonnet bowled along the quayside, with no one in pursuit.

I found Mr Walker in conversation with two other gentlemen of his party, at the top of a flight of steps cut into the quay. He had removed his own hat as a precaution, although he might have been advised to keep it on: his hair appeared to have been blasted to the extremities of his head, and but for a few tenacious strands clinging to the crown would have been halfway to Bangor. His chin fitted neatly, almost mathematically between the wings of his shirt collar, with only a very little remainder for a mouth. A smile would have been beyond it. I waited for a sufficiently long pause in which to introduce myself. And waited. And eventually cleared my throat. "Gilbert Rice," I said, "sent from the Ballast Office." Mr Walker nodded in my direction, turned to resume the conversation, then turned back to take in my garb. His mouth contracted still nearer to absolute zero.

I had been expecting – hoping for, indeed – some kind of floating workshop or laboratory, with at least a modicum of shelter. For this first trip, however, Mr Walker had requested that he be taken in a simple skiff, "the better to understand the opponent". One of the gentlemen went first down the steps into the boat. Mr Walker went second and I, with infinite care, third, taking my seat, in the only place where I could see to take it, in the prow, facing backwards, whereupon the first man, having addressed some further remarks to Mr Walker, climbed out on to the dock again.

The boat registered every step of the ballet as a roll, now to this side, now to that, which my stomach took up and exaggerated further. I clasped my hands together between my knees, praying that the turmoil would stop, that the slop of the water in the bottom of the boat would stop. Mr Walker, who had not yet spoken one word to me, consulted a chart folded small in his lap. After half a minute he looked up at me curiously. His eyes under all that forehead had a peculiar intensity, as though they too were instruments of his profession and not attributes of nature. He regarded my hands, idle in my lap. Only then did I realise that I was expected to row. I was about to tell him that there had been a dreadful misunderstanding when he turned and shouted an instruction to the gentlemen on the quay – another chart was wanted, showing the soundings that Rennie had taken.

"A good thing after all we had not already taken to the water," he told me before resuming his study.

While we waited for the soundings chart to be delivered I watched a neighbouring boat detach itself from the safety of the harbour wall. The boat was, at a guess, three feet longer than our own, its lone oarsman possibly the same number of years younger than me. I followed his movements closely as with only a few glances over his shoulder he steered a path through the skiffs and gabbards and shallow-bottomed coalmen. If nothing else I was a quick learner. I placed the oars in the rowlocks and when the chart had been handed down into the boat, the rope untied, I leaned forward, dipped the blades in the water and pulled. The oars jumped back at me. I steadied them, shuffled my bottom, as much as to say it had been the fault of an unfamiliar seat; tried again. We moved. I leaned forward a third time, as close to Mr Walker's knees as I dared, and back, we moved further, faster. Mr Walker had taken out a stub of cedar pencil and was writing in a notebook as though settled behind the desk of his London office.

Forward, pull ... Forward, pull ... Forward, pull ... Within a very few strokes I had found a rhythm. If anything, the wind was less bothersome this close to the water. I could do this, provided I did not think too much about the water itself, or the fact that every stroke was carrying me further out of my depth, i.e. the shallows of the Mill Dam at Cromac. I became almost detached from the effort, not an actor, but an observer. It was an extraordinary sensation to leave the town behind, although looking back from the prow the impression was rather that the town, all its rooftops and spires, its two conspicuous clock towers, had come adrift from me. I watched it move in regular stages, further and further south. Soon it would be bearing down on Lisburn, Banbridge, Newry, pushing them before it across the rucked landscape: Dundalk, Drogheda, Dublin, Wexford and – with an almighty splash – off the edge of the island altogether.

"Port!" Mr Walker said, with the urgency of one who had said it once already without response. "Hard to port!"

In my confusion I pulled with all my strength on both oars and almost at once felt a jolt run through me from tailbone to gullet. The charts, the notebook and the pencil spilled from Mr Walker's lap. I had rowed us into the mud.

"Did you not hear me? I said *port, port*!"

I made as though to stand.

"Sit!" said Mr Walker, holding tight to the gunwales to keep the boat from tipping over.

I sat heavily. I imagined Sir Clueless in his tower, snatching the glass from his eye in anger. "I am sorry," I said. "I should have spoken up earlier, I do not know the first thing about boats or rowing."

"I had guessed as much. I still hoped you were endowed with basic common sense," Walker said. He loosened his grip experimentally, one finger at a time. The boat was quite steady. "But we are where we are."

He had recovered his belongings (the notebook fortunately had an oilcloth backing) along with his composure. He looked about him.

"In fact," he mused, "we are, by wonderful accident, almost exactly where we need to be." Which was to say at the point, a little beyond Mr Ritchie's shipyard and the Corporation Docks, where the Lagan made its first sharp bend to the right. Some few hundred yards distant on the starboard or County Down side was the salt works at Ballymacarrett. Nearer to hand, on the port side, and of rather more interest to Mr Walker (I looked, belatedly, over my shoulder to see it), was a timber pond. The green wood formed a shifting, clunking floor. "Here," he said, and looked down at his chart and then up, "is our first obstruction."

He produced from his pocket a small bone-handled knife with which – three deft flicks – he sharpened the point of his pencil and commenced to make a sketch, no longer the great engineer, but the enthusiast intent, you might have thought, on a landscape for his library wall.

"Now," he said when he had finished, a matter of five minutes at most, "push back with the left oar on the bank – that's the way – and quick strokes with the right – and more, and more . . ." The boat came away from the mud, like a spoon from a jelly: *slurp*. He sat back, pleased with himself, or with me. "And row."

I followed the twists and turns of the river, encountering few other vessels, until we were just short of the Pool of Garmoyle, where the mudflats, more waterlogged by the yard, finally disappeared below the surface and the Lagan lost itself in Belfast Lough. The sun had come out a few minutes before, casting jewels on the surface and silhouetting the ships sailing towards us from the open water. Even at a distance they were vast in comparison to our skiff. I understood then something of the pull of the sea on men's imaginations; and I felt more pro-foundly than ever I had in all the church services I had attended how tenuous was our hold on this world of ours.

Mr Walker's eyes narrowed and widened and closed and opened in their turn, and when they had imprinted the view on his memory he nodded. "I think that will do for the first day."

As quickly as it had appeared the bright spell passed. The clouds building above the hills to the west were again black with rain. It had been an adventure, but I was keen to be back on solid ground. The tide too was on the turn and that, coupled with my urgency, helped speed us home. His work complete, Mr Walker was a little more expansive than on the outward journey. He told me that once as a lad, not much older than I was now, he had made a visit from his home in Falkirk to the west of Scotland. A friend of the family, a clergyman, had pointed out to him the Antrim coast, only fifteen miles distant. Terrible events were occurring in that country and he was to be sure to keep it in his prayers. And indeed Mr Walker had, long after the terrible events had run their course; and now this op-portunity had arisen, almost as though in recognition of his re-membrance.

"The river is the key to prosperity," he said, "and prosperity the key to the common good."

I was not obliged to say much, concerned as I was with get-ting us back to shore, which was perhaps as well, given the chasm in my knowledge of the events in question, always sup-posing they were the ones that had ended with Henry Joy McCracken hanging from a gibbet in High Street. Still, I sig-nalled my interest and – at the appropriate moments – aston-ishment and quiet reflection by means of nods and shakes and raised eyebrows, which seemed to satisfy my companion well enough. After I had cast up the rope, at the second attempt, on to the quayside, he shook me by the hand.

"Thank you for your efforts, young man," he said, and his mouth rose above the constraints of his collar to produce a smile of two seconds' duration. "Another time, I trust."

And with that he was off up the steps at the top of which the two gentlemen were waiting to whom he had been talking when we set out, three or more hours before, and with whom he began now, without breaking stride, to converse again.

I started to walk back to the Ballast Office, but after only a few steps, in the course of which my feet seemed unable to agree with one another, or either of them with me, had to find a wall to cling to – a ship chandler's, it so happened. The owner used a boat hook to reach across the coils of rope in the window and rap the glass: "Away on o' that with you, you lazy so-and-so!"

It was the oddest sensation, and one that, though I have been to sea many, many times in the seven decades since, I have never again experienced. I believe that what I was that March afternoon by the Town Dock was land-sick.

I had still not fully recovered by the time I quit the office at the day's end, although that did not prevent me from taking my preferred, less direct route home, along Rosemary Street.

Some few months earlier my friend Millar had presented himself at the door of my grandfather's house. We had not been entire strangers all this time: the size that Belfast was then did not allow for that, any more than did the prominence that Millar had early begun to enjoy in it.

He had been in London for some time, studying architecture

in the offices of Mr Thomas Hopper, and from there had been sent to Markethill, near to Armagh, where Mr Hopper was building for the Earl of Gosford a castle – in the eighteen hundred and twenties: a castle – that was the talk of the entire country. Rumour told of two hundred rooms, of keeps and stone passages with veritable dungeons beneath. The work had been going on then for upwards of ten years, and would go on – perhaps only Hopper himself was aware of it – for twenty more.

Millar, meanwhile, had found the time to build a pair of villas at Holywood, on the County Down shore of Belfast Lough, which had won him so many admirers that, although still not twenty, he had been encouraged to enter the competition for the design of a church on Rosemary Street, the Third Presbyterian, it being a special feature of our denomination that no sooner had one congregation been established that a schism would occur over a point of theology – a point, sometimes, of typography – resulting in the building of a new church, often within sight of the first. (First Presbyterian, in fact, was to be found fifty yards further up Rosemary Street from Third.) It was my grandfather himself who drew my attention to the announcement of Millar's success, which had prompted me to write a letter of congratulation, which had in turn prompted him to chance a call.

My grandfather received him with perfect civility. (You would have thought it was my hand he was asking for, not my company.) Not a word passed between them about our childish escapade, but then for my grandfather actions had always spoken louder. It might have surprised Millar to know it, but to my grandfather's eyes his life had acquired the arc of a grand act of atonement.

He had left town again soon afterwards, being expected back first in Markethill then in London, and having, after much deliberation, decided to entrust the execution of his design for a "pure and massive" edifice to the architects Thomas Duff – who had lately completed the Roman Catholic cathedral at Armagh and who had also worked under Hopper at Gosford Castle – and Thomas Jackson, a former pupil of Duff's.

I was not altogether sure what was intended by "pure", but the edifice I saw taking shape day by day was undoubtedly massive, if a little less trustworthily so on the afternoon of my land-sickness.

The "other time" to which Mr Walker had looked forward when taking his leave of me did not come to pass. Despite Ferris's lurid imaginings the sickly apprentice made a full recovery (further testimony to Dr Murray's fluid of Magnesia), the survey of the port was completed and its findings were launched on the perilous voyage through boardrooms and debating chambers, which none before had survived, while I returned for twelve uneventful months to the daily deception of Sir Clueless that was the inauspicious start to my own career.

❧❧❧

Besides the waterways, the Ballast Board introduced me to what was, in effect, a whole other town, Belfast after dark. Night did not any more, of course, hold quite the terrors that it had for previous generations of our townsfolk. We were early converts to the virtues of coal-gas lighting. I had been taken along myself, the autumn of my tenth birthday, to witness the ignition of the first jets, on a lamp standard at the dock end of

High Street, and still remembered the gasps of astonishment at the brightness of the flames, and the howl from somewhere in the vast assembly of one much younger child, who was expecting perhaps brimstone to follow. The main streets were now all well lit – second only to London was our boast, although those few I knew who had visited there doubted even that inferiority – and the gas network penetrated deep into the alleys and courts in which the town abounded.

Not everyone was overjoyed by the improvement. Hard on the heels of the gas-lamps came the by-laws protecting them from interference and destruction, by those whose trades had depended on the rule of darkness (and whose Sunday services in the House of Correction I had often attended) and those, as unlike the first group as it was possible to be, who feared that street lighting exposed to the public gaze what nature, and God, had intended to remain private.

As for diversion amidst all this effulgence . . .

"The playhouse!"

"We went the night before last."

"For the first half only."

"Which was more of our attention than it deserved."

"You say that every time we go."

"Except when we arrive at the interval."

"There is a ball in the Exchange."

"When is there not a ball in the Exchange?"

. . . planning for it consumed the greater part of our mental energies on the ground floor of the Ballast Office. The only limits were stamina and wherewithal, although among the circle I became acquainted with through Ferris and Bright it was almost a mark of pride to have been pursued for debt: "had up before the Manor Court", was what they said. For some it was as much a part of their economy as the Bank or the Pawn; but not for me. My first salary was forty-five pounds per annum, or a little more than seventeen shillings in the week. Half I gave straight away to my grandfather, who in turn gave half to Molly. Out of the remainder I had to provide for all other needs – a concept of which I now had a firm grasp, even if it was not one I could share with my grandfather. I was not niggardly, but neither was I profligate. Far from the Manor Court, I ended most weeks a shilling or two to the good.

A handsome new gymnasium had recently opened on Montgomery Street (Bright swore by it for the musculature) and there were any number of dancing classes from which to choose, although Monsieur Perois's was by common consent the pick of them. (I was always intending to go *next* week.) And everywhere there were taverns and public houses, of all conceivable sizes and varieties. Some were known chiefly for their singing, others for their games; for others the dining room was the draw, or the cellar, or indeed the promise of a particular kind of company. Oftener, however, the attraction escaped definition. It had an air about it, was as much as could be said. "Not the worst place to pass an evening."

It was the custom in those days, among the younger townsfolk in particular, to make an excursion on Easter Monday to the Cave Hill, the last and most prominent of the hills, stretching from Colfin through Black Mountain and Divis, walling us in on the west. Ferris and Bright were astonished to learn that these festivities had so far passed me by. "But where did you go as a lad to trundle your egg?" Bright asked, and was even more astonished by my reply. "Not once?" he cried. "You poor little orphaned mite."

They were adamant that they would not go that next Easter without me, should they have to take me there in chains and with my egg . . .

Well, let it be hoped that I would consent to come willingly.

The Cave Hill was then far removed from the town limits, or they from it. What are now the northern suburbs were still distant hamlets in the hill's considerable shadow. When viewed from the town side it was famously said to look like the Emperor Napoleon in repose, or at least like the Emperor Napoleon's brow and nose. I confess I had always struggled to see it, just as I had struggled to see in the profile the shipwrecked giant that impressed itself on Dean Swift's imagination when as a young man he was prebendary at Kilroot, a few miles further north along the Lough shore. Still, on the night before the day in question I had Molly boil me an egg, which I painted to resemble the Duke of Wellington, brooding and braided, off to do battle again with the Little Corporal.

I was probably more exact than I needed to be with a hard-boiled egg: a plate commemorating the victory in the Waterloo Campaign and decorated with the Duke's face had hung throughout my childhood on the wall of the stairwell outside my grandfather's study, and though it had met with an accident around the time of the Catholic Relief Act (Nisbet, taking it down for Agnes to dust, had let it slip through his fingers) I had long since committed its every line to memory.

Ferris and Bright called for me before it was quite eight o'clock, Ferris sporting a fine new pair of white duck trousers and carrying a large haversack, the contents of which, he assured

Bright and me, we would thank him for later. The freezing fog that had descended overnight had not yet cleared and there was frost still on the setts of Hercules Street, which on any other Monday at that hour would already have been thick with sawdust from the butchers' shops that stretched from one end of the street to the other. (Some said there were forty-seven, others forty-nine, others that there was no point in counting: by the time you had finished another would already have opened somewhere back along the street.) We stopped for a "warmer" at an inn, the Lamb and Flag, near the junction of North Street and Carrick Hill.

I had, as I have intimated, until I started to work, been as ignorant of alcohol as I was of egg-trundling, but the Ballast Office stood right next to a tavern and, never mind the nights, scarcely a daytime passed now without me finding myself in there or in one of its numerous siblings within spitting distance: the Lady of the Lake, the Rob Roy, the Red Cross, the Cumberland, Mrs Hainen's, Mrs Henry's, Martha Kennedy's, Flood's . . .

I knew my limits, though, in more ways than one.

As we sat that morning in the Lamb and Flag, with our glasses of rum punch, Bright drew our attention to some business being transacted at, or rather, as he said, *under* a table in the corner. "The big fellow with the wavy hair – don't both turn at once – appears to be some kind of fence or fixer. You know the sort, will buy from you what never was yours to begin with and sell you what by honest means you never could have got." I managed to get an angle on him in a mirror set behind the counter – "big" did not come close: he was as broad-shouldered as two men – then looked away when his eyes found mine out, as if he had been all along conscious of the scrutiny. Even in that instant, even with the mirror between us, I felt he had the measure of me. (Of all things, it was the red hen I thought about. The red hen and the green potato.) Ferris leaned across the table and whispered with evident relish that this was where the weavers had met who had exploded the bomb outside the house of their employer on Peter's Hill.

"You were barely off your mother's t— then," Bright interjected. Ferris shook his head. That was as may be, but this was still not a place to be found drinking alone later in the day. The thought, though, would not have occurred to me. Drinking on its own (and therefore on my own) did not interest me in the least: it was the company it brought that I craved. Besides which, I had not entirely forgotten my grandfather's lectures those years before: other people's worlds did not a playground make.

By the time we emerged, warmed twice over, just to be sure, the fog had dispersed and the sun broken through, adding a further, unnecessary, festive touch to the procession we saw making its way along North Street towards us. There could not have been a person between the ages of twelve and twenty left anywhere in Belfast. It was as though the doors of every costumier and milliner in the town had sprung open and their wares simply danced out. All were dressed for the impression they would create on the journey, rather than the steep climb that awaited them at its end. A fellow linked my arm as the multitude passed in front of the Lamb and Flag; Ferris linked my other arm, and Bright Ferris's, and in this way we were swept along into the countryside in the direction of Carrickfergus. Hucksters weaved in and out calling "willicks" and "yellow man", jostling with the preachers ("a new nuisance", according to Ferris, a veteran of two years) for whom the road to the Hill was rather a road to the temptations of Hell. The famous Tantra Barbus, far removed from his usual haunt at the foot of the Long Bridge, danced attendance, with his hand out and his mouth open: "Give a man a drink, there, sirs. Give a man a drink." Cockybendy the fiddler, too, who could usually be relied on to pop up wherever two or more were gathered, walked alongside us for a couple of reels, then retired a penny the richer to start again further down the line.

Bright leaned in across Ferris to ask me what I thought.

"Who is thinking?" I said, and took a bite from a cinnamon bun that had been passed to me over the shoulder of the person in front.

Near the Deer Park my companions and I broke away to stand for a time before the spectacle of a man in a red coatee, missing an epaulette and all but one of its buttons, balancing a young girl above his head, her left foot resting on the open palm of his raised right hand. No one we asked could tell us how long the pair had been there already. They looked straight ahead, neither of them moving, save for the faintest of trembles in his upper arm and, now and then, a twitch in her calf. That, it seemed, was the whole of their act, if act it was: he might just have been holding her up as lost in the hope that her kin could see her, and unlike the other performers we had encountered since the Lamb and Flag they had no tin cup before them in which to collect coins. Of course, it would not have been possible for a crowd of any size to gather before such a spectacle, on that raucous day of all days, without comment being passed ("Your wee woman's not real, he stole her out of the waxworks") and without someone in it feeling compelled to throw something our acrobats' way – a ball of paper as it happened – not with any great intent, but rather speculatively, to determine the likely effect. Which was, a deeper tremble, an accelerated twitch, then afterwards as impassive as before. An apple core followed the paper, arcing over my head and the girl's and landing, innocuously, in the long grass behind. A second later a stick cut the air, end over end, missing the man's left ear by inches, and who knows what other missiles might have been thrown had not a piper perched on a stile a little way up the lane put his elbow to the bellows in that instant, drawing the major part of the crowd to him, Ferris, Bright and me included.

I told my friends I had feared for a moment that something dreadful had been about to occur, at which Ferris confessed, laughing, that it was he who had thrown the paper ball, and Bright and I chased after him calling him all the scoundrels of the day.

The lower slopes of the hill, when we arrived there, breathless, a quarter of an hour later, were dotted with the less energetic revellers at their rest: parents perhaps, prevailed upon to wait by sons and daughters who were even now halfway to the summit and, if what I had heard was true, all the promise of licence that that held out. Higher up, the path got rougher, the undergrowth thicker, and the overhanging branches became more of a hindrance. In some of the dimmer recesses campfires burned. There was laughter, here and there a flash of vivid colour among the black tree trunks. We three pressed on, without a word, emerging eventually a little below the first and largest of the caves (already colonised), some few hundred winding feet from the plateau. Even from this vantage point it was possible to descry the contours of Mann to the south-east and further north, and more solidly, Scotland's western coastline.

"I think here would be as good a place as any for our picnic lunch," Ferris announced, and when I remonstrated that we still had not reached our goal – that it was not yet, in any case, eleven o'clock – gave me an extravagant wink. I saw then that behind us three young women had already spread their rug. In fact, so unusually flat and green was the ground round about it, they might have brought their own square of lawn. Bright, affecting not to have noticed, cast his eye over the terrain and declared it ideal for trundling eggs, by which he might have meant only that it did not encompass any rival group of unaccompanied young men.

The haversack being opened, Bright and I duly gave thanks to Ferris and to Mrs Divin, his landlady, who had wrapped beef, sausage, cheese, and cut bread, in separate linen napkins. Her bounty had run to apples too, the last of the winter store, hazelnuts and walnuts already shelled. And there was beer, of course, three pint bottles from which we wasted no time in drawing the corks.

I was conscious all at once of a rise in the volume of our voices. The young women behind us, in contrast, managed to conduct their conversations without a single word carrying to our ears, a combination of their bonnets' natural shielding and their own intentionally raised hands. That they were talking about us, however, we were in no doubt.

When we had eaten our fill (less than half of what "Ma" Divin had prepared) and drunk our bottles dry, Ferris, Bright and I stood and with great ceremony marched a dozen steps to the right where we formed a line facing down into the valley: the

Duke of Wellington, an unspecified bald man (Ferris's minimal effort) and (Bright's idea: "more conundrum than decoration") a chicken.

"Eggs at the ready!" Ferris commanded. "On a count of three. One . . . two . . . *three*!"

His egg rolled half a yard and stopped. The Duke of Wellington meanwhile had raced ahead of the chicken. Bright and I followed after them, whooping our encouragement. His conundrum was brought to a halt, if not a resolution, by a clump of docken leaves. My own egg carried on a few feet more then veered left into a gorse bush. I should just have let it lie, but, no, nothing would do me but that I would retrieve it. The hard-boiled Duke had won! I practically skipped. And then while I was still some two or three yards off I lost my footing entirely and slid forward on the seat of my trousers. I raised my hands to protect my face, but I seemed to pass right through the bush and out the other side, into a free-fall. I let out a scream – I had no idea how far the drop was – and my arms shot up above my head, with the result that when I did hit the ground, no more than a second later, I was almost upright. My right foot took the full weight and buckled beneath me. The second after that the egg too came out and struck me on the head. Ferris and Bright arrived on either side of the gorse just in time to see it. Their faces, which had been all alarm, broke into companion grins.

"'The trundler shall be disqualified,'" Ferris read from an imaginary rule-book, "'if he shall reach the end of the course *before* his egg.'"

I made a lunge for the object in question and would have brained him with it, but the sudden movement caused the pain to flare along my ankle so that I cried out, worse than before, and the concern returned to their faces.

Bright instructed me not to attempt to move: there was a track leading down from the gorse to my level; he would be with me presently. Ferris meanwhile was calling to the young women we had been so keen to impress – the young women who, despite their petticoats and dainty shoes, had succeeded in reaching here, staying here, without mishap – asking that they go and find "a couple of strong-looking fellows" willing to help.

Their skirts made a greater sound in their departing than did their voices.

Ferris joined Bright in standing over me: talking over me. "We could knot together two coats," said one to the other. "Yes," returned the other to the one, "and tie them somehow to branches, with creepers, perhaps – I have my knife with me."

"It is only my leg that is hurt," I called up at them. "My understanding is not impaired."

The young women returned within minutes – the same rustle of skirts, the same barely audible whispers – accompanied by a pair of brothers whose family farmed at nearby Glengormley and who had, they said, "poked their heads over the hill this morning to see was there any sport". They poked their heads now over the gorse. After listening for some moments while Ferris and Bright outlined their plan for effecting a stretcher, the older of the brothers lifted me, without ceremony, but with a good deal of delicacy, on to his back and – four great strides – up the track. It was how they carried the lame sheep off the hillsides, his younger brother explained.

The last things I saw before we descended into the woods

again were the young women, standing so close together on their patch of lawn that their bonnets resembled three blossoms on the one slender stem, gently nodding.

The brothers – their name was Kelly – told Ferris and Bright that there was an inn at the Lough end of the Buttermilk Loney where I could rest until a carriage could be got to take me back to town. Once we were on a gentler incline I insisted on trying to walk. After two or three excruciating steps, however, I admitted defeat. Bright said, without much conviction, despite his attendance at the gymnasium, that he and Ferris between them could carry me the rest of the way, but the older Kelly, "Dan", would hear none of it. Sure, the day was young yet, and was not this a bit of sport in itself? And so down the Buttermilk Loney to the inn I was carried, like a lame Glengormley sheep.

It was Bright who commented, when we had arrived at our destination, on the sign, which I would otherwise have passed under oblivious.

"Ha!" he cried. "What better place!"

I lifted my head from Dan Kelly's back to see depicted on the wooden board a procession of stooped individuals approaching a hopper, from the bottom of which a troop of youth danced gaily away; and above it all the legend "The Mill for Grinding Old People Young".

It might have been a page torn from that book I used to look at in Hodgson's, *The World Turned Upside Down*, with its strange news of dogs that played flutes and rats that built houses and geese that cooked cooks.

"Let us hope that the mill can perform its miracles on the crippled as well as the decrepit," said Bright.

Ferris had gone ahead to rouse the master of the place, or as it turned out the mistress, a small woman of sixty or so in a widow's black tulle cap, who directed us towards a snug on the left of the door, where I was laid out on a bench with Ferris's haversack for a pillow.

I asked Bright to look in my pockets for my purse, but the Kellys would accept no payment for their trouble; a drink to set them up for the journey back up the hill was all that they asked. The mistress led them off towards the tap-room, promising to send someone directly to attend to my ankle. When next the door opened, therefore, it was to admit a pale, serious-looking creature with the blackest of hair, hanging in two long curls either side of her eyes, which were unexpectedly blue, I noticed, then for the second time that day glanced away so as not to be thought to be looking too closely. She had brought with her a tray bearing three tumblers half full of brandy, of which Ferris straight away relieved her.

Bright asked her name and she told him, "Maria."

He asked her had no one taught her to curtsy. She seemed to think a moment before bobbing. Bright waved his hands to stop her. "No, no, no, I was only having a little fun," he said. Ferris followed with some fun of his own. Had Maria, he wondered, as she set about rolling my trouser leg, much experience of men's ankles? The girl, two ankles among eight, made no reply, but concentrated on removing my shoe and the stocking beneath – no easy task, as it proved. Now that I was able to see the ankle properly I was alarmed by the degree of swelling, which had spread almost to my toes. The girl probed it with her fingertips, stopping when I winced, despite myself, before probing again, more gently. I winced again. She made a noise through her nose, turned and left the room.

Ferris and Bright laughed so hard as the door closed that they had to hold on to one another's shoulders to keep from falling over: that expression . . . that *snort* just now! They stopped when Maria returned with her mistress a minute later: two naughty schoolboys with buttoned lips and brandy tumblers behind their backs.

"Maria is going to put on an ointment," the mistress said, and handed the girl an earthenware pot. "It has been in my family for generations."

Bright's eyes suggested that he had a further smart comment, but his lips remained tight shut.

I lay back against the haversack and closed my eyes, feeling the flat of Maria's hand now as well as her fingers: first the ointment (which did in truth smell more than a little mouldy) then a bandage. I tried to think of something I could say to her, but nothing came.

Ferris all the while was telling the mistress the whole story: my first Easter Monday on the Cave Hill, our choice of spot beneath the summit, our picnic; our egg race . . .

I heard a snigger and opened my eyes. Maria's hair had fallen across her face, but I was sure I could see a smile through its veil.

"You are tying that too tight," I said, more sharply than I had intended.

"It is too tight," Bright repeated.

Maria made as though to adjust the knot. "It will do," I said, brisk now rather than sharp. Still, her face when she stepped back towards the door – a final curtsy for Bright's benefit, or for mine – was flushed with anger.

The mistress was apparently oblivious to all of this. She told us that a boy had gone on horseback to Whiteabbey to order a carriage. She hoped that I would be comfortable in the mean time; and if I wished for more brandy I was only to say the word. Ferris said the word for me, for the three of us, but it was not Maria who answered the summons on this occasion. Indeed, though we ordered another tumbler after that, the carriage arrived before I saw her again, before I could make good my fault.

The Kellys, hearing I was to depart, came out to the front of the inn, with the look on them now of men who might after all tarry a while before attempting Glengormley again. Ferris and Bright supervised the footmen transferring me to the vehicle. They ordered the driver to take it gently and keep the shocks to a minimum.

"Do you know this road at all, sirs?" the driver asked. "The potholes are the major part of it."

Already revellers were beginning to trickle back to town from the Cave Hill, the very young, the very old and the prematurely very drunk. At sunset, and hazardous though it sounded, a blind harpist would lead those who had stayed the course down from the summit. My friends' eyes as they looked out of the carriage window were wistful: all those pretty bonnets left unplucked. Bright patted Ferris's thigh. The duck trousers were a sorry sight. "There is always the summer and the Maze Races to look forward to," he said, stoically.

A church bell tolled the hour as we rattled into the town: one, two, three, four. Given all that had happened since I left home that morning I would not have been surprised to hear four strikes more.

I was brought into Donegall Place amid great fuss, most of it of Ferris and Bright's making, and was carried again, by footmen and driver combined, up to my room. (Bright: "Look, a proper 'sky parlour'!") My grandfather was still out on his visits, Easter Monday not being explicitly referred to in the Scriptures, but was soon found, at an extemporised prayer meeting in Hudson's Entry, and persuaded home. He sent at once for Dr McDonnell, whose house stood a short distance down the street, towards the White Linen Hall, and who although retired now from day-to-day practice could nevertheless be depended upon to attend on a neighbour in an emergency. Just as dependable were the knee breeches and white stockings that, almost alone of the men in Belfast, he persisted in wearing. He arrived within the quarter hour with his man Mick, as constant a companion as Nisbet was to my grandfather, and like his master an opponent of the full-length trouser leg.

"So!" the doctor said and rubbed his hands together. He was reputed to have begun his education in a cave in the Glens of Antrim, Dr McDonnell, which might be where his voice had acquired its permanent echo. "So."

My grandfather's nose and brow wrinkled at the scent of the ointment as the doctor rolled back the trouser leg. McDonnell too drew in a sharp breath before complimenting whoever had applied the bandage. Bright told him that I feared it had been tied too tightly. "No, just right," said the doctor and began to unravel it. "Just right."

The examination lasted barely a minute, making up in brevity for what it lacked in lightness of touch. (Oh, the contrast with the last fingers to have lingered there!) There was, he assured me at the end of it, no breakage, or even tearing of the ligament, but the ankle had been very badly sprained. He would wait twenty-four hours to see if the swelling went down before making any further diagnosis. In the meantime I was not on any account to stir from my bed, and was to have as little excitement as possible while I remained there – this with a glance towards Ferris and Bright, who straight away began to gather their belongings, and with many elaborate bows – not reciprocated – and wishes for my speedy recovery, departed.

The pain was tolerable for the first part of the night, but gradually grew more severe as the laudanum wore off that Dr McDonnell had given me before he left. I lay in a state between sleep and true wakefulness, fancying one minute I could hear a harp being played below on the Flags and the next that there was a tapping at my window, that the circus act I had seen that morning at the Deer Park had found me out and the man's hand become monstrously extended; except it was not the little waxwork creature who was offered up on his palm, but my nurse from the Mill for Grinding Old People Young; it was Maria. She clasped a knife in one hand, a book in the other. "To hear of a Frenchman eating a frog is no news," she read aloud, "but to see a butcher stuck by a hog is strange indeed."

By morning, however, the pain, like the imaginings, had faded to almost nothing. Molly, the housekeeper, whom I had rarely before seen this high up in the house, came in person with my breakfast, or at least held the door for the girl – utterly unknown to me – who did the actual carrying.

"Where is Agnes?" I asked, trying to sit up. The bed sagged beneath me. The struts would need a turn or two.

"A nunnery," said Molly and pulled back the right-hand curtain. I knew by the force of the light it was something after ten o'clock.

"A nunnery?"

"She might be for all I care." Molly gave the other curtain a sharp tug, lest it should think for a moment of displeasing her too. "This is Hannah."

Hannah set the tray on the bedside table, with evident relief: no mishaps. Molly stood by the door and watched the girl withdraw, holding up her dress – or Agnes's dress, as it most likely was – as she went, so as not to tread on the hem.

Molly sighed.

I decided I would wait a while before asking her to tighten the bed struts.

Dr McDonnell and Mick, their knee breeches and stockings, returned as promised in the late afternoon. "So" – Mick, I noticed, rubbed his hands in time with his master's – "so, how have we been?"

"Bearing up," I said, and Mick gripped my shoulder, as though the leg had been in danger of falling off.

On completing this second examination, as briskly and efficiently as the first, as briskly and efficiently as one who had once been used to seeing forty or fifty patients a day, Dr McDonnell was pleased to tell me that his prognosis had been correct: a sprain rather than a tearing of the ligament. There would be no need for "surgical stabilisation". Rest was all that was required now.

In the end I remained a week confined to the house. I suffered no recurrence of the first night's frightful dreams, but still Maria's face came to me, day as well as night. In truth, although I went through the motions of reading books or playing patience, I found as the days progressed I was able to think of little else: the hair as black as black, the unexpected blue of her eyes, the touch of her fingertips . . . the flush of anger on her cheeks as she left the snug in which she had ministered to me.

Ferris and Bright visited in the middle of the week, bringing along with the anticipated tittle-tattle from the Ballast Office and Environs a less expected piece of news, gleaned from the minutes of the previous evening's Board meeting. Mr Walker's surveys and explorations, in which I had played such a small part, had already fared better than the majority of their predecessors. In short, they had given rise to a plan for the creation of a straight channel between the town and Garmoyle by means of staged cuts across the bends of the river. The harbour was to be maintained at a minimum of twelve feet as far as the Long Bridge, with the present quays built over and extended further into the river, while the material dredged up in the creation of the channel was to be formed into an "island", which might be put afterwards to any number of uses. A sub-committee of the Board had already been to London to procure a Parliamentary Bill whose passage into law, it was held, no right-thinking person with the town's best interests at heart could possibly obstruct.

So who should be obstructing it but our own Lord Belfast?

Bright, on his feet, said we must have Reform, with the same passion with which he would normally have said we must all have some new stuff he had seen in the window of John Johnson and Son for waistcoats. It was intolerable that the town's progress should depend on a man elected by *twelve* voters, all of whom he had, in one way or another, in his pocket.

"Can we expect then to hear of you at future Reform Society meetings?" Ferris asked him.

Bright sat again, and crossed his legs. "I would go, except that the Society meets on the night that I attend my gymnasium."

A second elapsed of utter silence before Ferris guffawed, and Bright not far behind him.

My grandfather, when I related all this that evening at dinner, said, yes, yes, let every man have the franchise, although much good it would do them. The votes would continue to be bought; only the currency would change, become still baser. Perceval had it right: before we reformed the system we should reform the morals of all classes.

"Perceval" was the one prime minister – the one politician of any rank – of whom my grandfather spoke with unqualified regard, being the one prime minister openly to have espoused a "vital" religion while in office. We might already have been living in a truly reformed land had not John Bellingham, a disgruntled businessman, brought Perceval's premiership, his life indeed, to an untimely end, the year before my birth, stepping up to him in the lobby of the House of Commons and opening fire at point-blank range.

I had come across an engraving once of Perceval's assassination in a much-perused copy of the *Newgate Calendar* on a stall in Smithfield Market. I had a vivid recollection of the victim's arching back, his assailant's right arm extended to within inches of its target, and, between the two, the door standing open into the Commons, although in my mind it had become confused with the door into Death itself: unrelieved black. The text below laid out the whole case, from Bellingham's imprisonment in Russia over an unpaid debt, through his many petitions, on his release, to the prime minister himself for compensation, to his crazed resolution to act when those petitions were ignored.

He had wanted to hand a serious lesson to the upper ranks, was what he said: that they could not do wrong with impunity. After firing the fatal shot he had sat down calmly on a bench in the House of Commons lobby to await arrest, preferring to appeal to the sense of fair play of any twelve of his fellow Englishmen than to flee.

His fellow Englishmen voted twelve to nil in favour of hanging him.

Back at the table, I tried to draw my grandfather out further on the Reform question, but he blocked me with a request for the salt, which he applied copiously to his mutton, so copiously in the end that he was unable to manage a mouthful more and gave the plate to Hannah with instructions to fry it up for him for breakfast. (From her expression he might have entrusted her with the formula for eternal life.) "Every last crumb," he said unhappily, wasting not.

≈.≈.≈

My return to work coincided with a great excitement in the town, brought on by another dreadful murder, closer to home and the present moment, confirmation of which had only just reached us: five policemen slain in County Clare on Easter Monday.

The miles that the story had travelled, the hands, and mouths, it had passed through might have added to the grisliness – the talk was of mutilations and other abuses of the corpses – but the bald facts were unsettling enough. A sergeant and four constables from the station house at Doolin had come upon a large body of peasantry, near the chapel at Toohavara, clearly intent on some mischief, for all were armed and all wore straw hats by way of uniform. When the policemen tried to take one of this company into custody the countrymen overpowered them, separated them from one another, and either shot them in the fields round about or beat them to death with clubs. The murderers were supposed to be "Terry Alts", provoked to their ghastly deed, and a succession of lesser outrages in recent times, by last year's poor harvest in that part of the world. The fear that day in Belfast, however – a fear expressed only among pockets of friends, and then not without a glance over the shoulder – was that land and crops were mere excuses. One of the policemen in his final throes had cried out to his assailants, "Clare boys, I am a Catholic!" He had articulated what many of the people I spoke to held to be true, and many of those presumably whom I saw crowding at the doors of the town's gun shops: that the real targets of the Terry Alts were Protestants at large.

Belfast then, thirty years after the Act of Union, did not have much of religious strife, still less of violence. St Patrick's Day and the Orangemen's march on the Twelfth of July could, it is true, be occasions for mayhem, even murder, and were as a consequence regularly suppressed, but the confrontations seemed of a piece with the parades' air of Carnival, an interruption to everyday relations (a *hazardous* interruption, but no more than was, say, the running of the bulls at Pamplona), relations which if not wholly cordial were neither consistently hostile. It was not unheard of for Catholics to reside in Brown

Square or Sandy Row, or Protestants in the Pound. By far the most alarming incident in my lifetime, to that point, was the bomb to which Ferris had alluded in the Lamb and Flag – and which had spread the name of our town far and wide for several days – and *that* had arisen out of a dispute over combinations, not religion.

In more recent times, however, the "monster meetings" that had accompanied Mr O'Connell's campaign for Emancipation had reawakened in some Protestant townsfolk ancient fears of encirclement and extirpation by "Papes". (Remember Portadown! Remember 1641!) "Clare boys, I am a Catholic!" ensured those fears did not fall back into a slumber.

Only much later did I connect these events, and fears, to the "baser currency", the thought of which had, in a roundabout way, spoiled my grandfather's dinner.

❧❦❧

For those first few days back at the Ballast Office I relied on the use of a bow crutch (when I could wrest it back from Ferris and Bright), which Mick had delivered on Dr McDonnell's behalf to my grandfather's house, with the injunction that even after I had left it aside I should not, for a few days more, overexert myself. It was not until the beginning of the following week, therefore, that I felt able to return to the Mill for Grinding Old People Young to thank Maria for the care that she had shown me, and to ask her forgiveness for the ingratitude that I had shown her in return. I told no one that I was going, not my grandfather, who nevertheless called to me from the top of the staircase as I opened the street door that I was to remember what Dr McDonnell had said about exertion, not Dr McDonnell himself, and very particularly not Ferris and Bright.

I walked again, at a fraction of the pace, the route of the Easter procession out the road to Carrickfergus, as congested a district as any in the town, where North Street, Mustard Street, Little Donegall Street flowed into it, but in short order less densely populated. Already by Great George's Street there were wide open spaces on either side of the road, although there were numerous scaffoldings to be seen too, terraces of weavers' cottages taking shape behind them to serve Mulholland's Mill, which having burned down some years before had recently been rebuilt at twice the size and converted – foolishly, some still said – from cotton to linen. North Thomas Street was little more than a name, the last before the Milewater Bridge and the town's northern limits. It was from here on Easter Monday that we had struck out, westward, for the Cave Hill. A little further on lay Lilliput Farm – how puny those who built the house here must have felt in the shadow of a giant; how puny and yet how elevated to be able to appropriate such a name – with the Lough now running to shore directly behind. A little further on again was Ringan's Point, which I passed with all the haste I could muster, that bleak spot being where the town's suicides and unbaptised foundlings were disposed of; then, within sight of my destination, I made the last of my frequent halts since leaving home. A few years before a man named Livingstone had flown in a hot-air balloon from the town to Fortwilliam, not far from here, in less than five minutes. On foot, or on two good feet at least, it was a journey of at most three-quarters of an hour. That night it had taken me more than half as long again. It was not discomfort or tiredness that forced me to stop this final time, however, but a shortness of breath brought on by the anticipation – or as it had suddenly become, the dread – of seeing Maria again. What if she were still angry with me? And how exactly would I explain my petulance that day?

I would have turned about then and there and started for home, but for the certainty that I could not endure another week like the two weeks just past, constructing conversations in my head, taking them apart word by word, starting all over again. For good or ill, I must go on.

I had for obvious reasons not been particularly sensible of my surroundings on my previous visit. A closer inspection revealed the Mill for Grinding Old People Young to be a building of some dozen windows fronting on to the road, with a double gateway on one side through to the stables and outhouses and, on the other, a small garden almost totally taken up by a clump of blue-flowered hydrangeas. Curtains drawn on some of the upstairs windows suggested paying guests, or more extensive private quarters than a widow living on her own might be thought to have need of.

From somewhere in the rear came the sound of fowl disputing with one another their order in the roost, a pig arguing with itself.

Having entered again beneath that curious sign, I passed the snug in which the Kelly brothers had deposited me, this evening occupied by four men, advanced in years, arms folded, and engaged in what appeared to be a pipe-smoking contest. (They were neck and neck, and neck and scrawny neck.) I looked, in vain, for Maria in the tap-room that served the snug and then tried a dining room further along the corridor, again without success. Immediately I pushed open the door of the next room, however, I saw her, standing as though deep in thought by the counter. There was a brief moment in which I had to merge the face before me with the one I had carried in my memory since Easter Monday: an adjustment to the advantage of the living face, which was perhaps a little thinner than I had remembered, careworn, even, but more beautiful than any I had ever beheld. If I had not known it before I knew then that I had become properly infatuated. She looked at me equably as I came into the room, even answered my smile with one of her own, but it was clear from the speed with which the smile faded and her eyes slid away from my face, that she did not know me from Adam. I shrank into a corner between a window and a high stone hearth.

I might not have known what I would say to her – what, that is, of the one hundred and fifty versions I had rehearsed and abandoned during my convalescence – but it had not once occurred to me that I might be deprived of the opportunity to say anything at all.

The room was oddly proportioned, as though the original had at some stage, and at whim, been divided. The hearth dominated, as it would have dominated a room two or three times the size, although the turf fire that smoked and very occasionally flared in its grate was barely adequate to the task of warming even that reduced space. There were perhaps eight other customers, including the first women I had seen about the place who were not in its employ: a mother and daughter, was my instant surmise, the elder stroking the hand of the younger, who held a balled handkerchief to her nose throughout the time that I remained there, like a plug to a dam of tears.

I had been sitting, trying to appear at my ease, for several minutes, before another, auburn-haired girl came to take my order of a glass of rum and water, which she brought after the passage of several minutes more, having served two other customers in the interim. Maria, meanwhile, did as close to nothing as any living, breathing human being can do. She might just that moment have dropped from the sky, so detached was she from the activity around her. Perhaps she was still new to the trade. If so, she risked having her career terminated before it had properly begun. To judge by the looks she cast, the auburn-haired girl would have dismissed her on the spot had she but the authority. She it was who, when my drink was finished and I held my glass aloft, coaxed Maria – actually, shoved her – into bringing me another.

"I am sorry," she said when she arrived with the bottle and the jug for my water.

"I do not think you can remember me," I said. She finished pouring, looked at me a second or two; shook her head. I raised my leg a little by way of prompt. "At Easter time? You bandaged my ankle for me. I came to say thank you."

This drew a more genuine smile. "The young gentleman who chases eggs," she said, or as it sounded, "who chases ex." She had said so little at our last meeting, and that so quietly, that I had failed to notice that her accent was not native. I took the jibe in better part this time. "My egg-chasing days are over once and for all," I said.

"You were embarrassed, I think," she said then. "Such a *silly* thing to have happened."

The stress on "silly", I chose to believe, was another peculiarity of her speech.

She apologised that she had not recognised me sooner. She

had been so intent that day on treating my injury, and my features, as she recalled it, were contorted with pain for much of the time. And then there were the other people present. It had begun to feel a little – what was the word? Like "crowded", only worse.

Still I could not place that accent. I asked her, if it was not too impertinent a question, where she was from. "Poland," she said emphatically, as though expecting me to contradict her. "Near the town of Łuków." The name meant nothing to me, although had I first seen it written down rather than heard it said – "Wukuf" – I might have had a dim recollection of encountering it not long since in the newspapers: a battle; the kind of thing then that was inclined to catch my eye.

"I must return to my duties now," Maria said, apparently oblivious to the fact that to the observer her duties seemed to consist of standing very still and counting the brasses above the fireplace. "Thank you for coming back. It was not necessary."

"Oh, but it was," I said. "Believe me."

It was brief, but a look passed between us, a meeting of more than eyes alone. She nodded. "I am very glad", she said, "that you have recovered."

"Maria!" She had got halfway to the counter when I called her back. "You forgot something."

She returned, puzzled, to the corner, then saw the coins in my palm. Her expression as she took them said she was never going to learn this trade.

I had no further opportunity to talk to her that evening. Shortly after Maria had brought me the second glass of rum, the mistress appeared in her widow's cap – it seemed as much a part of her head as her hair – and summoned her to another part of the inn. The auburn-haired girl looked daggers at Maria's retreating back. After half an hour she still had not returned. I wondered about going to look for her again, but, no, I had done what I had set out to do, and more, there had been a moment of clear understanding. In any case, whether because of the rum itself or of the fresh air that had preceded it after so long confined to the town, I was suddenly very weary and still had the walk home ahead of me.

The mother of the tearful girl smiled up at me as I squeezed past her table. I think that were I to have offered, as the first halfway presentable young man to happen by, she would gladly have had me take her daughter off her hands. I did not offer and she called instead to the auburn-haired girl for another quartern of gin.

Twenty feet from the door of the inn the way became (how had I not thought to take this into account?) almost completely black. The April evening had given way to a February night, a chill northerly wind pressing against my back. I stuck to the land side of the road, twice narrowly avoiding a ditch, until I judged I was well clear of Ringan's Point, then crossed to the shoreline, where the darkness seemed a little less dense, and where the lapping of the water acted as a warning and a guide both: "not this way, that . . . not this way, that . . ." Before long I began to discern an occasional light in the distance, like a coal fallen from the banked-up fire of the town, I thought, and was pleased enough with the notion to try to work it up into a line or two of verse. Bright could do that sort of thing very tidily, was forever passing pieces of paper between our desks with couplets written on them, often utterly scurrilous. I on the other hand soon found myself thinking more about the impulse to compose than the words themselves.

Poetry! What on earth – or who – had possessed me?

I had come alongside Lilliput Farm again, and was seized by the vision of Dean Swift riding this very road on his way from Kilroot to Belfast and his beloved "Varina": four long years, waiting and hoping. I thought of him, in his dejection at her refusal, finally abandoning this part of the world altogether. That was what I would do in the same circumstance. In the early hours, before anyone else was stirring. A last look back over my shoulder at the town of my birth, before spurring my horse on to whatever now fortune held in store for me.

So caught up was I with fleeing and passionate letters sent post-haste that I scarcely noticed the wind any longer, or indeed registered the remaining half a mile to the outskirts of town. Even at this hour, the sensation as the buildings closed in around me was much as I imagined it would be being taken up from the ocean into a great ship, its passengers all unconcerned by the vastness that surrounded them and that only a few minutes before had threatened to swallow you.

Coming in by Carrick Hill and North Street, I saw once more on the opposite side from me the Lamb and Flag, where Ferris, Bright and I had had our warmers en route to the Cave Hill. It looked tonight to have burst at the seams, men crowding the footpath before its doors, slouching against its walls, the lamp standards, whatever solid surface they could find. The man Bright had pointed out on our last visit, the wavy-haired "fixer", was instantly recognisable among them, in conversation with a man in an oilskin coat, although not so deep as to prevent him from keeping an eye too on everything that was going on around him – on me as, for the first time since Lilliput, I broke my stride.

I had walked off my earlier weariness, and having regained the deck, as it were, a part of me had no wish to retire yet to my cabin. I remembered Ferris's caution against drinking here alone at night, but at that moment I did not care, any more than I cared that I would be obliged to rise for work at first light, five or six hours hence. Tonight nothing bad could befall me. Not here. Not in my town. I crossed over and with a little effort made my way inside.

And nothing bad did befall me, or nothing worse than that when day did break – a minute, as it seemed, after my head touched the bolster – my eyes could not be persuaded to open. My grandfather paused on the landing outside my room half an hour later.

"Are you not about yet?" he called.

"I was at my prayers," I replied, my mouth only just above the bedclothes.

"I see." He stood a moment or two more and then walked back down the landing to the stairs. I prayed then, all right, silently, that I might be excused that one small lie, which I fully intended would be my last.

Two nights later I walked out along the shore road again, feeling stronger in body, more resolute in spirit, and pleased with myself that I had remembered to bring a tin lantern for the journey home. So of course – because God, it appears, punishes self-satisfaction before all other sins – when I arrived at the Mill, and though I looked in every tap-room, dining room, snug and hidey-hole, Maria was nowhere to be seen.

I returned from my search to the room with the outsized

hearth, around which tonight were crowded men with clay packed, vividly orange, about the soles of their boots. (They had walked in them, perhaps, from the building sites around Mulholland's Mill.) The auburn-haired girl was serving here with a second girl, plumper, and prettier, if a little wall-eyed on the left side. It was of this girl that I enquired about Maria, but the auburn-haired one, whose name, it soon came out, was Dorothy, and whose ears, such was the force of her antipathy, were attuned to pick out Maria's name above all other competing sounds, straight away intervened.

"You are looking in the wrong place for that one. This is a place of *work*," she said. The wall-eyed girl covered a smile with her hand. "And work and her do not exactly agree."

I had seen the evidence of it myself and could offer no defence.

"And now it seems she is 'indisposed'." Dorothy appeared to be offering the word up for my inspection. I nodded, which satisfied her and left me none the wiser. "As if the rest of us did not have indispositions of our own."

Here the other girl nodded firmly, perplexing me further. "Murder, she is let get away with," the girl said.

Dorothy poured two measures of gin for a man with a palsied hand and wiped her palms on the underside of her apron. "Of course, you know she is to leave us as soon as her letter arrives."

Her words were ostensibly addressed to the other girl, but I was in no doubt they were intended for me.

"What letter?" I asked.

"From her gentleman, who else?" She made a play of stopping herself. "Oh, dear," she said then, "had you been hoping . . . ?"

My face must have told its own story. "Oh, dear, Louisa, I think he had and all."

Louisa covered her mouth with her hand again. "Dorothy," she said into it, thrilled and appalled in equal measure. I turned on my heel. As I reached the door I heard Dorothy call to me. "Don't look so miserable, she is too old for you anyhow: four and twenty, if she's a day. You want a good Belfast girl like Louisa here." The men around the fire laughed, whether at me or at some joke that had passed between them I neither knew nor cared to discover. And then I was outside, breathing heavily, purging myself of the very air I had swallowed in there.

I had stomped, in my rage, some distance down the road before I realised that I had forgotten my lantern, but nothing – not the ditches, not the potholes, not the stillborn or the suicides – would induce me to go back for it.

In fact I might never have gone back again had I not, quite by chance, spotted Maria several mornings later on Hanover Quay, on the opposite side of the Town Dock from the Ballast Office. At least, I thought that it was Maria. I was standing with Sir Clueless, who was talking to the skipper of a Maryport coal freighter lately docked, negotiating with him the length of his stay. (Till the last shovelful was sold out of the hold, was what the skippers usually angled for, should that mean their vessels being tied up from one year's end to the next.) It was her proximity to the water's edge that attracted my attention – another step and she would have been treading air – before the turn of the head that afforded me a glimpse of her face, framed today by a lace-trimmed bonnet.

The emigration season was just getting going in good and earnest; a ship bound for Montreal lay at anchor further down the Lough, and my first thought (if that twist in the gut counted as thought) was that she meant to join it. Her costume, however, I told myself in the next second, was not that of a lady about to embark on a sea journey of any length, even the length of Belfast Lough, its greatest protection from the elements being the lace pelerine covering the shoulders that her dress otherwise left bare. And I am ashamed to say it crossed my mind then that her business there was the same as that of the other girls who waited on the quays for a boat – any boat – to come in, until I noticed, beneath the hitched hem of her skirts, that she was wearing wooden pattens on her feet, although we had not had rain for several days past. Unlike those other girls, she dared not, for whatever reason, have her shoes or her dress soiled.

No sooner had I remarked them than the pattens turned about, towards the town, and the face was lost to me in the multitude.

Sir Clueless was asking me the date of the third Tuesday after next.

"Third Tuesday after next? The seventeenth of May," I said, and he repeated it to the coal boat's skipper. I picked up Maria's bonnet again as it weaved in and out of the carters and the bagmen and the families waiting with their trunks and bundles for the gabbards that would carry them on the first leg of their journey to a new world. At the bottom of Princes Street the bonnet came to rest again briefly. I had the impression of a man's head nodding in close proximity to it, or perhaps shaking – I could not be sure, only that the movement was vigorous.

Beside me, Sir Clueless had finished with business and moved on to pleasantries: who had died, who fallen sick, and who had lost his fortune since the last time the skipper put in at Belfast.

"If you have no further need of me at present . . ." I said.

Sir Clueless cast a sidelong look at me and stroked his lapels with his thumbs, a tic of which he alone in the Ballast Office appeared wholly unaware.

"Keen boy, this," said the skipper. His smile had more of gold in it than all the Meeting Houses of Belfast put together. "Eager to get on with his work."

"Yes," said Sir Clueless.

"So what of Batt?" the skipper asked, voice rising in anticipation.

"Which Batt?" The stroking stopped.

"Thomas, or Samuel: he had invested in a steamer, the last I heard."

"That Batt," said Sir Clueless, and to me, "You may go."

As soon as he turned his back again I slipped away in the opposite direction. At the High Street end of the dock I saw coming towards me Roddy McCluskey, a satchel draped right to left across his body, and recognised him as the man with whom Maria had been in conversation. Roddy had been deprived by nature of both his arms, but in all of the town there was no better messenger, or guide. He was a living, breathing gazetteer.

"Roddy!" I hailed him. "That lady you were talking to just now . . ."

"Prussian," he said, as though he had been debating it with himself, and I did not correct him, nor have to ask then if he had met her before. I understood now too the vigorous movements of his head.

"Was she looking for directions somewhere?" I asked.

"A pawnshop. I told her she was on the wrong side of town, she would have a better choice in Smithfield, or Hill Street, even Academy Street." Roddy tipped his chin, inclined his head to the right then jabbed it backwards, doing the work of ten fingers. "But if she must take her chances here then she could have her pick of Philips or Johnston in Princes Street."

I clapped his shoulders. "Thank you."

When I arrived at Princes Street, however, the place was in uproar. A horse drawing a cart of manure had caught its hoof in an abandoned lobster pot and stumbled, tipping its load across the roadway. The manure steamed. It stank. The horse neighed and thrashed on the cobbles, trying to drag itself up. Its owner was too preoccupied to help, jabbing his finger into the chest of the man who had left the lobster pot lying, asking him had he dropped another pot somewhere with his brains in it. Seconds had already volunteered themselves, thirds and fourths, even. Over their heads and along the street I could see the twinned clusters of golden balls, for the pawnshops Roddy had recommended were exact neighbours. The obstacles between them and me, however, were suddenly too daunting.

The horse, summoning who knows what reserves, righted itself and reared up at the same moment as the fisherman clouted the cart owner with another lobster pot. Everyone else scattered, me included. I overtook Roddy as I hurried back along the quays to the Ballast Office.

"Will you tell me if you see her again?" I called, and he nodded, eloquently.

I did succeed in reaching both Philips and Johnston later that day (the manure had been swept into heaps at the sides of the street; of the horse, the cart, the lobster pot there was no sign), but neither Miss P nor Mr J nor a single one of their assistants claimed any memory of a lady answering Maria's description, or indeed speaking in her uncommon voice. "It is not impossible that she was here," was as near to an affirmative as I could get, this from Johnston. "But only the docket can prove it for certain."

A police bill to the right of his head warned brokers of the theft of a load of plate from a house in Hannahstown on the night of the 5th *inst*. A reward was offered, a pen picture painted of an individual of low character observed in the neighbourhood earlier the same day, "missing the top portion of the left ear".

"Can you check?" I asked.

"Not my docket, hers."

Several dozen clocks ticked against the tock of several dozen more.

"That is most helpful," I said.

The pawnbroker leaned his weight on fingertips spread on the glass counter between us: a hothouse for silk handkerchiefs and scarves of every imaginable hue. "I am sure", he said, with a smile as second-hand-looking as anything in the shop, "you would want me to be as helpful were someone to enquire after you. And now," behind me an assistant had already opened the door, "good day."

The thought of how close I had come to meeting Maria again continued to tantalise me. If only I had slipped away from Sir Clueless sooner; if only I had not stopped to talk to Roddy McCluskey; if only I had got to Princes Street a fraction of a second before the horse met with the lobster pot . . .

So it was in a state more of distraction than desire that I

found myself once again, on the second-last evening of April, back on the road to the Mill. It had been a fine day, the spring dressed in its richest colours, which were deepening now as the sun slid slowly towards Black Mountain. A platoon of infantry added their scarlet as they marched along Great George's Street towards the North Queen Street barracks. Filthy-faced children of the kind Belfast seemed to specialise in fell into step beside them, their chests and stomachs puffed out, their chins pulled in against their necks. The drummer boy found the mimicry particularly hard to bear, being not more than a year or two older than the biggest of his tormentors. His face flared to a shade just short of his tunic. The sticks in his hands beat like fury.

Further along the shoreline, beyond the pigs let loose nightly upon the wrack (they were practically cured before they were slaughtered, the pigs of Belfast), oystercatchers provided the spectacle, returned in their thousands to carry out manoeuvres on the mudflats where they had built their nests of stones and eggshells. The emigrant ship had already sailed from the Pool of Garmoyle, across the estuary; a three-master was anchored there in its stead, waiting for the morning tide to carry it up to the town. Around it the gabbards and rowboats clustered, the former taking on urgent cargo, the latter passengers whose affairs or emotions, or indeed ailments (I saw one man being handed down behind his bath chair) would not permit them another night aboard ship. "A sixpence to take you up the Lough..." And around all of these the customs vessels prowled, making sure that whatever freight left the ship reached the shore at the place decreed by the Revenue.

Forcade, the Superintendent of Quarantine, would be in

among them, too. At the beginning of the year the Board, as though in answer to Ferris's desire for drama, had circulated to all who worked in the Ballast Office a memorandum on an outbreak of the cholera, which, it was feared, from its first stirrings in Bengal, was making its way inexorably across the continent of Europe to our shores. Ships wanting to dock in the town were obliged under threat of the severest penalties to make known all unexplained illnesses among passengers and crew, and could if necessary be quarantined at Garmoyle or even returned to their port of origin. We, on land, were likewise to be vigilant. A description of the symptoms of the disease was appended, from the increased heart rate to the fishy odour of the flux it brought on. (Ferris whispered to me that whoever did not hold his nose, as a matter of course, on entering a privy deserved all the fishy odours he got.) Bulletins were issued at intervals throughout the remainder of the winter and into spring: the cholera was in Sebastopol, St Petersburg, Vienna, Prague; a ship from Cadiz bound for Liverpool had put in at San Sebastián with all on board dead or dying... We marked each new location with a pin on a map, next to the cabinet where the Harbour Constable's pistols were kept. It was the pin that broke the established patterns for which we were to be most on the alert.

Some of the older clerks remembered the previous panic, a dozen years before, and how that had passed without a single case being reported in the whole of the island, which did not prevent one or two of them carrying little muslin pouches of lavender to keep at bay any noxious airs – that is, any more noxious than usual airs – that might be carried through our door. And still the bulletins continued to come in, of outbreaks in Leipzig and Hamburg to the north, in Sicily and Sardinia to the south. The newspapers were now beginning to take an interest in this "Hindoostanee menace". The day they verified a fishy flux west of Calais there would not be lavender enough in all of Ireland.

The shore road was more congested than I had yet seen it on my evening excursions. The good weather had brought the people out to walk off an early tea, or work up an appetite for a later one, or simply to clear their heads of the noise of the day. Not a few of them, I realised, the closer I drew to it, were intent like me on the Mill. Men and women both sat on benches on either side of the entrance, gentlefolk and working folk, enjoying the warmth of the sun, watching their children play at marbles and hopscotch in the dusty forecourt, and lending the scene the air of a *tableau vivant* of a country that had never had to concern itself with Terry Alts or the threat of cholera.

For all that it was busy inside, I had no difficulty on this occasion locating Maria, in the main room of the inn, and Maria, it pleased me to observe, had no difficulty recognising me, nor, to judge by her look of confusion the moment after, the import of my returning there a third time. For I did not doubt that Dorothy had made known to her my last visit, in her own very particular way.

We were unable to exchange much more than glances, because this was the room presided over by the innkeeper herself: "Peggy", as I heard the older patrons call her, although to the less seasoned she was "Mrs Barclay", when they could summon the courage to address her at all.

I had seen it before, this power of landlords and ladies (utter despots some of them), although not perhaps in one so advanced in years – the "sixty or so" I had first allowed was undoubtedly conservative – or so quiet and genial in manner. Even Maria was "galvanised" in her presence.

I was obliged to wait until the very end of the evening for the chance to speak, when the lamps had been let burn low and Mrs Barclay had retired upstairs, leaving only the determined few, and the half asleep, hugging their tankards and tumblers. I had hugged my own tumbler since I arrived to keep myself from drinking more again in my agitated state than I was accustomed to holding.

Maria stopped before my table. Her hair had been tied back earlier, but was now working itself loose at the sides. There was a warmth came off her, a smell like fresh-baked biscuits.

"You came again," she said simply, although I thought I detected in the tone admiration for my perseverance.

"The air agrees with me," I said, and she smiled – a smile like something being let go within: the air at that moment was yellow with pipe smoke, too befuddled to disperse. Maria took herself off down the room and picked up a bowl piled high with oyster shells, which she still carried when she returned.

"I know what Dorothy told you," she said.

"I thought that you would," I said.

"It is true." A shell slipped from the summit, unsettling the pile. She steadied it with the heel of her hand.

"I thought that it was."

"And?"

She was being obliged to bend a little towards me, which meant – I had not been aware until then that I had done it – I must at some point in our exchange have cast my eyes down. I lifted them now.

"And I wish only to offer you my friendship, and protection if you should ever need it."

The thought evidently amused her. "Protection?"

"When you are in town," I said. "I saw you there the other day."

Her demeanour changed. She looked down angrily at the oyster shells and I thought for a moment she meant to tip them over my head, but a burst of singing then from another part of the inn seemed to give her pause. "You were *spying* on me?"

"No, not spying. The Ballast Office where I work is on the quays. It was pure chance that our paths crossed. Nearly crossed."

Her knuckles were white. I explained to her that the streets around the docks were not the safest for a young woman on her own. Even on High Street ladies going to church on a Sunday evening often walked in pairs. She was, perhaps, not familiar with our town.

"I am familiar with other towns, thank you," she said, "towns bigger than this." She began to say something more, but evidently thought better of it. Instead she took the bowl of oyster shells to the counter and stood for half a minute with her back to me, shoulders rising and falling, rising and falling. The singing had started up again, outside now. Never mind the words (and forget about the tune entirely), it was hard to make out whether the singer was a woman or a man, old or young. He – she – was drunk, that was all. Maria's shoulders rose a final time, fell again.

"All right," she said when she had returned. "You will be my Irish Protector."

She held out her hand. I went to give her mine.

"Your glass," she said.

A couple of days after this I heard that Millar was back in town, or more specifically, back in Rosemary Street, where, it seemed, all had not been proceeding to his satisfaction. Indeed, so appalled was he by the discovery of what Duff and Jackson had "done" to the Third Presbyterian Church in his absence that he had quite literally not been able to quit the building site. It was there that I eventually found him, in his shirtsleeves, at the top of the broad granite steps leading up from the street, talking to a stonemason and his apprentice. He looked, when he turned at the sound of his name, what he was, a man who had not slept, or even shaved, in more than forty-eight hours.

"I suppose," I said, wanting to lighten the mood, "you wouldn't have time for a game of handball?"

"Gilbert," he said, and straight away took hold of my arm and pulled me further inside. "Look at this . . . and this . . . and this . . ."

I did not know how to tell my friend that I had looked at his church several times a week since the first stone was laid and had noticed nothing untoward, any more, in truth, than I did when I was standing in the middle of the skeleton with him, despite his gesticulations and an accompanying catalogue of errors and omissions that finally left him at a loss for words.

"If I had got here even a day later the damage would have been too great to repair," he managed at length. "Hopper drummed it into us daily that as architects our duty was to be prejudiced in favour of no style, but to understand them all. This *Duff* has evidently forgotten the second part, and Jackson, if Duff was his teacher, can never have known it."

"You know that they have the building of the new Museum, the two of them," I said. I might have added that I had had rather more company on those occasions when I had stopped before that site, on the north side of the square with the Academical Institution at its centre, than when I stopped here. Less pure and massive they might have been, and erected at considerably less than the ten thousand pounds Millar's was rumoured to be costing, but we had no shortage of churches in the town; we had never yet, on the other hand, had a museum.

Millar shook his head. "I had heard," he said, then, something catching his eye, ran to the foot of a ladder at the top of which, some thirty feet distant, a man worked on the architrave of an enormous window arch. "Do you think perhaps a narrower chisel for that angle?" he called up.

He declined the invitation to dine with me that evening, but promised he would see me on Sunday, when no amount of vandalism to his project would persuade the workmen to forgo their day of leisure (he did not think from listening to their talk that they were too much concerned with worship), and when we might go for a walk together instead.

We met in front of the bank on Castle Place directly after morning service, under skies at once overcast and brighter than where I had just been. I had had it in mind to suggest the Cave Hill for our walk, and perhaps afterwards a stroll down Buttermilk Loney, but Millar, although he was not in the strictest sense working, was not wholly at rest either.

"I thought we might go to the Giant's Ring," he told me.

I had only the vaguest sense of where it lay: in the parish of Drumbo, several miles to the south of the town, and therefore, from my point of view, entirely in the wrong direction;

but "lead on", I said, making light of my disappointment, "to the Giant's Ring!"

There was not a town in this island or the next, Millar said as we walked, more convenient than ours to a site of such antiquity – not less than three millennia, most of those expert in these matters agreed – or such mystery, as the Giant's Ring, with this one suggesting a burial site, that one a place of sacrifice, and still another a connection to the worship of a sun god.

And what did the people of Belfast do? Why, they raced horses there, of course.

He had touched on the two reasons why my sense of the monument's whereabouts had remained so long untested. My grandfather would not easily have been reconciled to the fact that it had once been used for pagan ritual, and never mind that there had been then no other, which is to say no more Christian, ritual of which to partake. "A thing can strike you as inherently wrong, even if you do not know yet what is right."

As for the race meetings, which for a number of years had been held there at Whitsuntide, in my grandfather's system of values they ranked only a little above pagan ritual.

It was a walk of more than an hour and a half from the White Linen Hall along the Dublin Road, and took me – had I but known it – past the spot where I would eventually build my own house, although at the time it was nothing but farmland, among the richest in the county, if not the entire country. (The winter barley was coming into ear; I plucked a couple of beardy stalks for us to chew on as we went.) We interrupted our journey at Shaw's Bridge, coming off the road so that Millar could inspect the bridge's underside from the vantage point of the towpath, which ran alongside the River Lagan as far as Lisburn. A captain in Cromwell's army was supposed to have built a bridge of oak here, and to have left his name attached, even though that bridge had been replaced by a stone one and that stone one washed away by a flood before the bridge we stood under was built, and was lucky still to be standing, said Millar, pointing out several areas of recent repair.

"It is perhaps best not to know these things," I said.

"It is perhaps advisable then that you never accompany me under the Long Bridge."

The Long Bridge had spanned the Lagan then for the past one hundred and fifty years. For at least the last fifty of them there had been calls to tear it down and start again.

I thanked Millar kindly for the caution. "Now all I will be able to think about as I cross it is what is under there that I am *not* seeing."

From Shaw's Bridge to the Ring it was country lanes and paths so winding and perplexing that at one point we convinced ourselves we had passed the same stand of birch trees twice in five minutes. We called out to a farm lad we glimpsed across a hedge asking if he would lead us to the Ring for a penny and he immediately turned and ran, which puzzled us a great deal. At length, however, and more by luck than design, we found the right track and almost unexpectedly in the end stood on a broad earthen rampart, a near-perfect circle (around, it had to be admitted, a near-perfect racetrack) some six hundred feet in diameter, in the utter stillness of that spring afternoon, trying to accommodate to our understanding the evidence of our eyes. Millar it was who broke the silence. The so-called Primitives who had constructed this rampart three thousand years ago had, he said, more sense of harmony and proportion, to say nothing of natural drama, than all but a handful of the people now permitted to practise their craft upon the towns and cities of our realm. I accepted without question, without him even having to state it, that my friend was to be numbered among that handful.

At the centre of the arena and entirely screened by the rampart from all but the birds of the air, the balloonists and the deity (God the Father, or god the Sun), was a cluster of large stones, perhaps a dozen in all, including those lying flat and at a little distance from the main formation: a *cromlech*, Millar called it. Large quantities of bones had in the recent past been found in the fields round about, lending credence to the view that these stones had formed the entrance to a passage grave, and that the Ring had, over time, attracted to it lesser, satellite graves. To the eyes of a great many others, however – to my eyes seeing them for the first time – the stones had the appearance of a collapsed Druidical altar. It was difficult to disentangle the foreboding from the awe as we walked out towards them, difficult to walk rather than slow march.

The topmost slab came to just below my shoulder, which, in the years since our first meeting in Smithfield, had pulled away a good three inches above Millar's. For him the slab was a perfect pillow on which to dream ladders into heaven. He closed his eyes and moved his hands over the stone, as though it were communicating with him through a form of geological Braille.

"Do you ever have the feeling that your life to this point has been nothing more than a prologue?" he asked me suddenly. "A preparation for the thing for which you will be remembered?"

"I do not imagine that I will be remembered for anything at

all," I said, with a laugh that sounded false even to my own ears. What I ought to have said was, so far removed was I from the child who had expected very soon to join his father and mothers, and despite the odd presentiment of a few moments before, I did not truly imagine that afternoon that I would ever die.

Millar opened his eyes and took the measure of the site again. There were in the rampart seven distinct dips or breaches, which might at one time have been the points of entry for great processions of our ancestors, whatever they were intent on on arrival here at the centre. "All that I have done up to now has been but a sketch for what I intend," he said. "Even Rosemary Street. Even before those clots got at it." I had begun to circle the *cromlech* while he talked so that now we faced each other over the top of one of the more upright stones. "I have been talking to the Presbytery of a congregation near to Lisnabreeny, on the road to Ballygowan," Millar said. "Do you know where I mean?"

I did, in the gentler hills of Castlereagh, across the Lagan Valley from the Cave Hill and Black Mountain. My grandfather had a cousin, the manager of La Mon's Mill in Gransha, further out that road, whom he entertained once a year and to whom he paid in return precisely one visit, on a horse borrowed for the day from Dr McDonnell. It was what he liked to call his holiday.

"Are you then to be the official architect of the Presbyterian Church in Ireland?" I asked Millar.

"Well, that was one of my misgivings," he said. "Even as I was pacing out the plot with two of the elders, nodding at their assurances that I should be given free rein, I was asking myself was this really the time to be taking on another church. And then the *elder* elder mentioned, by way of aside, Conn O'Neill's castle. Half the walls in the neighbourhood, he told me, were built from its leftovers."

"Conn O'Neill?" I said.

"My reaction exactly," said Millar. He had joined me by now on my side of the stone. We sat with our backs to it. I thought of us outside Billy Pollard's handball alley, with our pennies and our slabs of honeycomb. "The elder said to me, 'You know the story, don't you?' And when I told him I did not he shook his head. 'Man, dear,' he said."

I confessed I did not know it either. Millar shook his own head. "Man, dear."

Conn O'Neill, as the elder elder's story was passed on to me, was the last of the great Gaelic chieftains of Clandeboye, whose lands ran down to the banks of the River Lagan, at the opposite side of the ford from which Belfast eventually grew. There had been a castle of sorts at Castlereagh since the time of the Normans, although never as grand as under the O'Neills, when, so great an advantage did it enjoy over the surrounding countryside, it had acquired the name of "Eagle's Nest". Belfast itself would have appeared an insignificant huddle of huts and hurdles in those early years of its settlement, even its castle a plaything, and indeed to begin with Conn was not greatly perturbed by the latest newcomers to the valley. Then he made the fateful decision to entertain his family and friends at a grand feast, which, as grand feasts then were inclined to, degenerated into an orgy of drunkenness (this was a Presbyterian elder speaking through my friend), so prolonged that eventually there was no wine, no whiskey, no porter, no intoxicating liquor of any description to be had in the entire castle, whereupon Conn, with his reputation as host at stake, dispatched a wagon down to the settlers' town for fresh supplies. As his men were beginning their ascent again to the Eagle's Nest, however, a party of English soldiers obstructed them and tried to confiscate their wagon and all its cargo. Fearful of returning empty-handed, the servants drew their swords and in the scuffle that ensued one of the English fell, mortally wounded. Sir Arthur Chichester – the original Sir Arthur, the Charter Chichester – was incensed . . . and perhaps secretly pleased at the opportunity that now presented itself. Hardly had the wine been broken open in Conn's Castle, the famous victory toasted, when more English soldiers arrived with a warrant for the arrest of Conn himself, on charges of levying war against the Crown, and the great debauch ended with the chieftain of Clandeboye nursing his head in Carrickfergus gaol.

And that was the beginning of the end of him. Some months later a Scottish lord, Montgomery, arranged to have him smuggled out of the prison in return for a share of his lands, which, such was the mire of indebtedness that Conn found himself in, quickly turned into the greater portion of them. At his death, a dozen or so years later, he owned nothing beyond his castle walls. And once he was gone they too fell.

"Conn might have been a fool," Millar said, stepping outside the elder's tale, "but swindling a fool is hardly a heritage of which we can be proud."

"And so . . . ?" There was clearly an "and so".

"And so I began to wonder if that might not be the place to lay down a marker, a reminder to the great-great-to-the-power-of-however-many-grandchildren of the land-grabbers that there is more to us than simple avarice . . . or ought to be."

I was accustomed to Millar's way of talking, his striving for a kind of purity, but I felt the need to introduce a grain, at least, of doubt.

"Can one building do that?" I asked.

"If it is the right one, it can."

"I would not expect you to give them the wrong one," I said, and he laughed.

The day had continued overcast, but there was warmth beneath the cloud. We sat for a time, a pair of drowsy-heads, making only fitful attempts at conversation. I dipped my toe into the troubled waters of the Harbour improvements, but in the matter of leisure I was closer in those days to the artisans than to my architect friend: such talk was finally too much like work for a Sunday afternoon. The grass when we started to our feet was grown damp around us. We stretched, pulling down handfuls of air, letting out long groans that began in pain and ended in an ecstasy of release. A strange performance, although the stones had no doubt witnessed stranger, and who was to say but that they would witness stranger again.

As we walked back towards the town, Millar, reinvigorated by the rest, or the stretching, pumped me for anything I might tell him about the Museum, which, as to the building itself, was not much beyond what might be observed by anyone stopping on the pavement opposite with twenty minutes on his hands. I was a little more familiar with the Natural History Society whose members had almost willed the Museum into being as a home for their meetings and for the curios from the different kingdoms of nature that they brought along to them. My grandfather, with his fondness for societies, had as a matter of course attended an early meeting, in the Library at the White Linen Hall. "Clever," was his verdict, "but too young."

I did know from having heard it discussed in the Ballast
Office that a bottle had been inserted at the architects' suggestion into the Museum's foundation stone, which Lord Donegall
himself had laid the year previous. Included in it were examples
of the coins then current on the island, copies of all five local
newspapers, an almanac (this was clearly some size of bottle: a
Nebuchadnezzar, a Melchior), and a portion of the Scriptures,
the book of Job, the twelfth chapter – "Who knoweth not in all
these that the hand of the Lord hath wrought this?" etc. – tran-
scribed in fifteen languages, as a guide for future generations, a
sort of Rosetta Stone.

Millar stopped as abruptly as if he had walked into a post.
He looked at me, his eyebrows inverted Vs of bemusement.

"I am only repeating what I heard said," I told him.

"I know," he said and shook the Vs away. "I know." But several times after that, in the companionable silence that once
again descended on us, I plainly heard a tut escape him. Rosetta
Stone!

I tired considerably in the final half mile and by the time
the White Linen Hall's cupola came into view I was close to
limping.

"Have you hurt yourself?" Millar asked.

Given his lambasting of Duff and Jackson I could only imagine what he would make of Ferris and Bright, of me for con-
sorting with them.

"I twisted my ankle coming down the stairs," I told him,
and tried to disguise my discomfort. "It really is not anything
much."

I did not tell him either, therefore, about Maria and my
walks to the Mill for Grinding Old People Young. All the

things that had been so consuming me in recent weeks indeed seemed, when I was alone that night and lying in bed, embarrassingly trivial.

What would I be remembered for? What was the act to which my life till now had served merely as prologue?

I could not see anything other than a succession of days at the Ballast Board and I knew in that instant that a succession of days like that would finally be unendurable.

ও.ৼ.ৎ

I awoke at not much after half past five to the baying of dogs. Mr Sinclair, who had the house next to Dr McDonnell's, had lately been keeping his hunting pack kennelled in his gardens, which stretched back, like our own, on to Fountain Street, and two or three times in the week would run the dogs through the streets before the town was fully roused. I drew the curtain back a few inches from the left edge of the window frame and with my fingertips made a porthole in the condensation. The very first sight I met with was Lord Belfast astride a grey mare, talking to Mr Sinclair's master of hounds by the wall of the old Castle gardens and appraising the dogs as they flowed past, a limited palette of white, black and tan.

Lord Donegall was often to be met with about the town, "acting", some shopkeepers, familiar with his terms, were moved to complain, "as if he owned the place" – except that even with the leases he had sold of late it is moot whether he was in fact acting. I had never before, though, had the opportunity to view the "older son" at such close quarters. I do not mind saying that he cut an impressive figure, at once straight-backed and relaxed in the saddle, as befitted one who had been a captain in Hussars before his entry into Parliament. He had for some time sported a pair of small moustaches, indeed had provoked quite a "craze" for them among the young men of the town, which had still not fully abated, but this morning his lip was as bare as if it had all his life been innocent of hair; his side-whiskers too had been trimmed back to just below the ear. He wore a top hat and a coat with an astrakhan collar, so that it was difficult to determine whether he was making his way home very late, or had set out from it unusually early. It was said that in looks he resembled more his mother, but in his habits and the hours he kept he was incontrovertibly his father's son.

When the Marquis finally resolved to live only at Ormeau, the family's former butler, a man called Kerns, had taken over the house at the end of Donegall Place and turned it into the Royal Hotel, which by location and imprimatur quickly became the foremost establishment in the town. According to rumour, Lord Belfast had a room kept in it in permanent readiness – the same room he had slept in as a child – for those nights when the prospect of the journey to Ormeau, or of the reception awaiting him at the end of it, was too much to contemplate. There were other rumours, of the sort that men who would like to have an hotel room of their own to avail of will always put about, although on one occasion, it is true, I had seen – all who were abroad that noontime had seen – the Earl's wife, Lady Harriet, leave the Royal in a fury, infant son and daughter hurrying to keep pace with her, and get into the carriage in which she had drawn up just minutes before. I heard her voice, too, would wager I would have heard it had I been instead in my grandfather's house at the opposite end of the street. "What are you waiting for, you imbecile?" she shouted to the coach-man. "Go!"

≈.✿.≋

A falcon, also belonging to Mr Sinclair, was perched on the branch of a pear tree, overhanging the Castle wall, a matter of feet from Lord Belfast's top hat, as though waiting on him for its commands rather than on the falconer, wherever he had got to. It was as curious a grouping as could be imagined and for a moment, hearing the barking of the dogs echo off the narrow ravines of the streets, I had the uncomfortable sensation that any one of us shut up in our houses could be the quarry, so that when his lordship glanced up, in laughing, towards my grand-father's house I instinctively let go of the curtain and stepped back from the window. Would he notice where my fingers had wiped the glass and know that I had been watching?

When I dared to look again, some minutes later, the hounds, their master, the Earl and his mare were all gone from the street. Only the falcon remained, perched in the pear tree, pecking at the jesses attached to its ankle. Then the falconer at last arrived and held up his glove for the bird to hop on to and the street for an hour or two more was empty again.

≈.✿.≋

A Cantonese merchantman had anchored during the night at Garmoyle.

Davidson, one of the deputy dock masters, had rowed out at first light with Dr Forcade and reported back that there was no sign whatever of illness or infection among the crew, who should therefore be allowed to come ashore. In the course of the morning, however, word spread throughout the town that we were about to be invaded. Shortly after midday a delegation of weavers from Sandy Row arrived at the Ballast Office to demand that the ship be turned away. (They had been brought up perhaps on stories of the Rabbi who was kept from lecturing at the Exchange by an earlier generation of townsfolk concerned about "infection".)

Sir Clueless came down at length from his lookout post and after a few minutes more of pacing up and down and stroking his lapels went out on to the street to offer his reassurance. All on board were in excellent health, we heard him say (to the casual observer Ferris, Bright and I might have looked as though we had been nailed by the ears to the door): the weavers were welcome to ask Dr Forcade themselves. They, though, did not care a jot (though neither did they say "jot") for anything the doctor might have to tell them: Orientals were Orientals. Sir C said something else that was lost to us in the roar that greeted this piece of self-proving logic. There was a sound as of the handles of shovels or sledgehammers, whatever weavers were doing with shovels and sledgehammers, being struck on the ground. Gelston, the Harbour Constable, had meanwhile let himself in at the back door. "You boys look like you have been nailed up there," he observed, casually. He selected from the iron ring at his belt the key to the cabinet where his pistols were kept. I watched as, one after the other, he took them down and went through the business of loading – powder, wadding, ball . . . rod to ram the whole lot home – as briskly as if he were filling and tamping a pipe. I watched him tap a small measure of powder into each of the frizzen pans and set the firing pins from half-cock to full. He saw me staring. "The first one goes over their heads," he said, and after a moment smiled. Fortunately, before I could discover whether the joke was that both shots went over the heads, or that the first one in fact did not, Sir Clueless succeeded in making himself heard.

"Gentlemen, gentlemen! *Please!*"

It would go very ill for the town, he said, if merchant ships were to be turned away from it without good cause. We were an island nation, with an island nation's weaknesses as well as strengths. Where was the cotton to come from to feed their looms in the event of a retaliatory action? "We will all go over to flax," said one voice, and was roundly cheered for it. How, Sir Clueless persevered, would they otherwise get their finished goods, cotton or linen, to market? The cheering died. They were all, he knew, reasonable men; surely they must be able to arrive at some compromise.

Two hours later a small flotilla of rowboats began to land the crew at the head of the dock. In fact, there were as many Portuguese as Chinese among the sailors, although the former had to a man adopted the latter's long "queues" at the backs of their heads, their black silk caps and slippers, and the whole lot together had taken on that weathered hue common to seafarers the world over. They set up camp where they landed – such was the compromise – creating tents out of broom handles and sailcloth weighed down with barrels. In the course of the afternoon they washed their shirts and hung them to dry on the dock rail, and cooked food in shallow cauldrons that smelled like no food any of us had ever in our lives eaten and few of us ever would.

Ferris, who had gone out to take a closer look, reported back that several among the Chinese had passable English, and one had used his to express his bemusement at the hostility they had encountered: he had a brother living near to Pennyfields in London, who had previously visited Belfast without comment being passed. "But not with so many of his fellows," Ferris suggested to us, "and in all likelihood not during a cholera scare."

Towards evening the weavers returned to satisfy themselves that their terms were being adhered to. Gelston had kept the pistols loaded all day as a precaution, although, as he explained to us, once the balls were in, it was easier to row out and discharge them into the mud than try to unload them by hand.

While the weavers were there, a party of butchers, as Catholic as the others were Protestant, arrived from Hercules Street to ensure that Sandy Row did not imagine it had the sole right of refusal. (The Sailortown dockhands had fewer qualms. Some of the silk garments bartered for in the days that followed were features of the Belfast streets for years to come.) Mr John Hanlon had shown up too, a merchant who by virtue of his trade with that part of the world had assumed for himself the role of Vice Consul for Portugal and – by virtue of Portugal's recently ended interest there – Brazil. He, though, could neither engineer a lifting of the dock-head blockade, nor persuade any of the Europeans to abandon their comrades in favour of a night in his servants' quarters. They accepted, though, his offer of a barrel of port wine, which being opened without delay added greatly to the air of revelry.

As I walked away from the quays at the end of my day's work I passed the two younger daughters of my grandfather's immediate neighbour, who just happened to be on their way from the Flags to their singing master's house on Hamilton Street, a quarter of a mile in the opposite direction, and who wanted to know if it was true that the heathen sailors had been running around all afternoon (their mouths could scarcely sound the words) *half naked*.

"Yes," I said, leaning in towards them. "And do you know which half?"

Millar had sent me a letter in the course of the afternoon telling me that he had been called back to Gosford Castle, and asking if we might meet. We made a poor tea of ox tongue in aspic – poorer still with the memory so fresh of what I had earlier smelt cooking – in Magee's on High Street, where Millar had brought his boxes for the following morning's five o'clock coach to Enniskillen by way of Armagh. (For one who had so little regard for appearance he had an impressive amount of luggage: "I take my world with me each time I travel," he said with a shrug.) He was entirely ignorant of the excitement at the docks, but had spent the greater part of his day at Boyd's foundry on Donegall Street, where the columns were to be cast for the peripteral portico that would, he hoped, complete the rescue of the Third Presbyterian Church: ten of them in all, each weighing two tons.

"It will not, of course, be a feat to compare with dragging megaliths down from the hills to Ballynahatty" (as I now knew to be the name of that portion of Drumbo parish where stood the Giant's Ring), "but it will still be a sight to behold when they are delivered."

"I wouldn't miss it for worlds," I said.

"I will see to it that you don't."

He picked up a piece of tongue with his fork. In the premature twilight of Magee's rear parlour it resembled more a piece of the furnishing fallen on to his plate.

"I have been giving more thought to the church at Castlereagh," he told the tongue. "When I was in London I saw some drawings of the Temple of Apollo Epicurius at Bassae in Arcadia." He looked past the fork at me. "You will not have heard of it," he said, then, before I could thank him for his confidence in me, went on. "Scarcely anyone has. It was so inaccessible few *Greeks* had set eyes on it until late in the last century. The Frenchman who discovered its ruins was murdered by bandits; the first surveys made of it were lost in a storm at sea."

"I am bound as your friend to recommend that you steer well clear of it." I laid my hand on his wrist. He batted it away for the joke that it was . . . mostly.

"There are things in those drawings as yet untried in the modern era, in this island or the next, in the whole continent of Europe, that I know of. Imagine if they were to be attempted first in Belfast."

"In Castlereagh!"

"Why not? It is a good deal more accessible, and visible, than Bassae," he said.

We parted early, for he had an eight-hour journey ahead of him and a final check to make, before he slept, on Rosemary Street.

"I have left instructions with the foremen that if either of those buffoons shows his face the police are to be sent for at once," he said, and I had to ask myself again whether it was not Duff and Jackson who were most in need of protection.

I came round by the Castle gardens on my way home and

paused a few moments under the pear tree where Lord Belfast had earlier sat astride his grey mare. Of the hounds there was not a whimper to be heard now: huddled safe in their numbers while the night dogs roamed and howled. The foliage, I noticed, was particularly dense directly overhead. Perhaps I had misinterpreted this morning's little scene. Perhaps his lordship had been no more aware of the falcon's proximity, its scrutiny, than he was of mine, for – this too was only now apparent to me – he would have had to lean so far back to see my window he would likely have fallen from his saddle. Perhaps he was, after all, not the hunter, but the hunted.

I would afterwards return to this thought many times and to the unexpected thrill it produced, and I would ask myself whether that was the moment, before anything further had passed between Maria and me, between the Earl and the town, at which I realised that my destiny and Lord Belfast's were somehow intertwined.

"To see a lady drinking of tea is no news. To see a bird shoot a man in a tree is news indeed."

⁂

What with one thing and another – one thing and *John Millar* – a full week had passed since I last took the road out to the Mill for Grinding Old People Young, an omission I rectified the very next evening. Maria, when she saw me come in at the door to the main room, nodded, to herself, as it seemed: "Good."

It had been in my mind as I went to ask her if we might take a walk together some time, with – I thought it would be the done thing to suggest – one of the other girls from the inn, the Lord alone knew which, for company, although as it transpired, having had to wait again until the end of the night for the opportunity to ask it, I got no further than the first half of the question. "Of course. I should be delighted," she answered, without hesitation. She would have the whole of Sunday afternoon to herself.

Accordingly on the following Sunday I presented myself at the side gate of the inn at the hour agreed. My grandfather had passed comment on this second consecutive Sabbath excursion with my friend (I did not disabuse him of the notion that Millar was still in town), and on my cravat, which he fancied must be new, although as he recalled I had a perfectly serviceable one, bought for me only last Christmas.

I might have been wearing an ass's yoke for all the notice Maria took.

"Let us walk then," she said, whatever of delight she had felt in accepting the invitation having clearly evaporated in the interim, and set off at such a clip that I had almost to run to get into step with her.

"Is something wrong?" I asked.

"What could possibly be wrong?" she said, and I decided to pursue it no further. She would talk when she was ready. This, it turned out, was when we had already got halfway to Whitehouse, having overtaken in the process a dozen pairs of young ladies and gentlemen, walking at love's more leisurely pace, dawdling being long recognised as more effective than sprinting for shaking off a chaperone (for we passed an equal number of that species too).

She stopped abruptly by a milestone: Greencastle 2 . . . Carrickfergus 4½.

"Louisa tells me she was taken to see a mermaid in Carrick-fergus when she was a girl," she said, as though that had been the very thing that had been troubling her all the while. I remembered having heard the mermaid story from somebody else whose cousin's friend had seen it—or "her"—caught in a fisherman's net. I had never had reason till now to doubt it. "Do you think she could be in earnest?" I asked. Maria looked at me for almost the first time since we left the inn. I laughed. "Of course not," I saved her the trouble of answering. "It is absurd."

"She can describe for you in great detail the hair," Maria said, "'beautiful golden tresses, cascading down her back.'" Her hands described the contours. "But ask her an important question, about the tail for instance, how it attaches to the waist, and she is like a fish herself."

She performed the flapping mouth. I tried to steer my thoughts away from waists and tails, and, for different reasons, from the casual cruelty of Maria's mimicry.

"You must think us a very credulous lot."

I wondered had Louisa told her too about the people who went prospecting at night for the gold the Danes were supposed to have abandoned on the Cave Hill; or about the Fairies who with mists and spells made sure they did not find it. The Fairies at any rate were patent nonsense.

"No more credulous than people where I come from," Maria said, then paused. "It is just that I had been depending so much on the Reason of the people of Belfast."

I laughed again. I thought it was another test. She peered at me more nearly still.

"Why else would I have travelled halfway across Europe to reach here?"

A fat raindrop landed at that moment on the road between us, then another, and another.

"For the gentle climate?" I said, and she let out such an exclamation that a curlew, turning stones down by the shoreline, some thirty yards distant, took sudden flight, calling its name as it went.

As the raindrops continued to come down we fled ourselves for the cover of a nearby chestnut tree, whose lowest branches, growing out almost at right angles to the trunk, offered us in addition convenient seats on which to carry on our conversation. Because now that she had started to speak Maria was in no mood to stop.

Her family, she told me, were *szlachta*, members of the Polish nobility, which might have signified something for generations gone by, but by the time Maria was born, in terms of wealth and status, was all but meaningless. Every second or third family in the district where she lived were *szlachta*, and like Maria's the majority had no land to farm or to let; for some the coat of arms was the nearest thing to a coat that they possessed. "I have tried to explain this to Dorothy at the inn, but she is interested only in the first part. Every day it is, 'Pardon me, your *ladyship* ... If it is not too much trouble for you, *highness*.' I tell her what my father told us growing up: nobody ever ate a title. Better that they were all abolished."

Her father brought up Maria and her siblings to expect nothing and work for everything and above all to stand up for one another. I did not confess to my own doubts about her capacity for work, and of her "activities" in her current position she herself said only that, although she had been introduced to the English language at an early age, the dialect of the people here, and the speed at which they unleashed it, on occasion overwhelmed her.

When Maria was five her father showed her how to form a proper fist. "Do not make the childish mistake of tucking your thumb under the other fingers," he said. "Place it on the out side, like this: the lock that holds it all together. And, remember, when the punch connects, *grind* your knuckles. Whoever is on the receiving end will not be back to bother you in a hurry."

The word "mother" did not appear in any of these stories. Beyond a certain point "father", too, began to flit in and out. The Poland her father was born into had, before his childhood was at an end, been carved up between the Russians, the Prussians, and the Austrians. Several times when he was a young man he had chosen exile over foreign rule, but always he would find himself drawn back. Why should he have to be the one to leave, after all? His native country?

Maria was twelve when the Russian soldiers arrived at their house on the edge of the village and arrested him on charges of sedition. More than nine years would pass before she saw him again.

One day, not long after the arrest, a group of boys followed Maria and her brother Jan through the village, shouting taunts and insults. Maria ignored them for as long as she could possibly bear, then turned, thumb already pressing her fingernails into her palm. She singled out the biggest of her tormentors – Tomas, the carpenter's son – and before he even had a chance to retract his slanders, or repeat them to her face, caught him with her fist in the left eye, giving her knuckles a twist for good measure. The boy staggered backwards, yelling that he was blinded. She hit him again, on the side of his head, and felt the gristle of his ear yield. Where the third and fourth punches landed she could not have said, such was the rage that had now possessed her, but blood spattered her smock, her face and her hair. Jan pulled her off, urging her to run, fast, before the carpenter himself was alerted by his son's screams.

Her father was wrong, though. Tomas did come back to bother her, the next time she and Jan were in the village: he and seven others, older and bigger again. Together they dragged Maria off the path into the undergrowth beyond the forge. Jan managed to struggle free of the boy pinning his arms and ran for help. It was a quarter of an hour before he returned.

The teasing and name-calling got worse after that, but Maria went to the village regardless. Even if she had wanted to, she could not hide away for ever. Every now and then as the months passed she would come across Tomas, sitting on his own, pulling the legs off a grasshopper or something equally worthy of his talents, and she would look him in the eye – the eye she had ground her fist into, leaving him writhing on the dust and dirt – and the sneer would shrivel on his face. And she was satisfied then that, deep down, he knew it was he, not she, who had lost.

"I am sorry," I said into the silence she left after these words, although sorrow scarcely felt adequate.

"For what?" she asked. "For that? It saved me early on from a belief in mermaids and angels. There are in this world only people and dumb animals."

The rain had not amounted to much in the end, although the clouds had succeeded for a time in blotting out the County

Down side of the Lough. We remained where we were, underneath the tree, watching as pair by pair, chaperone by chaperone, those slower walkers we had earlier overtaken passed us by; watching and, on Maria's part at least, talking more.

I own that I did not always follow her story with ease. So complicated were the affairs of Poland – so numerous even were the names by which it had been known – that Ireland's history was made to seem straightforward, the history of the *Presbyterian Church* in Ireland, a model of harmony and decorum in comparison. I gathered, however, that at some stage in the tenth year after his arrest her father had been allowed to return to his family, and almost at once had joined with a clandestine group plotting to overthrow their ever more oppressive Russian rulers. Maria had been visiting an elderly and infirm aunt in Toruń when the Uprising finally occurred the previous November. Her first thought was to return home, but her father counselled against it. She should see out the winter where she was. Hard though it must be for Maria to accept, her aunt's call on her must take precedence for now. Besides which, the campaign against the Russians was progressing splendidly: by spring all of Poland would be liberated. Then two things happened at almost the same time. Maria's aunt suffered a fatal haemorrhage and the Russian army entered free Polish territory in overwhelming numbers. All around her in Toruń people were packing their belongings and closing up their houses. Maria, as the daughter of a known agitator, was in particular peril. Her aunt's friends and neighbours were anxious that she waste no time in escaping further west: her father could not be expected to write in the midst of such turmoil. But it was not her father's word she was waiting for.

"Ah," I said.

She looked at me askance. "I have never made a secret of him."

"No, you have not, although neither have you spoken of him directly, or even given him a name."

"I did not see how his name could possibly have meant anything to you, but as you wish: Colonel Ludwik Branicski."

"Colonel!"

"Please do not," she said.

"Do not what?"

"Do not say anything to make me regret coming here with you today."

She took from some fold or pocket in her dress a small cylindrical object – I had no name for it then, scarcely even a reference point – which she placed between her lips. From somewhere else she produced a "Lucifer" match (these at least I had seen, although not often) and, leaning forward, struck it against a stone at her feet. The fire positively roared from the tip, but by tilting the stem this way and that, Maria brought it under control, making of it a precise blade of flame. She touched it to the cylinder in her mouth and disappeared in a cloud of smoke.

Colonel Branicski, she said, when she re-emerged, was one of her father's fellow conspirators, twenty years older than Maria, a veteran of the Polish corps of the Grande Armée, and already married to a woman he no longer loved.

(She did not have to tell me to refrain from saying anything, for – between the smoke and the married man – my tongue by that stage had failed me utterly. I wondered could anyone see, or hear us from the road.)

He had sworn to her, had the Colonel, that once Poland was

freed he would complete the separation from his wife – for what were the bonds of marriage, after all, when set against the shackles of Empire? He told her that that was the secret meaning for him of the cockade he wore on his lancer's cap, the crimson and the white: their two lives entwined.

So she waited in Toruń, and waited, and waited, and waited. And the letter when it came was from her father. She was to go to Paris. No one was thinking of failure, even now, but it was important to prepare for all possible outcomes. There were people in Paris, loyal friends, with whom she was to make contact; they would instruct her how best now she could serve the cause. (Those were the words that tipped the balance for Maria.) He omitted from the list he gave her the name of Mme Branicski, yet hers was the first Polish face that Maria saw when she arrived in that city. She came down the staircase, into the hallway, of the house off the Place de l'Odéon to which Maria had been directed. "My dear child," she said, and laying her hands on Maria's shoulders placed three kisses on her cheeks. And Maria felt in the coldness of that embrace the certainty that her rival knew everything, had somehow arranged it that Maria would be summoned here, out of the Colonel's reach.

She lasted there for five days and nights. Five days and nights of false smiles and brittle conversations and meals left untouched on her plate. (Five days and nights in the course of which she had discovered for herself the habit of tobacco-smoking and its – temporary – calming effects.) On the morning of the sixth day she booked a seat in a coach out of the city, travelling north. What money she had had the journey from Toruń had all but consumed, but she had a few pieces of jewellery that her aunt had left to her and her brothers and sisters, which she had been determined to use only as a last resort. The flight from Paris was achieved at the expense of a small lapis lazuli aigrette brooch.

If she had any thought in her head that morning it was that she would make her way to London, where there was also a community of Poles, but the closer to that community she drew the less the prospect of it appealed to her. Who was to say that she would not find there too friends of Mme Branicski? It was while in the state of agitation – desperation – this thought brought on that she remembered the stories that her father had told her of his own exile to Paris as a young man, remembered in particular his meeting with an Irishman called . . .

The name came out almost as a cough with the last of the smoke from her lips. I had to ask her to repeat herself to make sure I had heard it correctly – "Tone" – then straight away hushed her. If there was one name more calculated than Henry Joy McCracken's to provoke argument, or worse, in our town, it was Wolfe Tone's.

I glanced towards the road, which was thankfully at that moment empty. "You must take care where you utter that name," I said in a whisper.

"So far I have only met one spy here," she replied and narrowed her eyes at me.

"It is no laughing matter."

"Oh, but to see your face," she said. "It is."

I checked the road once more. "You know what was the end of him?" I asked.

She nodded, solemn again. "I was brought up on it," she said.

Tone had talked often to her father about Belfast where, together with his wife and children, he had spent the final weeks before he was forced, on pain of imprisonment, into exile from Ireland. A town more committed to the cause of Liberty was not to be imagined. *The Rights of Man* was its holy book, its Qur'an. On one memorable occasion he had climbed, with a handful of the leading Qur'anites, to the summit of the Cave Hill, and there sworn a solemn oath never to rest until Ireland was free.

Every day that he had been away he had dreamed of sailing back into Belfast Lough to signal the start of the rebellion that would unite all Irishmen, irrespective of class or creed, against English rule. He laughed as he related this, "My *friends* would hound me out of Dublin all over again for saying so, but Belfast is the key."

By the time the rebellion did start, two years after their meeting, Maria's father was back in Poland. It was to be some months, therefore, before he learned that his friend Tone had never accomplished his dreamed-of return to Belfast, but was instead captured in lonely Lough Swilly, to the north-west, in French officer's uniform, and brought to Dublin to be tried. He asked that he be shot as a soldier. He was told that he would hang as a common criminal. He denied his enemies the satisfaction by cutting his throat as he sat in his cell on the day before that set for his execution.

"There are people here would say he should have been hung for good measure," I told Maria.

"And what would you say?" she asked, but spared me the embarrassment of being found wanting for a reply by continuing with her story. She was not quite sure what she had been expecting that morning, driving through the French countryside, when she made her decision to pass by London and travel on instead to Belfast. Of course, more than three decades had passed since her father and Wolfe Tone had talked together in Paris, but she liked to think that places, like people – cities, like citizens – possessed an essential character, which they retained no matter what the circumstances.

"A cornfield beneath the snow is still a cornfield," she said. "A graveyard is still a graveyard. The snow melts, the corn rises again."

"And the corpses?" I asked.

She regarded me with a faint puzzlement, so that I wondered whether she had forgotten the second part of her opposition.

"They lie where they always lie," she said with a shrug. "They are corpses."

What she had certainly not been expecting to find in Belfast was a town so consumed by the desire to make and spend money. Did no one ever talk of anything but yields and tariffs and returns on investment? Even the young people she over-heard at the inn appeared to have room in their heads for noth-ing else, unless it was silk stockings and cravats.

I almost said – pulling my coat collar closer about my own cravat – that she should meet my friend Millar, and was sur-prised at the jealousy the thought of their meeting provoked in me. I began to recount instead my conversation with him at the Giant's Ring . . . She laughed at the first mention of "Giant's", she had heard the Causeway on the northern coast so described: everything marvellous the work of mythical creatures! (I was gladder than ever that I had not mentioned the "little people" guarding the Danish gold.) I persisted. The Giant's Ring was very much the work of human hands, Millar's ancestors and my own. I would take her there some day to see for herself. And to the Museum when it was open . . . the Museum, which, I was quick to add, had been raised entirely by public subscription, a boast no other town on the island could make. Before long I was telling her – as though I had actually read it – of the History of the town, published several years previously by the son of one of my grandfather's friends, who was at the time not much above one and twenty, and who was letting it be known that he intended soon to add a second volume (an intention on which he would not deliver for a further fifty years – I said a word or two at the dinner to mark the occasion – having a business to attend to in the mean time), but anyway, to get back to Millar and me at the Giant's Ring . . .

I stopped. She was smiling.

"I am sorry. I did not mean to talk on so," I said.

"The criticism clearly stings. That is nothing to apologise for," she said. "I was perhaps too rash in my judgement of your generation, at least. So long as they do not concern themselves only with history and monuments."

The County Down shore had emerged once more from its rain-shroud, the fields, the fir trees, the few slate roofs, rinsed clean.

We came down off our seats in the chestnut tree and started walking back slowly the way we had come. But even slowly we covered the distance much too soon. We had got to within sight of the Mill before I could bring myself to ask the question that had been pressing like a weight against my chest.

"What makes you so sure your Colonel will write to you even now?"

She turned to face me. "What age are you?"

"I do not see what that can have to do with anything," I

said, but this time she did not talk over my embarrassment. She waited. "All right, then, I am eighteen," I said, and walked on. "Or will be soon."

"Then I would expect you to know," she said quickly, but not unkindly. "'My Colonel', as you call him, will send for me because of how he looked into my eyes when he swore it. I cannot believe he will not."

The crimson to her white, or the white to her crimson . . . I was not sure which way round they were supposed to be; not sure either I wanted to think about it too much.

But the days passed, turned into weeks, and still he did not send.

In the countries united under the crosses of St Andrew, St George and St Patrick, meanwhile, those weeks coincided with a General Election, the second since the death of the old King the year before. The new King – the old Duke of Clarence – had yet to be crowned, although that had not stopped him going in person to the House of Lords at the end of April to dissolve Parliament, for the purpose, as he said, of ascertaining the sense of his People on the question of Reform. The round dozen of his People resident in Belfast and entitled to vote returned, as before, and before, and before, a Chichester, unopposed, whatever His Majesty was able to ascertain from that. For the fifty thousand others, resident but unentitled, the day was remarkable only for the hail shower that appeared out of nowhere about eleven o'clock in the morning and in two minutes filled the gutters and gullies with ice, which by half past the hour had melted away again as though it had never been.

I walked with Maria whenever she would let me, which, as time went on, became whenever she had a couple of hours to herself. The chestnut tree, our habitual destination, was a shade now from the sun more often than a shelter from the rain. Between one week and the next in the middle of May it flowered, looking, as we approached it, as though someone had spent the previous seven days and nights decking it out in beeswax candles: a tribute, a gift. I bowed and held the branches for her to pass under. She responded with an imperious tilt of her head, her fingers wafting before my lips, just out of reach.

I took to going to the Commercial Rooms in my spare time, searching in the newsroom for any item of comfort to bring her. We had then, besides the town's five newspapers, dozens more across the whole island, which were regularly delivered, in addition to those brought by boat every week from London, Manchester and Glasgow. Keeping abreast of them all would have been full-time employment for three men. (There were, curiously, always *exactly* three men in the newsroom any time I went in, although never exactly the *same three*; they clearly operated shifts.) I was interested, though, in one story only, and soon knew where in each paper was the most likely place to find it. The lines, in truth, were few and far between. As May was drawing to a close, a report appeared of a battle for the town of Ostrołęka. The report told of a redoubtable Polish defence, hand-to-hand fighting, of disarray in the Russian ranks. It merited a visit that very evening to Maria, who would, I think, have hugged me when I gave her the news, if she had not at that moment been drawing the third of four pints of ale being loudly demanded by a party of men all wearing lawyers' jabots. When she had returned from serving, she drew a map for me on the counter with her finger: "Here is Ostrołęka. See? To the west of the scorch mark – Białystok – and north of Warsaw. It was vital that we held on to it." But when I turned the pages of the next issue of the paper, two days later, the victory had turned to a defeat, with only the heroic rearguard action of the cavalry standing between the Poles and complete annihilation.

I did not rush this time to bring her the news. And the Colonel still did not write.

Often Maria and I would pass our time together in complete silence, reading the books we had brought along with us, or simply watching the traffic on the Lough, the passage of the clouds across the sun, although there were times too when we would carry on like children, playing "chasies" around the tree trunk, tumbling to the ground at the limit of our breath and laughing. We were at ease in one another's company, but never so much so that, secluded though we were, we forgot ourselves. Our consciences were our chaperones, even if at times conscience on my part was indistinguishable from awkwardness and lack of experience.

She shared with me her cigarettes (she was my introduction to the word as well as the habit), of which she had brought a small supply from Paris, where they had been imported from Spain, restricting herself to one every week or ten days. For this reason as much as any other I refused at first when she suggested I join her in smoking. But she kept on at me, asked me if I was perhaps afraid to try, and in the end I said all right, then, I would.

Although I had by then seen her do it several times I could

not when put to it myself work out how to hold the thing, and could never afterwards correct the hold I improvised. She struck the Lucifer herself and touched it to the cigarette while I sucked.

And, oh ... I had never experienced such euphoria. I seemed to step out of time entirely, was scarcely conscious of Maria's voice as she asked me how I liked it. Tendrils of smoke drifted from my lips like the ghosts of every care I had ever had, exorcised. When at last I was able to raise my hand to my mouth again the cigarette was all but extinguished.

"You must carry on drawing in the smoke." She took the cigarette from me and blew on the tip. Her supply of Lucifers was nearly as precious as the cigarettes.

"I do not think I should have any more just now," I said, and sat on the ground. I was a long time getting up again.

On other occasions Maria wanted to talk about nothing but home, simple things like food – she never would have thought she would miss the cabbage rolls – and the subtly different quality of an early summer's evening.

And sometimes she returned to the topics of our first walk together, which were, in brief, the multiple currents and cross winds, blowing down decades and across continents, that had picked her up and set her down here in a tree on the north shore of Belfast Lough, talking to me.

Her father had carried back with him to Poland the names that Wolfe Tone had recited of the people who so distinguished the town of Belfast and long afterwards was, in his turn, still able to recite them to his children. Maria had forgotten most of them during the years of his imprisonment (she had almost forgotten the sound of her father's voice), but a few remained.

McCracken was one, Barclay another. Why this last had lodged in Maria's head she could not say – there was none of the glamour attached to it that attached to "McCracken" – any more than she could rationally account for the fact that on her arrival in the town almost the first person she spoke to, the housekeeper of a boarding house on Gamble Street, sent by her mistress to tell Maria there were no rooms, had used to work for Peggy of that name and her husband James, although that piece of information was not elicited then and there on the doorstep: that would have been too unsettling a coincidence. The housekeeper, rather, had taken pity on Maria and told her to come back later in the evening when her mistress was at her whist party and when a bed might be found for her for the night in among the servants.

James Barclay, she discovered then, was many years dead, and the tavern that he and his wife had kept in the town – the tavern Wolfe Tone would have known, the Dr Franklin – had long since passed into other hands and suffered a change of name. The housekeeper, however, was able the next morning to direct Maria to the widow Barclay's door ("find the shoreline, keep to it, believe me, you will not miss the sign"), where Maria, who had been on the road now the better part of a fortnight, promptly fell into a faint from which she did not rouse for three days.

Another thing that had lodged in Maria's head was Wolfe Tone's dream of sailing into Belfast to stimulate the rebellion. Fate might still have intended a gallows somewhere for him to cheat, but to be able first to carry off that Grand Gesture . . . she could only imagine with him that it would have made a difference – a sigh almost as she said this – all the difference in the world.

"Assuming" (was it possible to envy the dead?) "he could depend on the tide," I said.

In Belfast all things great and small came back to the tide.

Besides the newsrooms, I had begun to frequent with a greater regularity in those weeks Bourdot and Galbraith's in Castle Lane, where I would have my hair trimmed, with particular attention to the side-whiskers, and such beard as I had managed to grow since my last visit removed from my chin and upper lip. Bourdot was then, at a guess, in his sixtieth year, and so well established in the town as to have featured in one of the first jokes its children ever learned: "Have you heard, have you heard? Bourdot isn't cutting hair any longer." "No?" "No, he's cutting it shorter."

His father had been ship's barber with a French squadron – if three frigates add up to a squadron – that had landed at Carrickfergus, under the command of a Commodore Thurot, back in the mists of the Seven Years War. Thurot, who was either mad to begin with or turned that way by the calamities that had befallen him since leaving Dunkirk several months earlier (there had been five frigates then; there had been food), had demanded of Belfast a ransom of fifty thousand pounds, in addition to fifty hogsheads of claret, thirty pipes of brandy, twenty-five tons of bread and two tons of onions, in return for his not attacking it, and had got instead five thousand militiamen descending on him and causing him to put out to sea again – or at least to put out to the Lough, there to sit at anchor waiting for a tide in his favour.

The tide, when it came, brought every English frigate within a hundred miles.

They chased him as far as the Isle of Man, where battle was finally engaged. Thurot, leading from the front (courageous as well as crazed), was struck by a ball and almost instantly died, at which the remainder of the squadron lost heart and, within a very short time, surrendered.

Several score of French, meanwhile, had been stranded in the hasty retreat from Carrickfergus and brought back as prisoners to Belfast where they were billeted for three months before being released. (We had nothing against the French uniform, only Irishmen in it.) In gratitude for the hospitality shown them, they requested, and were granted, permission to hold a ball in the Market House the night before their departure, to which more than two hundred townspeople came and danced and drank into the early hours. Some of the prisoners, indeed, were so grateful that they preferred not, when the moment came, to return home at all, but stayed to marry local girls, raise families, start businesses, or, as in the case of Bourdot *père*, dynasties.

It was while sitting in his son's chair that I heard it suggested that Lord Belfast had been responsible for one of the town's more unusual spectacles. As Bourdot tilted my head forward, this particular morning, to "clean up" my neck, I heard the slap of wet feet on the pavement outside, and glancing, awkwardly, left, saw Tantra Barbus, the pedlar, pass in front of the window, water streaming from beneath his hat – which was, as was so often the case, the only dry thing about him – and the look on his face of a man set on drink. The gentleman in the chair beside me, to whose ear hair at that moment Mr Galbraith was bending his full attention, wondered aloud that Tantra was still alive. The gentleman was an infrequent visitor to Belfast these days, but once upon a time he had done a lot of business with McGarrigle on Custom House Quay. (Gone now, too, McGarrigle, he shouldn't be surprised, though there was no one bigger then in barilla.) He remembered one day when he was coming away from the warehouse – he was going back fifteen years here, maybe more – happening upon a commotion at the foot of the Long Bridge. Through the gaps in the crowd of onlookers he could see Tantra Barbus (he did not know him yet by name, had never till that moment clapped eyes on him), knee-deep in the Lagan. He asked the man standing next to him what was going on and was told that young Lord Belfast and his friends – "that's them at the front in the 'toppers'" – had wagered the pedlar sixpence that he could not swim across the river. This Tantra had already done, there and back, and was boasting he could do again, even though he had already swallowed a quantity of gin by way of reward for the first swim, or reviver from it.

"Here was Lord Belfast to him, 'It can't be done.' Says Tantra, 'Ho, can it not?' And d— me if he didn't dive back in," the gentleman said and leaned a little towards me (Galbraith had moved on to his other ear). "He was like a *porpoise*. Under . . . then, just when you began to fear he was gone for good . . . up! He waved from the far bank before starting across again, could not have been more than half a minute getting his breath. When he arrived back he held out his hand and Lord Belfast put fivepence in it. 'What's this?' says Tantra. 'You gave me six the last time.' And Lord Belfast said, 'Yes, but last time it had the bonus of novelty.'"

Bourdot had come to stand before me and was raising my

chin on the point of his index finger to see that my side-whiskers were even.

"Are you quite sure", he said to the gentleman, directly into my face, "that was the first time?"

"As sure as I am sitting here," said the gentleman, and stood up, now that Galbraith had laid off his ears, to get his pipe from the shelf below the mirror.

Bourdot frowned at me, turned my head to the left, to the right. "I suppose it is a fi'penny he still asks," he said.

"Enough," said Galbraith, a man of fewer words than his partner, "for a half pint of gin."

"I am surprised he can command even that," said the gentleman, who had settled himself again in anticipation of the Bay Rum. "There is surely not a person in Belfast who has not seen it done by now. Unless, given the age of him, they pay in hope of seeing him one of these days drown."

It was while sitting in Bourdot's chair, too, on a morning early in June that I learned of the editorial carried by the newest of our newspapers, the *Northern Whig*, raging against the Chichesters' latest obstruction to the Harbour Bill. "Reformers of Belfast," Bourdot himself read aloud, a trace in his accent all of a sudden of his father and the Seven Years War, "Lord Belfast has refused to present your Petition for reform; merchants and freeholders of Belfast, his papa has ordered him to oppose the very first Bill you apply for, to mend your quays and improve your harbour. However the whole procedure admirably illustrates the base and villainous corruption on which our present representative system is founded; and ought to urge us all the more strenuously to procure such a Reform as will extricate the people out of the hands of the Aristocracy."

Bourdot lowered the paper. "Well, that is one way to get your newspaper noticed," he said.

Two nights later a pane of glass was broken at the front of the *Northern Whig* building on Calendar Street. The night constables, responding to the sound, gave chase to two men whom they had seen running from the street, but who, when the constables finally caught up with them on Bank Lane, were found to be the father of a dangerously sick child and the doctor he had summoned to attend her; so that the constables were still making their apologies and bickering among themselves when, at the far end of High Street from Bank Lane, a window was smashed in the Ballast Office too. A page tied to the brick found on the floor of the *Whig* proclaimed the perpetrators "Friends of the True Friends of Belfast". All we got was the brick. Bright, turning the missile over in his hands while I swept the debris from our desks, said he would bet his last farthing that these Friends of Friends were in fact lighter pilots whose trade to and from Garmoyle would be extinguished by an easier access to the town. Sir Clueless, he reminded us, had already had to deal with several delegations anxious for detail – not least of the amount of compensation proposed – and we could not, surely, have failed to notice ourselves a less than warm welcome these days in one or two of the taverns where we took our lunches, cheek by jowl with the boatmen. (If they had only known the part I had played in Mr Walker's investigations the welcome might have been several degrees cooler again.) Ferris, however, was of the opinion that the Donegalls themselves, if not actually putting bricks into the vandals' hands, had played an inciting role: witness the recent lavish dinner at Ormeau, to

which certain only of the town's merchants had been invited –
as clear an attempt to create dissension as you could wish to see.

"Or as obvious a means of gaining Lord Donegall a few more
weeks' grace from those gentlemen on his outstanding bills,"
said Bright, whose radicalism seemed to have peaked with the
outburst in my sickroom. He had arrived to work one Monday
morning not long before in high excitement, having on the previous Saturday evening attended a magnificent cock-match in
a pit at Hill Street. Over thirty pairs of birds had flown in the
course of the night and the spectators numbered four or five
times that. A group of students from the Academical Institution were there to cheer on their favourite, a Ginger – "Big
Red" – owned by McAdam that had the farm at Woodstock.
("Of course, *McAdam*," I said. "Never heard of him." "Ha,"
said Bright. "Ha and ha-ha.") At some point, that particular
match not going their favourite's way, the students accused his
adversary's owner of fighting Big Red's own blood against him.
One of them, the worse for drink, leapt into the pit and in
his confused state laid out *McAdam*'s man with a single punch,
which was the signal for a couple of Brown's Square boys to
leap in and exact retribution and things might have gone very
badly indeed for the student and his friends, who were threatening to call down the constabulary, had not Lord Belfast himself at that moment stepped forward from an alcove where he
had been watching with friends of his own. No one present, he
was sure, wanted to involve the police in this matter. No one,
suddenly, did. He enquired of the rival cock's owner whether
there was any truth in the allegation made by Red's support-
ers, which as all sportsmen knew was a very serious one. The
man swore on his mother's grave, his wife's good name, his chil-

dren's eyes, that he would never wittingly fight blood against blood, to which Lord Belfast responded by asking the scholar if he would accept a fellow sportsman's word of honour, and that he readily agreed to do, or as readily as anyone can whose lip is split and swollen and whose blood is running pure whiskey. Next, his lordship had the Brown's Square boys shake the student's hand. "Fair does to you, Mucker," said one (Bright overdid the accent), "you have some punch on you" – before finally he knelt by McAdam's man to whom salts had been in the mean time administered. The man was soon on his feet again – positively sprang to them in his surprise at finding a Member of Parliament squinting down at him – and having received the thick-lipped apology of his assailant, pronounced himself fit to carry on. No sooner was the match resumed than Big Red flew, spurs up, at the other bird's head, knocking him off his feet. In another minute Red had him finished off, to Lord Belfast's evident satisfaction. He had stood to lose twenty-five guineas had the contest gone the other way.

"A fly man and no mistake," was Bright's admiring verdict on the whole performance.

Ferris was contemptuous. "I was only at one cockfight in my life. The spectators squawked worse than the chickens. And the stink of blood for days after . . ."

"So speaks the man," Bright retorted, "whose idea of sport is to *blast* duck and snipe to kingdom come with a blunderbuss."

"Fowling piece. And at least we hunters give the birds a chance; at least we have to exercise some skill. We are confined to barrels half the time, for goodness' sake. The cocks are pure savagery. I am with the Prevention of Cruelty people on that."

The Society had made its first appearance in the town a year or two before (with too much to combat in the present – I am, in one sense only, glad to say – to be concerned with past misdeeds). Unless I was greatly mistaken, Miss McCracken was at the centre of it.

"They were there, too, on Saturday," said Bright, and tried to suppress a smile. "The students and the Brown's Square boys chased them up Hill Street swinging the corpses of the vanquished by the feet."

He flapped his arms at Ferris, who recoiled. "Ugh!"

"Lord Belfast," I said to myself.

"What about him?" asked Bright.

"Lord Belfast," I *thought* I said to myself.

"He is a fortunate man," said Ferris, "that wife . . ."

"That temper!" said Bright.

"That challenge!"

And from here the conversation veered off again and my own blushes were spared at the expense of the women of Belfast, young and not so young.

꙯

In the wake of the glass-breaking, Sir Clueless gathered us all together one afternoon in the Ballast Office, masters, deputy masters, constable and clerks. Even the cat was there, at least in body. (From the twitches of its paws and whiskers, it seemed its sleeping soul was somewhere else entirely.) The higher-ups sat on chairs arranged in a semicircle in front of the desks, on which the lower-downs knelt, becoming for that briefest of interludes, and in that most meaningless of ways, the higher-ups themselves. My head – as the lowest and therefore the highest in the Office – was level with the top of the chart displaying the progress of the cholera. The day before I had been tasked with placing a pin next to the Russian port of Riga, from where, it was reported, sixty vessels had earlier in the week fled before they could be impounded. At least four of them were intent on Sunderland in the north-east of England, giving rise to calls for a general quarantine on all Baltic shipping.

"Gentlemen," Sir Clueless said, and applied his thumbs with vigour to his lapels. A few more such speeches and he would be right through to his shirt. "Feelings are running high in the town. I need not enumerate the reasons why. You will all undoubtedly have your own opinions on where we find ourselves at present, I would not want men here who did not, but it is not for us to become involved in debates or speculation." (Bright, in front of me, nudged Ferris a moment before Ferris could nudge Bright.) "Our duty is clear. We are to carry out the directions of the Board and, ultimately, of the Parliament. Both of these, I need hardly add, are subject to the change that all the institutions of Man are subject to." A sound outside of a rope snapping quickly followed by a crash, the splintering of wood, all accompanied by a lexicon of curses. This sort of "violence", at least, we were used to on the docks. The Master of all Ballast pitched his next line a fraction higher. "We have another duty, however, which is to the river and the quays, to maintain them for the use of generations yet to come. It is on this that we must concentrate our efforts. However ill advised we might in private think are the plans – any plans – we are asked to execute, we must execute them in such a way as causes the least injury. Let us . . ." he coughed. "Let us be the men for the small details."

Somewhere around "generations yet to come" he had exceeded in duration anything we had ever heard him say, even to the Sandy Row weavers. Still, we waited for him to exceed it in distinction, and when no more was forthcoming, bar another "Gentlemen" as he turned to climb the stairs again, the whole company of us, high and low, fell to debating and speculating. We carried it on into the tavern next door, entering more like a band of brothers – or at least of uncles and nephews – than a group of men assembled by the mere circumstance of employment for attention to small details: *Now, who dares say anything agin us?*

My last memory is of singing "Sally in Our Alley" under a lamp near to Corn Market. Courtney, the north-side Harbour Master, had his arm around my shoulder, heavy as an anchor, his voice so far off-key as now and then to be approaching it again by the back door.

"Of all the days that's in the week, I dearly love but one day, and that's the day that comes betwixt a Saturday and Monday . . ."

I was woken in the dead of night by a hand on the same shoulder. I recoiled from the shock of it so that I would have tumbled out of bed on the other side had there been more than a foot between it and the wall. The new girl, Hannah, leaned over me shielding a candle.

"I am sorry, sir," she said, her voice not much above a whisper. "I knocked and knocked as loud as I dared. Only there is a lady in the kitchen wishing to speak to you."

"In the kitchen?"

"Yes, sir." Hannah turned her back and I realised that I had without thinking swung my legs out of the bed. I pulled the counterpane over them again, but was conscious of my shins and feet still being uncovered. Hannah addressed the wall. "The lady came in by the gardens, sir, and rapped on the window." Her voice grew fainter still. "I thought for a moment she was a ghost."

I asked Hannah was my grandfather roused too, but, no, she said, there was no one else awake but her. The house was still new to her, she had not yet learned to reconcile herself to its creaks and groans, and for that reason preferred to make up a bed in the kitchen, where she had the fire for comfort, otherwise she might never have heard the lady herself. Besides – she said it again – the lady had asked very particularly if she could speak to me.

I thanked her then for taking such care in delivering the message, as though a lady clambering over the back gardens in the middle of the night was an occurrence of no great irregularity or impropriety with us, and asked her to see to it that the lady was comfortably installed. "You are right," I said, "there is no need for anyone else to be disturbed."

My clothes lay where I had dropped them when Courtney had finally weighed anchor and I was able to stagger home. As soon as Hannah had closed the door behind her, I dressed to my waistcoat and, taking my boots in my hand, descended through the house in stockinged feet. My laces were still not tied when I eased open the door into the kitchen.

Hannah was standing just inside, looking at her hands crossed on her skirts. She did not wait for me to ask her to withdraw.

Maria sat, very still, very upright, at the table where Hannah and Molly took their meals (Nisbet was rarely to be found back here these days), a tin cup before her, a candle to one side. She was wearing, I was almost certain, the same dress and lace pelerine as she had worn on the last occasion that I had seen her in town. The bonnet she had had on then nestled in her lap, the brim peeping over the table edge.

"Hannah has looked after you?" I said.

"Yes, thank you."

Were it not for the candle, we might have been talking at three in the afternoon rather than in the morning.

She tilted the cup towards her. "*Máslanka*," she said. "I forget what the word is in English."

I came to stand beside her. Two strings of onions hung down from the beam above the table, rendered so many shrunken heads by the candlelight. "May I?" I lifted the cup to my nose and straight away withdrew it again. "Buttermilk," I said (I had never been able to stomach the stuff), "like the lane – the 'loney'," and Maria nodded, then all at once began to sob, burying her face in her hands. She was so dreadfully, dreadfully sorry for turning up at my house at such an hour, she said through the tears, but since I had once offered her my protection while she was in Belfast . . . Of course, I said, of course. I dropped to my knees by her chair.

"Whatever can have happened to you?" I asked.

She stood up, spilling her bonnet on to the floor, drawing the candle flame behind her. It was all so foolish and embarrassing, she who had teased me for my inexperience, to have been trapped as she had been trapped tonight.

"Maria!" I exclaimed then, collecting myself, whispered urgently. "In the name of G—, tell me what has happened."

"You must not think ill of me," she said as she sat. I promised her I would not, though in truth the images already cavorting across my mind were more grotesque than anything the candle-light could conjure.

She had, she said, when the flame had settled again, come to town tonight hoping to meet a gentleman – she gave the word some consideration before deciding it was the one she wanted who had offered to help her with her passage to the free port of Odessa, which – I would forgive her, she hoped, if she did not attempt a map tonight – lay fewer than five hundred miles from her home in Łuków.

"So, he has written at last," I said.

She drew a sigh: I was breaking the thread. "No, 'he' has not, but it was never my intention to stay here for ever. Lately I had tried to put hopes of leaving soon out of my head, but then a few nights ago I found myself in conversation with this . . ." – gentleman the second time was too much – "person . . ."

"At the inn?" I knew how petulant I must sound, but I could not help myself. The thought of her talking to anyone else there as she had talked to me filled me with a jealousy close to ungovernable.

She stopped. She had got the better of her tears completely now. "Perhaps I should not have come after all."

"Please," I said, "go on."

"I had met him first when I was in town on other business," she proceeded, as slowly as if she were testing ice with her toe. "Looking for a pawnbroker to take more of your aunt's jewels," I thought, but bit down on my lip, determined not to "crack" again. "He said he had an interest in a merchant ship, which sailed regularly to the Black Sea. He even had a friend in Odessa, a Turk, who could assist me with the onward journey by coach." For a moment she was transported by the mere word. "Perhaps even less than five hundred miles . . ." She shook her head, returning to the kitchen in Donegall Place, to the handle of the mug of *máslanka*, which she turned this way and that. "He would not listen to talk of money. He said, 'I am sure we can come to some arrangement.'" She paused; seemed for a moment to grow a little smaller. "What would you think if a person said this to you, 'we can come to some arrangement'?"

"Only that," I said feebly. "An arrangement."

She shook her head again, as though appalled anew at her own naivety, at the slipperiness of our language. She drew herself up once more to her full height. On her arrival at the "person's" house tonight (she would not name even the street, although I was narrowing it down to one of two or three), the arrangement had been laid before her in the most explicit terms imaginable and by then it was too late for her easily to extricate herself. So she had tried to keep him talking, and drinking (for that, at least, he needed little persuasion), drinking and talking, until, just when she had begun to fear that she would run out of things to say, or he of things to drink, he had finally got up to relieve himself – for one heart-sinking moment she had thought he meant to use the fireplace, but no, some vestige of decorum lived on within him; he carried on out to the privy – and she had fled.

"My hands were trembling so much I thought I would not be able to turn the key in the lock. Once I was outside I did not stop or look back. I was afraid that if I took the road to the inn he would catch up with me out there in the darkness. I was saying your name over and over as I ran. All I could think of was finding you."

I had started to raise myself up off my knees, but stopped. "How did you know where I lived?"

"The day you were carried into the inn. Your friends gave instructions when they were sending for the carriage to take you back to town."

"You have a good memory."

"It is the exile's refuge," she came back at once.

"And a very good sense of direction to come in by the back way."

"I knew the gate," she said, then hesitated. "I mean, I had walked down there once before in the daytime."

"So, you have been doing some spying of your own?" The idea delighted me.

She frowned. "Not spying . . . Only looking."

Before the last word was out I had leaned forward and kissed her cheek. She averted her face, touching the spot where my lips had landed, then turned back to me. I kissed her mouth, which opened a little, as if in surprise, although it did not close again when the first moment passed, but pressed forward against my own, drawing on my tongue with hers, and now the surprise was all mine, that I was being admitted into this other being, to where her voice resided, her very breath. I felt as I had felt that far-off day when I had put out in the boat with the Second Greatest Engineer in the Empire, that everything I had up to then counted on as a certainty was drifting away from me. This time I did not care if it ever came back.

Maria placed her hand on my jaw, turning my head aside.

All at once I was appalled at myself: she had run to me for refuge from one brutish man and now I, too, was taking advantage.

"Forgive me," I said.

"No," the hand on my face softened to a caress, "I am the one who should ask you for forgiveness. Really, I should not have come here like this."

I started to protest: I would not have had her do otherwise. She stopped me with her fingers on my lips. I heard a movement, a scuffling, where the dresser stood, on the far side of the room. "Mouse," she whispered, close to my face, "too quiet for rat," then, drawing back, breathed out like one defeated. "This is not wise."

"If wise is all," I said and, acting on I knew not what, took one of her fingertips between my teeth. Her arm went rigid, as though I had discovered a paralysing nerve. I ran my tongue over the pad of that finger and the next, my eyes fixed firmly on hers, glittering in the candlelight. The third finger was in my mouth, then the fourth. Her tongue moved behind her parted lips, mirroring the motion of my own. I placed an arm about her waist and drew her to me. She resisted only for as long as it took her to lean across and blow out the candle.

Light was already leaking into the sky beyond the kitchen window. We had minutes together, not hours, although I could scarcely have told you one from the other; it was nothing like enough time and it was time enough; the axis of my life had tilted.

At the first stirrings on the house side of the kitchen door, we drew apart. I held her face in my hands. Her eyes were closed. I had never seen her so at peace, had never felt myself so comfortable in another's presence, so unaware of where one of us ended and the other began. I kissed each eyelid in turn and felt the kisses as though the lips were hers, the eyelids mine. She

144

murmured something that I neither caught nor asked her to repeat. The expression on her face told me all that I needed to know. It looked how I imagined my own did at that moment.

And then, like the minutes that had led up to it, that moment too passed.

Maria adjusted her dress. I retrieved her pelerine from the foot of the chair, her bonnet from where it had come to rest under the table. The latter's lace trim had picked up dust, stray hairs, and a single grey down feather on its journey. I blew along it. The feather, and hairs, took harmless flight, but the dust, having soot in it too, left behind a smirch.

"I am afraid your bonnet has got a bit grubby," I said.

She took it from me and rubbed the mark carelessly between forefinger and thumb, which only had the effect of smudging it more. "There," she said. "All better."

I led her across the yard and through the gardens, past the midden, past the privy, past the hen run, past beds of scallions and peas and raspberry bushes just coming into flower, to the gate on to Fountain Street. Several gardens down, Mr Sinclair's dogs were baying to be let loose on the town. He had run them only the morning before; I knew, even if the dogs did not, that they would not be out again so soon.

"Take the next street on the right. I will meet you at the end of it in five minutes," I said. Maria rocked forward on her toes and placed a final kiss on my lips.

"I know the way. Remember?" she said, then slipped out through the gate. Dew had saturated the toe of my boots. It had seeped through the stitching of the soles. I might as well have been barefoot.

Hannah had returned to the kitchen in the time that I had

been out and was tending to the fire. She rose and curtsied as I came in. At almost the same moment, Molly entered the kitchen from the other end, fastening her apron, frowning. "Have you that fire never lit yet . . . ? Oh!" She held a hand theatrically to her breast. "I had not expected to see you at this hour, Master Gilbert."

"The birds woke me," I said.

Hannah, who had knelt again before the hearth, said nothing.

"It is the time of year for them, all right," said Molly. Her eyes lit on the remains of Maria's buttermilk. I picked up the cup and drank it off, squeezing my eyes shut against the tang. When I opened them, Molly's head was angled to one side. Could this be the same wee boy who had told her on more than one occasion when he was growing that she could keep her buttermilk for bleaching the table linen? I smacked my lips. She shook her head then took a basket from a hook by the door and continued into the yard. When she had gone I went out to the cloakroom where a search of the coat I had worn the night before yielded a farthing and two sixpences, and not, as the smell of the thing suggested, a couple of pipes with their ashes still in them. I came back to the kitchen and, bending down, placed the sixpences in the pocket of Hannah's apron. She acknowledged them with a bob of her head and shoulders.

"The lady was able to make her way home shortly after you retired," I told her; again the bob. Molly returned, her basket already in that short time four eggs the heavier, but lighter still than she could have hoped. "It is a wonder they have not stopped laying altogether," she said, "the sound of those dogs."

I asked her to tell my grandfather that I had gone to work early and would see him that evening at supper.

First the crack-of-dawn rising, then the buttermilk, now the haste to get to work . . . Molly's eyebrows signalled that no one could tell her there were not still surprises to be had in this world of ours.

The Flags were in shadow when I stepped outside, but a broad band of sunlight slanted across the front of the White Linen Hall to my right, a perfect demonstration of the points of the weathervane perched on its cupola, and a fair reflection of my altered outlook on the world. I turned left, north, and found Maria waiting where I had directed, at the junction with Castle Street. She fell in beside me without a word. I do not know that we so much as turned to look at one another directly. At some point, however, before we had reached the forty-seventh, or forty-ninth, butcher's shop on Hercules Street, she threaded a hand under my arm, which I crooked, laying my own hand on hers. It pleased me to think that no one seeing such a chaste arrangement of limbs would guess how intimately they had been entangled just a short time before, unless Maria's jaunty twirling of her bonnet, attached by its ribbons to her free wrist, was a signal, or be able to detect the currents that continued to flow beneath the surface of the skin, heightening every sense. The sky looked bluer, the breeze smelled fresher; when a child's laugh rang out from behind the door of one roadside cottage I would have sworn I had never before heard a sound as sweet.

On the Milewater Bridge an old woman tossed crusts for the gulls that manoeuvred for advantage in the air above her head. She smiled out from under her shawl as we passed, teeth insufficient to the scraps she gave away, told us we would do a body's heart the "power of good" – yes indeed, the power of good.

The Mill announced itself with columns of smoke from the largest of its chimneys: building up steam for another day's grinding. We stopped short of it, arms once more by our sides.

"Who would ever have dreamt this?" Maria said quietly, and I did not tell her that I had many times dreamt something like it, for in truth none of those dreams came close.

"I will come back tonight," I said.

"No, not tonight. It will be as much as I can do to fill up the pots without washing the floor with ale. And you, too," she said, "will want rest."

"Tomorrow, then."

She nodded. "Tomorrow."

Neither of us attempted to kiss the other, as though that had been an explicit agreement between us. I watched her walk away from me, wondering would she turn then wondering that she did not then wondering whether her not turning was an indication of her certainty that I was still there, or her fear that I had already left, or indeed of her complete indifference to my staying or going. She had arrived almost at the archway to the stables before she looked back. I saw her hand go to her lips. I saw it reach towards me, her head tip forward in the act of blowing.

She nearly knocked me off my feet.

Who had need of hot-air balloons? I *flew* back to town under the power of that kiss. I had had so little sleep and yet my legs were light – not the least trace now of hurt – my lungs seemingly inexhaustible. I felt as though I could run and run and run. I was seventeen! Why should I ever stop? I leapt bushes, I leapt logs, I leapt a three-legged dog that was too slow to get out of my path. I scattered the gulls on the Milewater Bridge, shouted "hello" to the old woman who had attracted them there. Down York Street, I ran, down Donegall Street, along the front of the Commercial Buildings, down Sugarhouse Entry, round a parked sedan chair from which a pair of legs stuck out (the sedan man's? a reveller's, too drunk to remember which way home lay?), left on to High Street, past Skipper Street, Bluebell Entry, Quay Lane, arriving at last at Chichester Quay and the door of the Ballast Office.

Bright had arrived just ahead of me. He looked as though he had just that moment stepped out of Bourdot and Galbraith's.

"Heavens!" he exclaimed, then glanced behind me. "Do you think you managed to shake off the hounds?"

An image came to me of Lord Belfast on his grey mare, amid the writhing mass of Sinclair's hunting pack. I stood, hands on hips, waiting for my breath at least to catch up with me. Bright narrowed one eye at me. "Another kind of pursuit? Two legs, cuckold's horns?"

He made the sign above his head – index finger and little finger extended – then quickly turned them into a comb, which he drew, needlessly, through his hair. Sir Clueless was coming towards us, nose stuck in the shipping news. There were boats in want of ballast, or very soon would be, there was silt and sand as yet undredged. "Boys," he said, more an identification of a species than a greeting. He selected a key from the ring at his waist. We entered behind him. The heels of his shoes were worn almost to the wooden block: all that pacing about he did in the course of a day.

"Do not think you can get away without telling me about it," Bright said out of the side of his mouth.

"You are the last person I would tell anything to," I replied, which in appealing to his sense of himself as a rake seemed to satisfy him.

The atmosphere in the office that day was especially close, but our Cantonese visitors and their skillets had gone from the head of the dock (they had left behind a quantity of tea and taken away a load of flax, so that Belfast was a hundred pounds the richer for having tolerated their presence) and, with the tide down, the only smells the windows would admit would be of the town's own making. It was preferable to stew. By mid-morning I was barely able to hold my head up. I found a reason to go to the chartroom, towards the rear of which was a broad lower shelf, marked "Abnormal Fluctuations Copeland Islands", where, it was common knowledge among the younger clerks, you could stretch out undetected for a quarter of – or even half – an hour.

When I opened my eyes that day I knew at once, from the foreshortening of the shadows on the floor, that something closer to two hours had elapsed. Ferris made a cutting motion with his finger across his throat as I took my seat again.

"Sir Clueless was here," he said in a stage whisper. "Twice."

A few minutes later he appeared a third time. "Mis-ter Rice," he said, and attempting a showman's sweep of his arm, indicated the stairs leading up to his office. "If you would be so kind."

I followed at his worn-down heels. The tide had turned while I slept. From the window facing his chair all that could be seen was water and masts – the port's problems in that moment utterly erased – and one flank of the steamer *Hibernia*, which plied the Liverpool route, and which had taken advantage of the favourable conditions to berth at Donegall Quay to the north of us, in the direction of Ritchie's Dock.

An earthenware jar of quills stood at one corner of the desk and next to it a case, lined with blue velvet, in which lay the pen Sir C reserved for his most important letters. He picked up this pen at moments while he spoke to me, testing the nib against his thumb, turning the ivory shaft in his fingers as though it were a flute and he was looking for the hole to blow into.

I had, he began, always given a good account of myself. Mr Walker, when he had visited last year, had spoken very highly of me: very highly. Of late, however, he, Sir C, had noticed something a little – rolling the pen between his fingertips – wayward in my behaviour. He did not know how to account for it, but at this critical time especially the Ballast Board was no place for idlers and scatterbrains. He placed the pen in its case and closed the lid, clasping his hands to dissuade them from further footering. Seconds, they lasted.

"I hope I will not have occasion to speak to you again, or indeed" – I was saying the words in my head before he spoke them – "to your grandfather."

I assured him I would give him no such occasion.

"And one other thing," he said. I turned, halfway to the door. A black-headed gull passed the length of the window, its beak red-inked, its eye on the bald-headed specimen and the tufted juvenile facing each other across the lacquered pool of the desk. "I have been here since I was not much older than you are now. The Copeland Islands Fluctuations shelf was there then. You might inform your fellow clerks."

"So?" Ferris wanted to know when I had come down. "What did he say?"

"Nothing important," I replied.

Somehow I got through the rest of that day with my eyes open, although of anything I might have done in it not a single memory survives.

On the morning of the following day a letter arrived for me as I was leaving the house. I had never seen Maria's handwriting before, but – something in the alien cast of the "l" and "r" – straight away recognised as hers the hand that had addressed the envelope. I tucked myself into an entry up the side of the Castle gardens to read it, although so eager was I for what I hoped to see that it was several moments before I could make sense of what I did.

My Dear Gilbert,

    The hour is late and my arm most weary. It is not this, however, that I refer to, but the pain in my heart, when I say I do not for one moment imagine that this letter will be easier for you to read than it is for me to write. But I do not know either what I can have been thinking, last night, putting myself in such a position, exposing the two of us to risk of discovery. I have pledged my love to another, who, I must continue to believe, will send for me soon. We have to be sure that we do not in future allow ourselves to be overtaken in that fashion. Therefore . . .

I tore the page in half, quarters, eighths, sixteenths, thirty-seconds, and in my fury at not being able to tear it more flung the pieces before me as I stepped out from the entry for the shoes and hooves and wheels of the town to finish off.

How could she? Addressing me as though I were some . . .

accident that she had let happen. The tip of my tongue had not yet ceased to smart where in a sudden paroxysm she had caught it between her teeth. Her scent was still ingrained in the lines of my hands, the creases between my fingers, and on other places to where those same fingers had, all through the night just past, time and again strayed.

How could she?

A greengrocer heading to Montgomery's market with a box of lettuces on his shoulder, and reading in the tearing and scattering what I had read in the letter itself, shouted his sympathy. "You're better off without, son. The lassies are as alike as these here butterheads."

Ferris and Bright were getting up a party to go that night to the theatre and on afterwards to whatever entertainment they could devise or divine. A bosom friend – they had no other kind – had been up before the Manor Court the previous day to agree a schedule for the repayment of his old debts and was in a mood to start running up a few new ones. But I had no desire whatever for company, was prepared to go to any length to avoid it. And there was no greater length in town than the Long Bridge, all twenty-five hundred feet of it, over the river into Ballymacarrett and County Down. I crossed directly I was finished work, when the traffic was mercifully all tending in the one direction, for the Long Bridge could with equal merit have borne the name of Narrow Bridge, and I still carried in my head Millar's hints as to the dire state of its undersides.

I started at the foot of the Donaghadee Road and worked my way up, which is to say east: Miscampbell, McComb, Armstrong, Beatty, Crossan, O'Kane . . . If a sign hung over the door I entered under it. I drank ale, I drank porter, I drank gin, I drank rum. I ate only that I might drink more: some bread and a piece of cheese that had been too long out of the larder, if indeed it had ever seen the inside of one, a plate of something resembling something that had once resembled beef; an egg, about which the less said the better. Between taverns, I passed cottage after cottage from which – even now that the age of great mills and manufactories was upon us, and, more immediately, that the dinner hour was upon us too – the sound of individual wheels and handlooms emanated. The smoke that came with it was pure turf; the floors, glimpsed over the half doors, were mud. I might rather have traversed decades of time than the twenty-one arches of the Long Bridge.

I was above two hours covering the mile to the lesser bridge over the Connswater River, which I now decided had all along been my ambition. I rested my elbows on the parapet, my head on my hands.

How could she?

"Hold steady there!" cried a voice.

Three boys – brothers as I took them to be, the youngest not more than four, the eldest, whose voice I had heard, maybe twice that – were balanced on a flat stone in the middle of the stream, fishing with a bent pin on a piece of string. I assumed at first that they had stripped down to their undergarments against the possibility – the probability, given the precariousness of their perch – of their falling in, but by degrees I recognised in their flimsy attire the vestiges of shirts and breeches, and what had seemed a summer evening's sport began to take on the aspect of dire necessity, with a twist, for me, of grim parody: "The river is the key to prosperity, and prosperity is the key to the common good . . ." Their bait was bread, which the eldest supplemented and moulded from a wad in his cheek between each cast. It seemed inconceivable that they should catch anything at all in this way and yet the middle brother toyed with a sharpened stick on which was already threaded one red-tailed specimen, a pound or two in weight.

I lost track of time watching the boys chew, mould, cast, wait, wait, wait more then start all over again. There was not so much as the hint of a bite, so that I began to wonder if they could really have caught the fish on their stick here and not simply brought it with them as a propitious charm. Eventually the midges found me out (they seemed not to bother the brothers) and I turned to begin drinking my way back to town. I had not gone more than a few dozen yards when I heard a smaller voice cry out – in alarm, I feared at first, then heard the other two join in with whoops of joy. However they had done it, the brothers had worked their trick again with the string and the bent pin. And I had not even had the patience to stand and watch.

It was as gloomy now within the cottages I passed as it was without, but the treadles and shuttles had not let up. I entered under a further three signs. Or four. Or, at least, not more than five. And after each stop I was more convinced than I had been before that I really did not care whether I ever saw Maria again. I had had an "Experience", that was all, with a woman older than I was. (And Dorothy was right: she was, I told myself now, much too old for me ever to have truly loved.) With time it would acquire the shape of Anecdote – I would hold back the rustling of the mouse in the corner by the dresser until . . . *later*, let us say – before one day becoming That Thing of Which I Did Not Wish to Speak to the young lady (I could almost picture her face, the searching look in her eyes) who was so desperately trying to understand the wound she detected somewhere at the very heart of me.

Crossing the river again, I was forced into the side of the Long Bridge for some minutes while the drivers of two carts that had passed too near to each other in the gathering darkness attempted to disengage their locked wheels: a common enough occurrence for pedestrians on that constricted thoroughfare. The only townsman never to have to give ground was Billy Massey, who was twice as wide as the coal barrow he pushed around all day. When Billy wanted to cross, people said, the horses stood on two legs to let him.

I managed at length to wriggle my way into one of the passing niches in time to see a head break the surface of the water at the foot of the next pier along. "Please let that not be a rat," I said aloud, for giant rat stories were the stock in trade of the docks and quays, "or even" – for it was swimming in the direction that I must go – "a dog."

The head disappeared and moments later reappeared, six feet closer to the town side, pale shoulders now visible beneath it. Of course. Neither rodent, nor canine, but human. Tantra Barbus was earning the pennies for the drink to send him to sleep until morning.

All that was left of him by the time I got across the bridge was a trail of wet footprints. I was able to follow them, past a rowboat recently beached, on to Ann Street, where there was, beneath a gas lamp, a mad confusion of prints, as though he had thrown in a dance for his benefactors, or had simply been so spoilt for choice for where to spend his money that he literally did not know which way to turn. I could not decide which was the more distasteful, nor rid myself of the thought that I was not one to be judging Tantra Barbus, having spent the evening as I had spent it, trying to render myself insensible. Tantra was an innocent compared to the *hallians* who provoked him to such self-abasement. I squeezed the words out between my teeth: "I could swing for that b— Lord Belfast," and was surprised enough at my vehemence that I forgot for the time it took me to walk through the next tavern door that I had intended to ring down the curtain on my own night's drinking.

My grandfather was most often shut up with his books or else already in bed by the time I came home in the evenings. As I tried to negotiate the stairs two drinks later, however, I noticed that his study door was ajar, a light burning within. I hesitated on the landing, my hand shielding the candle I had with difficulty lit in the hall.

"Gilbert?" he said. I thought about carrying on to my room. He might have called out ten times already tonight at imagined footfalls, and, besides, I did not trust my mouth and brain to be at all in harmony. I shifted my weight, to counteract a sudden list to the left, and a floorboard creaked. "Gilbert?" said my grandfather a second time. "Is that you?"

I pushed open the door, eleven years old again. The light from my candle fell first on his feet, which protruded from beneath his desk, having worked their way out of the slippers lying crossways on the floor. There was a hole in the toe of one stocking from which something more resembling horn than nail poked out. Who was it – Berris, Fright? – had said that parents were not another generation, but another species? How much more true was that for a *grand*parent? His own light was hard against the book he had been reading (too small to be the Bible: the Psalms, perhaps) and illuminated his face only to the bridge of his nose.

"'And the foolish man shall make of the night day and of the day night,'" he recited.

"It is only just gone a quarter past eleven," I said, or meant to; I managed to drop a *sh* sound somewhere in the middle. "And," (I would not be deterred) "you are still up."

"I am an old man, I have less need of sleep."

This seemed to me to be entirely the wrong way about. Surely it was the young, with so much still to see of the world, who ought to be the most wakeful? That, though, in my present state, would have been a sentence too far. My grandfather appeared anyway to have become absorbed in his book again.

"I will bid you good night," I said, or something approaching it.

He looked up, a frown forming, more of concentration than reproof. "Do you remember, one day we were walking on High Street – oh, I suppose you would not have been more than five at the time – and we met a pair of English gentlemen arguing together?"

For a moment I almost fancied that I did . . . for a moment. "No," I said.

"They had been making a tour of Scotland and crossed the day before from Portpatrick with the intention of walking to the Giant's Causeway," he went on, the appeal to my memory audibly dwindling with every word, "and had been assured, on stepping off the boat in Donaghadee, that it was not more than forty-five miles distant from Belfast. A few minutes before we came upon them they had learned that those forty-five miles were in fact Irish miles and to an Englishman would measure something closer to seventy."

I needed the chamber pot. I needed my bolster. I clenched my teeth and every muscle from my toes to my pelvis.

The two gentlemen, my grandfather was telling me, were divided between going part of the way to the north coast by coach – an expense that the younger, and shorter, did not think their purse could bear, despite their English shillings suddenly being worth thirteen pence – and turning about and walking back to Donaghadee, a mere eighteen miles, or twelve, according to how you looked at it. My grandfather had put himself at their service, offering to bring them back to his house, where they might carry on their discussion in more comfort and, if they did not mind him saying, with heat other than of their own making. The gentlemen, though, were determined to leave one way or the other.

"I do not think that they cared for the town, for anything they had met with in their short time here," he said, somewhat regretfully. "It surprised them that they felt so foreign in it. It surprised me. We could not even agree on the distance between us."

His attention seemed to have strayed again. I opened my mouth to speak, but only belched, softly, undetected, I thought, until my grandfather's eyes appeared suddenly in the lamplight.

"Keats," he said.

"I beg your pardon." I meant for the burp.

"John Keats."

I was confused.

"The younger of the English gentlemen we met on High Street. His name was not at all familiar to me then."

It was not at all familiar to me now.

"He and his friend, Brown, introduced themselves. He looked to me to be a troubled young man." Troubled, in my grandfather's lexicon, was cognate with "fallen out of Faith"; it was only one step away from Lost. "I went home and prayed very fervently that he might find peace. You prayed with me."

I summoned the remains of my sobriety (they did not amount to much) to say that I was sure Mr Keats would have thanked him for it. Thanked us.

"He died a short time later," my grandfather said, his fingers drumming on the Psalms, or whatever it was that he had been reading. "By all accounts still a stranger to God."

I was obviously invited to take with me up the remaining stairs to my room some moral from the tale. In fact on waking I was able to salvage only one phrase from the wreckage of the night before: "I could swing for that b— Lord Belfast"; and the only "John" on my mind was not Keats, but Bellingham, handing out his lesson to the upper ranks in the person of my grandfather's sainted Perceval.

⁂

That patient of Dr Breuer's in Vienna, who coined the term the "talking cure", nurtured, as I recall, daydreams to such a degree that they grew into a "private theatre", attendance at which she was able to combine with her everyday tasks and relationships. At the height of her hysteria, she was given to hallucinating in every particular the exact calendar day one year previously.

Though her body moved through the present moment her mind was not so much elsewhere as else*when*, the details that she let slip in the course of her conversations with Dr Breuer corroborated by her mother's secret diary. And yet, for all that, there were gaps too, areas of amnesia, just as there were hysterical symptoms that no amount of winding back could unravel: phobias for which no "governess's dog" could be found.

Something resembling a hysteria, I can only think, was incubating in me that early summer of 1831. (I have in the past deceived, and flattered, myself it was a contagion, every bit as virulent as the cholera: a few weeks before, Hector Berlioz had travelled hundreds of miles through the Italian states with a maid's costume in a parcel, intent on taking the lives of his fiancée, her mother, and the man who, with the mother's encouragement, his fiancée now proposed to marry.) I am trying to get as close as I can to its origin, or origins. At times, however, I have the impression that I am dealing not with an earlier version of myself but another person entirely.

My intention – my daydream – to begin with, though – of this I am certain – was not to harm, but to humble. If I had an image at all in my head that morning it was of Lord Belfast wading out into the waters of the Lagan, looking back over his shoulder at me, standing on the bank, gesturing grandly: "Swim."

"You are cheerier today," Ferris said, this at about half past ten. "You have scarcely let up whistling since you walked in the door."

Bright was asleep on the shelf in the chartroom. (Sir Clueless was out for the morning; I had a clear conscience on that score.) He had booked for himself an extra session in the gymnasium later in hopes of sweating off some of the previous night's excess.

"He was so drunk he raced Tantra Barbus across the river," Ferris said. "Over and back."

"*Bright* did?"

"Oh, he didn't swim against him, he rowed. If you had seen Tantra when he dragged himself from the water . . ." Ferris danced in the circle I had seen described beneath the lamp post on Ann Street.

I do not know that I whistled again the whole of that day, but it made no difference, finally. The seed was already planted. Not for Tantra alone, but for all of us, held by him in such contempt, Lord Belfast would have to be taught a lesson.

⊰♥⊱

I persuaded myself that I had need of a pistol. How else might I convince Lord Belfast to get into the water? How I might, even with it, was not a question I stopped to ask. I was, in that sense, following the lead of the men who had beat a path to the town's gunsmiths in the aftermath of the murders at Toohavara. Not that I could simply stroll into Messrs Braddell or Neill and pore over their wares, both of those men having known me since I was able to walk, and known my grandfather's principles no doubt a good deal longer. For notwithstanding that it was enshrined in the constitution that as a Protestant subject he had the right to possess arms for his own defence (as a Catholic subject he would have risked being transported), my grandfather would no more have a gun about the house than he would a bottle of gin.

Nor could I without inviting question enquire of a friend for the loan of something suitable. I did briefly consider asking Ferris, for the added cloak of legitimacy it would bestow, if I might join his duck-hunting fraternity, but, by his own account, the fowling piece was the preferred weapon on those afternoons spent in the barrel out on Belfast Lough; I wanted nothing so *obvious*. For a few days I kept a close watch on the comings and goings around the Ballast Office's gun cabinet, before concluding that there were indeed only two keys, one on Sir Clueless's key ring, the other on the constable, Gelston's. I had as much chance of removing their trousers without their noticing as removing those keys. Which did not stop me, when no one else was about, giving the cabinet doors a tug in passing. Locked fast every time.

And then I remembered the Lamb and Flag and the "fixer" Bright had pointed out to Ferris and me on Easter Monday, and whom I had seen again at work the first night I walked back from the Mill for Grinding Old People Young. "A man who would buy from you what never was yours to begin with and sell you what by honest means you never could have got." Was that not how Bright had described him? That was exactly the sort of man I needed now.

I think he must have come into the world attached to that tavern by means of an invisible cord, for he was once more at the table in the corner where I had first espied him, when I returned there on the evening of the day that his face had suddenly loomed up again in my mind. Either that or the tavern had taken shape around him. He was as focal a point as the fire, and to be treated with the same respect and caution.

I found a spot almost in the centre of the room from which

to observe him, hiding, as it were in plain view, becoming a part of whatever group temporarily coalesced around me. Men came and sat down beside him and a few minutes later got up and walked away; words were spoken out of the corners of mouths, curt nods exchanged, coins passed from palm to palm. His eyes never rested, but darted to the door, the counter, the table to the right, the table to the left, the door again, the counter . . . They lit on me as they had lit on me on Easter Monday, as they lit at regular intervals on every person and object in that room. ("What do you want of me?" they seemed to ask of the one, and of the other, "How might I turn you to profit?") I decided that there was nothing to be gained on this occasion by glancing away. Without any suspicious movement on my part his eyes would soon enough continue on their circuit.

After the fourth frank meeting of his gaze I saw an opportunity as one man got up from the seat next to his and was not instantly replaced by another, although someone else hiding in plain view would tell you the replacement was me.

Once I was beside him I was no longer a fit object of scrutiny. The only question now was "buy" or "sell"; already he was looking to see who would be next in my seat. For a moment I was granted a view of the world as he saw it, not as a marketplace alone, but also as a laboratory: he was a scientist and we were his subjects, the proof of his hypotheses as much a motivation as the profit deriving from them.

There was a smell of preserved lemons, overlaid on lard, which I attributed to the pomade that shaped the waves in his hair, or, as it seemed close to, kept them in check. Everything about him suggested a capacity to burst out suddenly.

He had a glass before him that I had not seen him lift more than twice in all the time I had been watching, and on one of those occasions he had set it down again without taking a drink. He was probably the soberest person in the whole house, apart from me.

"I have been told you might help me with something," I said.

"It depends on what the something is." The voice from such a hulk of a man was surprisingly reassuring, the words themselves scarcely less so: this was how I imagined a conversation of that nature would go. Still I could not bring myself to say the "something" outright, even in that hubbub and in the presence of so many diplomatically deaf years. I was obliged instead to fall back on hints and gestures, to which he nodded slowly. He stole but a single glance at my hands, as I specified "nothing too big".

There was scarcely any hesitation. "I will need a down payment," he said, and when I asked how much, laid his index finger on his coat sleeve: one would do it. I did not think he meant a shilling. I had succeeded in my year and a half at the Ballast Office in putting aside six pounds. I was already reconciled to having to part with a sizeable portion of it to get what I needed. I slipped a sovereign from my purse and passed it into his palm as I had seen the others do.

"All right," he said, although it might have been addressed to anyone, for the back of his head only was presented to me now. "Tomorrow night. Eight, not a minute after."

I could not settle to my work the next day any more than I could will the hours or even the minutes to pass. Several times I got up from my desk and put my ear to the clock on the back wall to check that it had not stopped altogether, until Ferris threatened to tie me to my seat if I did not leave off from it: the constant reminders were making the day go ten times slower for him. I was rescued at last from my torment late in the morning by a folder of documents, which Sir Clueless wanted taken to the Stamp Office on Arthur Street. He was as pleased to see me be first to my feet as the other clerks were envious. "I should have tied you down when I had the chance," said Ferris, as I passed him on my way out of the door.

The errand quickly accomplished, I took the opportunity to slip back to the house to satisfy myself that everything was in readiness for the conclusion of the evening's business, not least the hiding place, which after much deliberation I had decided ought to be behind the chest of drawers where the pennies had been hidden all those years before and where still, in all the years since, no human hand but my own had ventured.

It was a Thursday. I had spotted Molly as I left the office, making her way towards Tomb Street and the butter market, where she sometimes met and swapped news with her sister, who kept house for a minister off in Dundonald. My grandfather, I knew, would be out too – Thursday had for twenty years been his day for prison visits – and Nisbet with him. I had let myself in at the front door and was just stepping on to the stairs when I thought I heard a retching. I stopped, one foot suspended in mid-air, listening. There it was again, quite distinctly, from the far end of the hallway. I eased myself backwards off the stair and walked on tiptoe towards the door through to the kitchen. I called "hello", but got no response, save for the scrape of metal being dragged over the stone flags. I hesitated a moment longer then grasped the handle and flung the door wide . . . Hannah was busy about the fire. She looked back over her shoulder at me. Her face was flushed. Hanks of hair clung to her cheeks and forehead.

"Is everything all right?" I asked.

"Everything is fine," she said, but so weakly that my suspicions multiplied a hundredfold. I took a step into the room.

"Only I would have sworn I heard a noise just now like vomiting."

She cast her eyes here and there about the kitchen, frowning, as though someone might have crept in without her knowing.

A tin basin sat to one side of the hearth, a linen cloth covering it. I breathed in deeply through my nose. Hannah at the same moment opened the door of the oven, set into the wall above the fire, and a smell of fresh-baked bread overpowered the room.

I let the breath out again in a frustrated sigh. "You know if you are sick at all you are to go to your room and not leave it until a doctor has seen you?" In fact, if she had been concealing an infection of some kind we would have been within our rights to send her back to wherever she had come from and have the doctor see her there.

I had an image of a marker being pinned to a "cholera map" in the Ballast Office of some other port: "Outbreak confirmed in Belfast."

"I am quite well, thank you," she said, and set two loaves on a board on the table, next to a pot with a rabbit in it; the crusts were a deep chestnut, verging on black at the crest. "Just hot from working."

I looked again at the basin by the fire. I had to see in it.

"Don't!" she cried, so loudly that I jumped rather than halted, hardly aware that I had begun to translate thought into action. "I have another ball of dough in there," she said. "If the air gets in before it has finished rising it will spoil."

She held my gaze. We were probably – it had not struck me before – of a similar, if not an exact, age. Would she have dared to speak to my grandfather like that, or even to Nisbet? But then would I have considered for one moment checking in the basin if it had been Molly giving me the assurance?

"Of course," I said at length and turned away from the fire. I watched her face for signs of undue relief, and saw none. "I am sorry if I interrupted you."

She was occupied with a large kettle when I let myself out, using a poker wrapped in a cloth to push it closer to the coals; I paused in the hallway several moments more to ensure there was no repetition of the retching, then carried on up to my room.

The Lamb and Flag was, if possible, even busier that night than the one before. I arrived half an hour before the time appointed, which was as well, for it took ten minutes of jostling to get in at the door: my grandfather's prison-visit day was to the rest of the town "pay day". Or as Ferris once so succinctly described it, the start of the weekly race to drink your wages before you frittered them away on something altogether less fun. A race, he was proud to say, for which he was as fit as any man in Belfast, and no gymnasium required.

I was as many minutes again getting myself into a position to see, and be seen from, the table in the corner. As before, the buyers and sellers came and went, although in keeping with Ferris's formula the turnover this evening seemed twice as rapid; as before I waited until I judged that an opening had been made for me; as before the fixer did not turn to look at me once I had sat in the seat beside him.

"The man at the end of the bar," was all that he said.

I looked up. There were three men at the end of the bar nearest to us, none of whom was taking the slightest notice of me. A heartbeat later, however, the middle and, of course, *least* likely-looking one tossed off his drink and left by a side door. Not being directed what else to do, I stood up to follow. The fixer extended his arm as casually as if he were stretching into a yawn, barring my way. I pressed a sovereign into his hand and when his arm did not move had no option but to press another. The barrier was raised, the yawn, which appeared now entirely genuine, completed.

The door opened on to a dim and narrow yard with barrels, stacked three high, along one side and a choked drain along the other, slicking the cobbles with what I preferred not to think. The dominant smell of stale ale and cabbage was, in the circumstances, the best that could have been hoped for. I could see no one; could scarcely make out the far wall. I sensed, though, that it would not do to call out, and my mouth all at once was too dry to whistle. I tapped on the barrel nearest to me: once, twice, three times. A few moments later there came three answering taps from the shadowy end of the yard. I realised as I stepped with care towards it that there was a gap between the last of the barrel-stacks and the wall that finally took on definition beyond. The man I had followed was wedged in here. I stopped before him. He looked at me as though I was the one bringing something to him.

"I have already paid," I said. "In there."

"In there" was in fact as notional as where I was standing

now had been a few moments ago, the shadows having some-how given me the slip and regrouped behind me.

His lips moved, but nothing came out.

"Do you have it or do you not?" I asked, trying to keep my patience, and only then thought to look to see where his hands were all this time, which was down below his waist.

"In the name of G—!" I cried, and staggered backwards, one foot plunging into the drain. I dragged it free and fled, scatter-ing the shadows, into the bar. Shock made me lose all caution. I leaned across the fixer's table, with no regard for the person who had taken my place at his side.

"What kind of a man did you take me for?"

His eyebrows rose as he looked past me into the room, where every last customer was making a point of having seen nothing untoward; his voice, though, remained pitched low. "One who understood that there was less harm in that than in anything else that you might have been asking me for."

The man from the alley had come back in and taken up his position between his silent companions at the end of the counter, where a fresh drink had been set up for him. You would not have guessed from his expression as he supped, or from theirs, that he had stepped outside at all.

"You have three pounds of mine," I said. That got me for the first time the fixer's full attention, and his finger, springing up like a lock of hair, in my face. "*You* have three seconds to get out of this house," he said. "And as for anything else you might re-quire I would suggest you ask among your own class, for that is where the majority of such articles are to be found."

The finger between my eyes was joined by a second. "Two," he said, and I was gone.

My nostrils were still filled with the smell of cabbage a week and two visits to the Peter's Hill baths later.

On the evening of the second of those visits I was brooding in my room when there was a knock at the door. I called "Come in", expecting Nisbet, sent by my grandfather to ask what ailed me (I did not see how anyone else could have missed the stench I was giving off), and got instead Hannah. I noticed she closed the door behind her before curtsying.

"I needed to talk about yon time in the kitchen," she said.

It says much about what had been preoccupying me in the minutes before she knocked that I thought at first she meant on the night that Maria had come to see me. I feared – may God forgive me – an attempt to extort from me something more than the two sixpences with which I had rewarded her silence.

"I explained to you, the lady left," I began, getting to my feet, but Hannah shook her head.

"The other day, I mean, the boaking you heard" – she used the word as though it were the only fit one, which in that instant it became – "that was me."

"The basin by the hearth?" I said.

"No, no, that really was bread. I boaked in a bucket out the back door."

"I am glad to hear that you did not lie." I was inching towards the window: the air, I must have been thinking, remembering the cholera circulars; flush away the bad with the good. "But, with respect, the 'where' hardly matters: you are sick and risk infecting the entire household."

As I said this I was conscious that she did not actually look unwell. She looked, in fact, haler than I was used to seeing her.

"I am going to have a baby," she said simply.

"Oh." I stopped in the middle of the floor. I had not much experience of these situations, but I had enough to know that congratulations were not always in order. "When?"

"I cannot tell for sure. All Saints maybe. I feared I was before even I came to work here, but I feared more not getting the place, so I never let on to anybody."

She had not come further than that first step into the room. I asked her if she would like to sit down, which, after a moment's hesitation, she did, awkwardly, on the lip of the easy chair.

"Does my grandfather know of it now?" I cannot think what possessed me to ask. The answer, as I might have expected, was a shake of the head. "Nisbet? Molly?" Two more shakes. The truth was beginning to dawn on me. "Have you told anyone at all?" The movement of the head was slower this time and all the more emphatic for it. "Not even . . ." I was unsure how I should refer to the person in question: "the father", "your young man", "*lover*"?

Whatever I had chosen would not have been heard for her snort. "That twister? He is the last person I would want to know."

I was still trying to come to terms with the fact that I was the first. My earlier suspicion resurfaced. "Are you in need of money?" I asked carefully.

She shot me a glance of such anger my face flamed like a lamp.

"I mean," I said – I had regained the bed and sat upon it heavily – "is there *any* way at all I can be of assistance?"

She looked down at her palms, upturned on her lap. "Just being able to tell it is a weight lifted," she said. "It's enough to be thinking about carrying the baby without the secret forbye."

"Your own father and mother . . . ?"

"Mother only," she said. "She will be time enough finding out. I have a married sister up the country. I might be able to go there for a spell."

"I am sure there is no need. I will speak to my grandfather on your behalf."

She cut me short. "I have had plenty of nights already to think it through, and the air would be better for the baby out of town."

A thudding had got up on the street far below. Mrs Clarke, who kept the Hope Hotel in Hammond's Court, off High Street, had lately taken to placing a drummer at the entrance to the court as a lure to patrons.

"You must at least promise me you will wait until the last possible moment before leaving," I told Hannah.

"I'm only wee," she said, and standing up bunched the front of her dress in her fist to demonstrate the slack. "It will be a brave while yet before I am showing."

She looked towards the door as though she meant to go, but remained where she was, smoothing out the wrinkles she had made.

"And if you want to talk again, of course," I said, trying to coax from her whatever it was that kept her standing, "you know my door. I will be the soul of discretion."

She nodded. There was definitely something more. "Another thing I have been thinking, nights when I have been sitting by the kitchen fire, is what might happen to my baby when she is grown – I say 'she', I don't know why, it is just a feeling that

I have. When she, or maybe he, is grown will the world have changed, I ask myself, or will poor people always want? Will my child want? That is the question more than any other that keeps me awake."

For several moments more I sat on the bed, searching for words of reassurance, and finding none. She dropped me another curtsy and reached for the door handle.

"Hannah, wait!"

I crossed the room to the writing desk before my window and settling myself in the chair took from the uppermost drawer a sheet of paper. Even as I selected the quill, though, I was unsure what it was I would write, even as I dipped the nib into the inkstand. Looking out to my right I could see, between Mrs Bateson's house and Mr Shaw's, the offices of the Bank of Ireland, whose arrival on our street a few years before, hard on the heels of the Nelson Club, had been the occasion of outraged letters to the press: "What next, a *haberdasher's* on the Flags?" I had a sudden vision of banks and clubs and insurance brokers in an unbroken line from the White Linen Hall to Castle Street, on this side as well as that. (The haberdashery, I told myself, was hyperbole, but had I looked long enough and hard enough I might have seen any number of haberdasheries and silk mercers and gentlemen's outfitters, lit up for Christmas, might have seen too a brand-new brougham being driven up the middle, a face peering out of it, rendered unrecognisable by age.) One way or another, I would not be in this house many years longer. My hand, as I was thinking this, had begun to move across the page, left to right, left to right, coming back to the inkstand five or six times in the course of each line. I felt as though I was reviewing the words, rather than writing them, and was pleased when I had reached the end to discover that I would not have changed a one. I appended my name and pressed down on it with the blotter.

I offered the letter to Hannah to read before I sealed it. She shook her head. "I have not got to learning how yet," she said. "My sister knows. Maybe when I am in the country with the child she will teach us both."

"Well then," I was thrown for a moment, "it is addressed to the first-born daughter, or son, of Hannah . . ." Here I paused. "I did not know the surname to put to it, so I wrote 'currently in the employ of Mr Samuel Dawe Semple, Donegall Place, Belfast'." She nodded. We had each in our way grown up ahead of ourselves. "It sets out the means by which the child should seek me out if ever she, or he, is in need of assistance, me or my heirs and executors." I pointed to the middle of the page. "This, with the line under it, is the address of my grandfather's solicitor, and here below is the name of my friend Mr John Millar. I will make a copy for each of them in the morning and deposit them at the solicitor's office with the express instruction that they only be opened in the event that some calamity should befall me."

"Your finger is shaking," she said.

I reeled it in under my thumb. "I have been scribbling all day," I said, then regretting that I had made light of the ability to write, went back to the table for wax.

"I did not mean to come looking for charity," she said when at last she held the letter, sealed, in her hand.

"It is not charity," I said. "It is an offer of help with finding work. An insurance policy."

I opened the door for her.

"I hope that will allow you to sleep a little easier tonight."

"It will, when I have finished black-leading the grate," she said, as matter-of-factly as she had reported boaking in the bucket.

And I listened to her every step of the way through the house to the kitchen and the remainder of her chores.

　　　　　　　　　　　❧

There had been for several years past, on the Millfield side of Smithfield Market, a stallholder, an ancient Tyrone man, with cataracts in both eyes, who notwithstanding knew the place of every item laid out for sale on his stall, and knew too from long practice the exact position of each and every person who stopped there to browse.

"That is a solid silver knocker," he would say, before you had even stretched out a hand to it. "From a door in St James's in London that was persuaded it was no longer in need of it." Or, again, "Is it a garnet ring in particular you are looking for? There is an interesting tale goes with the one you have in your hand, which I will throw in for free."

Often it seemed as though the goods were only props, or prompts, and what he really traded in was the stories.

"That will be the Garrick, you are looking at there," he said to me on the afternoon following my interview with Hannah, when I paused – barely broke stride – before a coat, such as coachmen then sometimes still wore, with three layered capes at the shoulders. "You have to try it on to appreciate."

"Thank you," I said, "but . . ."

"No, do, try it."

His eyes were directed, sightlessly, to a point somewhere to the right of my head, but his ear was fixed firmly on my face. Whatever possessed me, I did as he suggested. It drowned me.

"There," said the blind man, smiling. "You will not get a better coat in all of Ireland – the weight of it."

I was about to excuse myself by saying that the weight, on as warm a summer's day as we had had that year, was half the problem, when I became aware of a specific bulk in the inner pocket below the left breast. I reached my hand in and pulled it out again quick, as though the metal object I had touched had been red-hot instead of cold.

"A box-lock, double-barrel, tap-action pistol," he said without the least alteration in tone. "From the reign of the last King but one, still in good order. Other necessities in the patch pocket front right."

I felt in there too; in number if not in detail the items accorded with what I understood the necessities to be. I withdrew my hand.

"Have you been in the Lamb and Flag?" I asked him.

"The what and what?"

I could think of no reason why he had singled me out other than that he had seen, or at least heard, me in dispute with the fixer. But then had he not accosted me just now before I had even opened my mouth? I came at the thing from another direction: "What made you so sure I would be interested?"

"I was not at all sure. As I recall, it was you who showed the interest."

"I glanced at it."

"And hesitated, as did a dozen others today, but none of

them put it on when I urged them to. There is always a good reason for our decisions, don't you think?"

I felt in the pockets again. My fingers closed around the twinned barrels. "How much?" I asked.

"For the coat as you stand up in it?"

Market-goers continued to push past in both directions, stallholders to call out their wares, yet we might have been the only two in the whole of that square.

"As I stand up in it."

"Five guineas."

I laughed. I had scarcely half of that left to my name.

"Two."

"Three."

"I will have to think."

"Two pounds twelve and six."

"I will still have to think," I said. Prudence prevented me from adding that I would do my thinking on the short walk to my house and back.

"I cannot say it will be here when you return," he shouted after me. "A coat the like of that."

I called back over my shoulder, "You said it yourself: no one else has tried it on." And yet the possibility that someone else *might*, the moment my back was turned, struck me as in every sense just. I stopped myself from rushing, if anything walked slower than I would have normally, took extra care removing the money from its tin box, replacing the box in the drawer, covering it again with shirts and linen. (The box itself was hidden not from my grandfather – he positively encouraged thrift – but from whichever enterprising burglar discovered his moral aversion to locked doors.) I was more than half hoping as I made my way back that the coat would indeed be gone. Already in those brief contacts between fingers and barrels I had felt a "charge", as might be said now. I had to remind myself that the gun was only one means to an end and not the end in itself.

But the coat was not gone, and as quickly as the doubt had entered it left again. I watched the old man as I approached, observing the telltale twitch of his head as he picked out my footsteps from the scores competing for his attention, coming closer, closer, stopping at last directly in front of him.

"So, you thought?" he said.

I placed the coins in his hand without another word. He weighed rather than counted them, giving them several flips in his cupped palm. They moved little, barely mustered a jingle.

"You had better look on the ground at your feet," he said. "You seem to be missing half a crown."

I did not even pretend to look, but placed that coin too in his hand. He gave the augmented pile another flip. He was satisfied.

"Health to wear," he said, and I put the coat over my arm.

"Health yourself."

A dozen yards on I stepped into a courtyard of blank walls and emptied the contents of the pockets into a felt bag that had formerly held a pair of my boots: a brass-topped ramrod, a tooled horn containing priming powder, a waxed wrap of what I assumed were flints, another, larger wrap of what I knew to be lead balls. The pistol came out last. The butt, as gently curving as the head of a walking stick, was of walnut, the barrels, which had been soldered one on top of the other, brass. The whole lot was not much longer than the powder flask. It was – down to the promise in the laurel wreath, engraved around the maker's name, that the bearer would prevail – perfect.

The transfer complete, I carried on to a clothes stall at the furthest corner of the square from the old man's – coats and trousers and breeches and dresses tumbled together as though they had been stripped from the victims of some catastrophe rather than traded. I showed the stallholder the coachman's coat. He turned up his impressively carbuncled nose. "These are not much in the fashion now, to say nothing of the season." Then, rubbing the nap of the collar between his fingers, "I will give you five shillings."

"Seven and six," I said.

"Six and that is my last."

So I added the Garrick to his mausoleum and continued on my way, let him smirk all he liked at the thought of getting one over on me. Let him smirk.

⁂

It was that time of the year when the sun in its pomp had to be dragged from the sky at day's end. I imagined Hyperion's horses, which Bright was so fond of invoking, somewhere on the western side of Black Mountain – Lough Neagh sounded about right – straining at their traces. Eleven o'clock would sound and still the mountain top was stained red from the struggle. The streets and lanes and fields round about were full of people who could not settle to bed while it was yet so light and who unwittingly became extras in the drama unfolding in my own private theatre. I felt as though I was getting to know the town a third time, not now through the eyes of a child, nor

180

of a youth given the licence of a wage and fellows his own age to spend it with, but through those of a man groping towards an understanding of the thing to which his life thus far had served merely as prologue. I was conscious suddenly of the opportunities that buildings presented, the archways, the buttresses, the shadows they cast, for the skip and a jump that could take you out of one street into another, as completely as if you had been translated into another plane of existence.

I mingled with my townsfolk on their circuit of the White Linen Hall, or at least on that half of it that afforded me a view of the Royal Hotel; I walked in their company the road out to Ormeau, joined them in their admiration of the Marquis's new house, now almost complete – all those chimneys! Those lights! – and stepped aside to allow them to pass in the entries around Hill Street, off one of which, as Bright had told it, cocks were sometimes fought. I squeezed and wriggled my way to the front of them as they lined the pavements of Donegall Square for the annual parade of the town's Masonic Lodges; the following evening, the final Saturday in June, I stood shoulder to shoulder with them in one of the largest public gatherings in years ("a hanging crowd," the man behind me said nostalgically, causing the hair on the back of my neck to stand on end), as Mr Wallace, Lord Belfast's solicitor, attended by the Seneschal and the Sovereign, Sir Stephen May, stepped on to a platform beneath a dolphin-headed lamp standard. The solicitor carried a letter, which, even before he had finished unfolding it, provoked such a tumult in the whole assembly that the Sovereign himself had to ring a bell to bring it to order.

"Please, gentlemen and ladies, ladies and gentlemen," he

called at the very top of his voice, then yielded the (temporary) floor to Mr Wallace.

"His lordship earnestly desired that I communicate the contents of this letter to you, so if you would have the courtesy to hear me out," the solicitor said, making no special effort to ensure that people could hear him even if they would. "He begins, 'I am most anxious that all opposition to the Belfast Harbour Improvements should cease, if possible' " – this to a few ironic cheers, quickly quelled – " 'but I cannot but give my most decided opposition to the intended Bill if the rights of the Lords of the Soil are not in some way protected.'" And this to catcalls so general and protracted that the solicitor was obliged once more to await the intervention of the bell.

(Many of those catcalling I had seen on parade the day before in their sashes, their aprons and their collar jewels; I had seen Wallace and the Sovereign too, several of the lesser Chichesters and others of the Mays, their in-laws; Brothers all in Masonry.)

When at last Wallace deemed it worth his while to try again it was to outline to the assembly a proposal that Lord Belfast hoped, should it meet with the concurrence of his father, would prevent him from being placed in the disagreeable situation of further obstructing the Bill: namely that the Lord of the Castle nominate half the members of any new Ballast Board that the Act might bring into being, and co-opt on to it besides the MPs for Belfast, Antrim, and Carrickfergus, which was to say – although he was much too coy actually to come out with it, even through this elaborate ventriloquism – his father's cousin, a neighbouring landlord, and himself.

Beyond these words the solicitor was not able to go, nor was there this time any let-up in the hullabaloo. (If the bell was rung again I did not hear it.) I roared as loudly as any gathered there my outrage that the Lords of the Soil and Castle should try to hold the town to ransom in this way. I wondered though how many others had right there in their pockets the means – should the need arise – to prevent it?

It was the last thing I looked at before going to bed. It was the first thing I looked at in the morning. I would kneel before the pistol and its "necessities" spread out on the carpet and call to mind Gelston, on the day of the protests against the Cantonese merchant ship, loading the Ballast Office's guns. Time and again I followed the routine – half-cock, powder, patch – up to the point of ramming the ball home. For I remembered too what Gelston had said that day, that after the ball was in it was easier to discharge the gun than unload it.

In the dawn light I peered along the topmost barrel to the wall of the Castle gardens, where weeks before Lord Belfast had sat on his grey mare, admiring Mr Sinclair's hunting pack. The dogs returned every second or third day, but of Lord Belfast there was no further sign, and each morning I would tap the powder back into its horn, shake the balls and patches into my palm and pack the pistol away again.

In fact I saw Lord Belfast just once during that time, leaning heavily on the shoulder of a footman as he left the Royal one particularly oppressive night, a little after ten o'clock; I saw his hand a few moments later flop out of the window of the carriage that bore him away from the kerb, but I was taken too much by surprise to do anything other than stare. I scolded myself that I would have to be more alert in the future, quicker to react.

And then, like that, he was gone altogether.

Ferris staggered into the Ballast Office one morning clutching his heart. "All is lost." He collapsed into a chair, scaring the cat out from under it. "Lady Harriet is leaving."

"Who says so?" I asked, startled up out of my own seat.

"I saw her with my own eyes, not two minutes ago, at the head of the dock."

I ran to the window, to the one pane not obscured by clutter or grime (thank you Friends of the True Friends of Belfast, replacing the glass was less trouble than cleaning it), and there she was, exactly as Ferris had said, looking not best pleased to have to wait for transport to her ship. There, too, struggling to keep their heads above the ruffs and ribbons of which their clothes appeared principally composed, were the son and daughter, together with their travelling circus of nannies and menservants and maidservants and enough hampers and trunks to provision a squadron of French adventurers.

Bright, at my shoulder, wondered did this betoken a rift in the marriage, then at once answered himself: if there had been a row the whole town would have heard it.

Anyway, he reminded Ferris, turning away from the window, the Maze Races were almost upon us. "Think of all those young ladies loosed from the town for the day," he told him. "Think of all that countryside round about. Think of the barns."

I rested my forehead against the glass, the smell in my nostrils of putty not yet dried. This was so unfair.

I did not see Lord Belfast that morning either. I knew, though, that there was little hope of his remaining behind without his family. More likely that he had already made the crossing on his own, leaving under my very nose. Sure enough, a notice appeared a few days later in one of the weeklies, just arrived from London, confirming that he and Lady Harriet would be spending the summer at their home in the Isle of Wight, where they had in recent years been in the habit of hosting a magnificent ball to mark the start of what in fashionable circles some were now calling "Cowes Week". Lord Belfast, however, was at pains to stress that he would still be travelling "up to town" for important Parliamentary business. Such as thwarting the desires of the town that gave him his title, he did not say.

For a day or two more I was at an utter loss. I had not until then understood – have not until now been able properly to put into words – how my feelings for Maria had become entangled with the Earl, my grief and anger, but also (how do I put this even now?) my longing. The shade I had been pursuing around the town these past weeks had been hers as much as his. Or perhaps it would be more accurate to say that her shade had been behind me, goading me on in pursuit of his. Either way, in losing him I had lost her all over again.

I had travelled too, in the restless thoughts that accompanied those wanderings, a long way from the watery scene I had first imagined being enacted at the foot of the Long Bridge. It had not taken me many nights to realise that I could do little in the town itself, in this season of all seasons, without bringing people in their tens, their hundreds possibly, spilling on to the street, alarmed, inquisitive, desperate for diversion. My vision now – and it was as vivid as if I had turned a corner in a museum or gallery and met with it executed on an immense canvas – was of a clump of trees, dark, mist-snagged, from out of which a horse was proceeding, its rider tall and straight-backed in the saddle, headed for a breach in an earthen rampart. A little to the right of centre, a second figure was bent over in the act of priming a box-lock tap-action double-barrel pistol in the lee of a broken altar – unmistakably, a broken altar, not a *cromlech* – of prehistoric stones.

There was a companion piece. Rooks taking to the air from the trees, the horse rearing up, its rider's head thrown back, and at the centre now, before the altar, the second figure, gun-arm outstretched, unbending.

That attitude – rather than that location – was the true measure of how far I had travelled.

I had been spending too much time on my own. I had been spending too much time with the gun. I had allowed myself to be seduced by it although all I could think then was that I had been thwarted. It was too late now to change tack.

But not, perhaps, too late to change target.

Afterwards I could not understand why I had allowed myself to become so focused on the son in the first place.

I was lying, forlorn, on my bed one evening, the pistol and its parts on my chest, when one after the other the phrases paraded through my head: "should the proposal meet the concurrence of my *father* . . . merchants and freeholders of Belfast, his *papa* has ordered him to oppose the very first Bill you apply for . . ."

I stood up. I made three circuits of the carpet. Stopped. Made three circuits more, my hands clasped in front of my face. It was all I could do to stop myself from laughing out loud.

All this time I had been pursuing the wrong Donegall.

⁂

The first and lasting cause of Lord Done'em all's debts went on four legs. As a young man not yet in possession of his inheritance, the Marquis had purchased five horses – at a cost of more than three thousand five hundred pounds, not one of which was paid in advance – from a certain Philip O'Kelly, the son of "Count" Dennis O'Kelly, or Colonel, as he sometimes styled himself. O'Kelly senior had arrived in London from Ireland thirty years before, penniless, illiterate, untitled and uncommissioned, and after a series of scrapes and misadventures had made two fortunes from the incomparable "Eclipse", the first on the turf, where the stallion was never beaten, the second at stud, where he was never found wanting. It can only have been the prospect of similar riches that caused the future Marquis to agree to spiralling interest terms for the five horses and to offer as security a percentage of the estates that he would one day inherit. His attempts at repayment fell at the first hurdle and by the time he came into his title his debt to the O'Kellys (for the debt had become a kind of shadow inheritance for that family) was, to hear some tell it, not far short of the net worth of Belfast. His life since then had been in large degree a working out of that early indiscretion, though not a learning from it. Horses were still his greatest love – he had lately been appointed steward of the Maze racecourse – and his greatest weakness.

I took it into my head that someone, I did not yet know who, should write the Marquis a letter.

Having already broken one great taboo by bringing a firearm under my grandfather's roof, I now broke a second, stealing a bottle of brandy into my room (on a Sunday, too) to help me discover the author. I set the bottle on the writing table next to the inkstand, although to start with I addressed myself only to the former. I was remembering how the last time I had sat down here to write, to Hannah, the words had flowed almost without my conscious intervention, although on that occasion there had seemed to be a connection still between *heart* and hand. In order for this letter to convince, I would have to take leave of Gilbert Rice altogether, or imprison him somewhere deep within, well away from the fingers he would claim as his, the voice he thought he commanded.

So I drank. Drank more.

As the level in the bottle dropped to the three-quarters mark a gentleman took up the quill and wrote "My Lord Marquis", then stopped. He made a ball of the paper and tossed it into the basket to the left of the desk. "Dear Lord Donegall," began a second gentleman, several mouthfuls later, "You will forgive, I hope, my presumption in writing, but I crave a meeting with you on a matter . . ." There was a snort: *my presumption in writing* indeed! *Crave a meeting*! That letter too was balled, tossed even further by the same hand that then slapped a clean sheet of paper on to the table. "Dear Lord Donegall." (A swig, straight from the bottle.)

> You have the reputation, fully justified, of being the first in this land in the appreciation of thoroughbreds. I recently had the good fortune (let us say it was "in the cards") to come by a yearling colt, fifteen hands high, that I intend to introduce a fort-night hence at the Maze meeting, after which his value is sure to soar. I am prepared, however, to show him beforehand to a select few investors, who will thereby "have the jump on" the crowd. I will put him through his paces at the Giant's Ring at full sunrise on Derby Day, a spectacle which, I am certain, a gentleman of your interests would find not only diverting, but profitable. I will

not pretend to altruism here (and you would doubtless be suspicious if I did). I am in a position where, not to be too delicate about it, I must see some early benefit from my windfall. I ask only that all concerned travel with an open mind and without attendants, or that they leave their attendants at some distance off, lest too great a gathering attract the attention of the less discerning and the merely curious.

I am, my lord, etc. etc., "Hippophile".

When this was blotted and folded I raised the sash window a foot or two and took several deep draughts of night air; then I felt my way to the tips of my fingers again and in a hand more recognisably my own, making allowance for a quarter – goodness, a *third* – of a bottle of brandy, began another letter.

They would say, when the discovery was made, that it had been the work of Terry Alts, which would be to my advantage in the immediate aftermath. Who would search for Terry Alts on the Flags, in the house of so respected a gentleman as my grandfather? At the same time, though, I was anxious that my role would not go undetected by everyone.

"Dear Maria," I wrote . . .

I told her that I knew what she thought about the triviality of our town in these times, but news would, I was confident, reach her within hours of receiving this letter that would perhaps cause her to think again; something involving the most prominent personage in Belfast, something, it would be no exaggeration to say, gigantic. (Was I pleased to have been able to unite deed and location in this way? As Punch.) Others might attribute the event to which I alluded to "mythical creatures" of one kind or another, but she, I knew, would have no trouble accepting a more mundane agency, an individual hand, even. If she could not find me worthy of her love, I hoped she would one day allow that I had been worthy of her regard.

That letter I put into a drawer. I would post it on the day before Derby Day.

The other I took with me the next morning when I left for work.

It was hot again, even at the Ballast Office end of the quays where we at least got the advantage in summer of whatever landward breezes were blowing. (In winter we just got battered.) In the middle of the morning Sir Clueless appeared among us and announced, to a general hurrah, that we might remove our topcoats. I, though, was careful to keep mine within sight at all times. We did not have pickpockets in the office, but we had pranksters for whom any item left too long unattended began to take on the appearance of a challenge. (The story of the mouse and the purse and the winning lottery ticket was the stuff of legend, the best part of the joke, of course, being that the ticket was all along hidden away in someone else's drawer.) At noon, while my colleagues were all in the tavern, I took a turn about the quays with the letter now transferred from breast pocket to coat sleeve: Chichester Quay, Hanover Quay, Custom House Quay, back; here and there a "how do you do?" or "another fine one, yes"; Chichester Quay, Hanover Quay, Custom House Quay, back.

I had been about this for half of my allotted hour when I picked out, under the sign of the European Life Insurance Company, Roddy McCluskey's head, holding forth. I watched a while, keeping my distance, then anticipating from the flicks and nods his intended route, ran along Store Lane, crossed a courtyard off that, another off that, and emerged at the top of Ireland's Entry half a step ahead of Roddy, coming, at speed, in the opposite direction. We collided. Roddy staggered backwards a pace or two and I feared for a moment that he would not be able to right himself at all, but carry on down, like a fir tree toppling. I put my hand to the small of his back and with the other hand reached round and tugged the letter from my sleeve, letting it fall.

"Roddy! I am so terribly, terribly, sorry."

He planted his feet wide apart, shook his head. "An accident only," he said. The satchel had got twisted round behind his back. He dipped and shrugged his shoulders until it hung down in front of him. "There is no harm done."

"I am relieved to hear it." I dusted the front of my coat then made as though to step away from him, but stopped in the act and pointed at the ground. "Look there," I said. "You have lost a letter."

He glanced at it, then at the satchel. A mother hen could not have known her brood better, nor have been more conscious of when something had befallen it. I bent down to pick up the letter. Even in the few seconds it had lain there it had succeeded in attracting to itself some of the dirt and detritus of the cobbles. I wiped it with my sleeve, took a step back in surprise.

"Lord Donegall!" (I really think I may have missed my calling.) "It would never have done to lose this." I tried to lift the flap of his satchel, but Roddy shrugged it again out of my reach.

"I don't remember being asked to carry anything there," he said, angling his head to read the address, which the (third) brandy drinker in me had marked as care of the Seneschal's Office, Castle Place.

If I am too insistent, I thought, it will only arouse his suspicions. I gambled in the opposite direction. I tossed the thing down on the ground again.

"What are you doing?" he cried.

"I am in a hurry back to work. Whoever has dropped this will discover his loss soon enough and retrace his steps," I said. "Or hers, indeed."

It was written all over his face, Roddy could not bear to see the letter lie. "Place it in my bag," he said at last. "Perhaps it did fall out. I will take it anyway."

"If you are sure," I said, but however he had managed it he already had the satchel open and ready to receive.

With a final hesitation for dramatic effect, I shoved the letter in with the others, bade Roddy the very best of days, and beat it on down the entry before he had the chance to change his mind.

꙳ꙮ꙳

The following day, Tuesday, was the Twelfth of July. The Orangemen's celebrations passed without much incident, in Belfast at any rate. (The countryside had always been another, bloodier story.) In the Ballast Office they passed almost without notice, except that they brought us one day closer to the Maze Races. As Wednesday gave way to Thursday, Thursday to Friday, that week to the next, there was talk, and thought, of little else. Even the progress of the Harbour Bill, due to be read before Parliament rose for the Coronation (itself due at the start of September), was relegated to a back room of the mind. Scarcely a one in the office, old or young, did not intend to take the road out to Hillsborough in the course of the festival. Hertford Livingstone, who kept the Dublin Hotel on Ann Street – a favourite with us, one of the many – erected every year a pavilion on the hill at the centre of the racetrack. All arrangements began with meeting under Hertford's canvas; quite a few of them ended there too, and got no further in between. On the Thursday, Derby Day, a bigger occasion by far than the Twelfth, or Election Day, bigger even than the Masonic parade, the office, like many another in town, would not open at all, although one or other of the Harbour Masters, decided by the tossing of a coin, would have to remain at his post. On our last night out all together – it seemed to me like years ago, not weeks – someone had proposed that a car be hired large enough to carry all who were interested in going to the big race. Someone else had proposed that the Ballast Board pay for it, which proposal was greeted with a great cheering and a rattling of pots and tumblers, then never mentioned after. A few days later a sheet of paper had appeared next to the cholera map, headed "Derby Glee" (the pin affixing it had been borrowed from the Ganges, which was too far back in the chain of contagion for it to be missed), with an invitation below it to sign your name for a place in the carriage. Ferris, or Bright, had added my name along with their own. I registered it without comment. I even joined in the counting down of the days, although we were counting down to two very different events.

≈☙≈

Millar was back in town, having managed to slip away from Armagh to oversee the installation of the staircase in Rosemary Street and to check on the progress of the portico, for which eight of the ten columns had already been cast. My grandfather passed on to me the report of an acquaintance who had seen him, "taking the front steps of the church three at a time, looking like he meant to finish the building single-handed".

"The opportunity arose very suddenly," Millar told me. "I would have overtaken any letter I might have sent to let you know I was coming. And then once I was here . . ." He spread his hands, apology and explanation both. We were talking in the coffee house on Waring Street. (I might have dispensed with the street name: we had but one coffee house then in the whole of the town.) It was not busy. It was not often. We were, despite the efforts of Mr Hanlon, as Vice Consul for Brazil and de facto coffee ambassador, a tea-drinking people – when we were not in our taverns, that is.

My friend looked as though he had been confined to the dungeons while he was in Gosford Castle. Either that or he had been kept all that time from sleeping. I knew the signs: I saw them each time I glanced in the mirror these days.

We had no sooner sat down and given our order than Millar began explaining to me in mathematical detail a problem he was having with the upper level of the church, which was intended to seat as much as half of the congregation: a floor with a hole cut out, was how he conceived of it, rather than a balcony, the idea being that at least as many would look down on the minister as looked up to him.

"You are nodding," I heard him say, and heard too the challenge in his voice.

"I agree with you."

"But I stopped talking half a minute ago."

"Which shows you how much I agree with you," I said, before turning in my seat to see if the waiter was coming with our coffee, which happily he was. Millar when I turned back was staring at me fixed.

"Something is amiss with you."

I hesitated. I knew Millar. He would not let this go until he had an answer. I had to offer him something. "A *miss* is right," I said, and when that drew no response, "a girl . . . a woman."

The waiter set the tray on our table, took from it the cups, the silver coffee pot, the cream, the sugar, and a dish of macaroons. He poured coffee for us – as black as molasses and almost as thick – then tucked the tray under his arm and made an abbreviated bow.

"A woman?" Millar said, the instant he was gone. He looked bemused. He would probably have struggled less if I had told him outright that I meant to ambush Lord Donegall. He excavated a Himalaya of sugar with his spoon and allowed it to dissolve in his coffee, then stirred, and stirred, and stirred. (Ferris, on the solitary occasion that I had been here in the past, had stirred his for a full five minutes before setting down the spoon and leaving. "How should I know whether it is good or not if I have nothing with which to compare it?" Ferris, in whatever realm you now find yourself, I am no connoisseur, but I have drunk enough coffee in the years since to tell you, you missed nothing that morning but the novelty.)

Millar stopped stirring, and with inordinate care, while he measured his words, replaced the spoon on his saucer. "You have not got her in a 'family way', have you?"

"John, please," I said, and only then wondered if it was possible, despite Maria's having at the critical moment in my grandfather's kitchen . . . No, I own that I was still unclear about the precise mechanics, less clear if anything than I had been before being inducted into the casual bawdiness of the Ballast Office clerks, but I was as certain as I could be that I was not to have a visit from her as I had had from Hannah.

I glanced behind me. If any of our fellow coffee-drinkers had heard, they were not letting it distract them from their sitting and looking glum.

"Well, then," said Millar. I was not sure whether the relief on his face was for me, or for him that he did not have to pursue this line of questioning further.

"She is in love with someone else," I said. He snatched up the spoon again, held it poised over the cup. "But I am almost over it," I added quickly.

Some friendships stay for ever in childhood, though the parties otherwise mature in mind and body. My friendship with Millar, I understood in that moment, was one such. I left it to him to choose the subject in which we might take refuge, and was not greatly surprised by it.

"I have been to see the Museum," he said. My "and", I trusted on this occasion, would be taken as read. "And", he went on, "I suppose it is good enough in its way." He took the merest sip from his cup; grimaced. "The laws of probability, of course, dictate that even a Duff and a Jackson must occasionally get it right, or at least not too far wrong."

This was tired stuff, and I thought for a moment I detected in it a softening of his attitude towards his rivals. I could not have been more mistaken.

"You remember the day we walked to the Giant's Ring?" I allowed that it had been much on my mind. "And mine," he said. "To tell you the truth, I have not been able to stop thinking about that bottle you told me was buried in the foundation stone of the Museum."

Said I, "It is a pity you are so far beyond foundation stones yourself."

"It is," he said, in such a way, however, as to suggest it was no great pity at all. "I went this afternoon to the foundry and asked Boyd himself if it might be possible to have something cast inside one of the remaining columns, a slate tablet, say." That "say" was a nice touch. "He said to me, 'The size of those columns, Mr Millar, you could cast a cow inside them and no one would be any the wiser.' A cow!" Millar slapped the table, rattling our cups and at last causing heads to turn our way. He laughed then stopped abruptly. "So I went straight from there to my grandfather's yard and found a cow's-length piece of slate. I have given the stonemason a text that I want engraved on it."

He took from the inside pocket of his coat a folded sheet of paper, which he opened and slid across the table to me, avoiding the coffee that had splashed out just now. I read it where it lay, my eyes – I could feel them and was powerless to stop them – growing wider with every word. Oh, my friend, my friend . . . I had thought he meant to outdo the Museum in rhetoric or ambition, but, never mind the "cow's length", what I read might have been cribbed from a *schoolboy*'s slate.

"You do not seriously mean to include this?" I said.

"The stonemason is at work on it as we speak, else I would not be sitting here taking coffee with you."

"But who will ever get to see it?" I asked. "Encased in all that iron?"

"Perhaps whichever future generation, or civilisation, unearths the bottle buried beneath the Museum. At least they will have their 'Rosetta Stone' to help them decipher my text." He slid the page back, around the coffee spill, and read it one more time himself, nodding at the aptness of this word or that, before folding it and returning it to his inside pocket. "Besides," he said then, "the fact that I know it is there is enough. I will rest easier in my grave."

"Let us hope you are a long time out of it." The words, by rote, had escaped my mouth before I could call them back. I could almost have spoken the response for him.

"The Lord knows we will be a long time in it."

"I think I have had all the coffee I want," I said.

He looked down at his cup. "I know what you mean," he said, and for once in our friendship I could say with a certainty that he was wrong.

Millar left a letter at the house for me a few days later. I did not acknowledge it, did not, in truth, even open it. His company at that precise moment was just too unsettling. I did not fear blurting something to him, I think, as much as I feared seeing myself reflected in him. It was important that I preserved the distinction I had made between the courses of action upon which we had each embarked, that I continued to convince myself that it was the casting of a slate in an iron pillar that was the act of a disordered mind. I avoided Rosemary Street, too. In so far as it was possible, I avoided anywhere that I thought would bring me into prolonged conversation with friends.

I left it until late in the afternoon of the day before Derby

Day, and what I thought was the opportunity of an empty office, to remove myself from the planned outing to the Maze.

"What are you doing?"

Ferris and Bright had, at the very moment I finished putting a line through my name, stepped in off the street, their arms full of the linen-backed rolls they had volunteered to go to Billy Blow's on Arthur Street to fetch. (I had been relying on them stopping somewhere along the way to drink a glass, or try on a hat, a pair of gloves. Why else would they have volunteered?) They stood in the doorway watching in astonishment.

"I am correcting an error," I said and sat again.

"Are you sure you are quite well, Gilbert?" Ferris asked.

"*Sane*?" said Bright, and dumped his cargo on the nearest desk. One of the rolls slipped out of the ribbon that had been holding it and opened a blank half-foot: a chart in search of its fluctuations.

They were as insistent with me as they had been on Easter Monday: the Cave Hill, I had to believe them, was tame in comparison with the *antics* I could expect at the Maze. Was I really going to let my grandfather deter me from the pleasures to which all young men had a right?

I, though, was not the person that I had been three months before. This had nothing to do with my grandfather, I told them, I had better uses for my time, that was all, and I did not even encourage the inference they drew, the same inference that they were, admittedly, capable of drawing from almost any combination of words in the English language (do not even mention French) . . . "There would not be seen, in the whole of this Mazy week, a darker horse than I," etc. etc.

I had already that day "put a line through" one other item on my list of final preparations, ducking into Church Street at the end of my dinner hour to leave Maria's letter at the post office.

The clerk, to whom I paid my penny, a little pudding of a man, or a little pudding topped with a littler, held the letter at arm's length. (It did not extend far.) "The Mill for Grinding Old People Young!" he read aloud. It was precisely this habit they had there of calling out addresses, like guards calling the destination of their coaches, that had led me to contrive the rendezvous with Roddy McCluskey for the dispatch of Lord Donegall's letter.

I was in luck, the clerk said. In the normal run of things it would be the morning before this could be delivered, but he lived out that direction himself and would gladly drop the letter off on his way home. I told him there was no great urgency and that the next morning would be soon enough, but he said I was not to worry on his account, the other clerks would do the same if an address lay in their way. "Tampering", they would probably call it now, may even have called it then in other parts of the kingdom. The clerk to the left of him looked up and nodded, sorry that he was not able to oblige me: "Anything around Edward Street, on the other hand . . ."

Besides, the littler pudding gave me a wink, it would be no hardship to have to stop off at an inn – and not just any inn, but that inn, where he had not stopped off in years, must be – and tell Her at Home that it was for work. And what was I to say to this, but "all right, then", and "thank you most kindly"? And, really, what difference could it possibly make now?

I did not go straight home myself when I left the Ballast Office that evening, but made my way instead up Donegall Street to cross off the last item on my list. Far ahead, three separate fires burned on the side of Black Mountain. It was the season for them, for gorse gone dry, and idle boys with glasses. The smoke plumes were angled in the breeze, a uniform forty-five degrees. It might have been a race from Cave Hill on the right to Collin on the left, the progress as stately as boats across a pond.

Past the Poorhouse, I walked, and the new lying-in hospital, until, beyond where Donegall Street became the Antrim Road, I came at last to the cemetery.

I had not visited my parents' grave for the better part of three years, had never visited it at all on my own. Without my grandfather to keep me right I wandered lost for some minutes before I succeeded even in locating the *New* Burying Ground. A guard hut stood just inside the gate, erected since last I was there, I can only think to dissuade the bereaved from mounting their own vigils and being tempted in the night, and in their fright at suspected grave-robbers, to discharge their blunderbusses, creating more graves, more vigils, more mishaps with firearms and so on in a never-ending cycle.

I found my family at length, wedged between Jane Brigs, remembered with respect and affection by all those who had the opportunity of observing her amiable disposition, and Michael Atkins, Esq., for forty years the manager of the Northern Theatre, who having strutted his hour upon this earth finished the last scene in the great drama of life on the 13th of April 1812, aged sixty-six years.

My parents' headstone was considerably less forthcoming than either of their neighbours' on character and achievements. Names, dates, and the coordinates of their three-way relationship were all that were inscribed ("wife of the below-named and also sister of the above"), along with the assertion that they were all gone to a better place.

A chanting had started up behind me. "A sailor went to sea, sea, sea, to see what he could see, see, see . . ." Across a field and over another wall the Poorhouse children had been let out to play. Looking back towards the town, I could make out the tip of a pole, garlanded with coloured ropes or ribbons. Hands clapped out the rhythm: "but all that he could see, see, see was the bottom of the deep blue sea, sea, sea." I turned again and bowed my head, trying to conjure the smallest memory of the people in the deep, dark grave before me – a hand tousling my hair, a face looming as I drifted into sleep. Not a single one came. It was an effort even to hold in my mind that the sister-wives could not be entwined in death as I had only ever seen them in life, or at least likeness.

It was an effort to think that if all went wrong tomorrow I might be returning here sooner rather than later.

What would the gravestone say about me? Hero? Hothead? Hanged?

I had not shied away from the possibility that I would share John Bellingham's fate, or imagined that I had not, the average Irishman's sense of fair play, to my knowledge, being no more reliable than the average Englishman's. (As for *Belfast* men, you might chance to fall among friends, or you might fall among "friends of true friends".) Always, though, it had been the drama of the moment I had dwelt on. I would find out Maria in the crowd, be it as large as the one that had gathered for the reading of Lord Belfast's letter – the ignition of the first gas lights. I would hold her gaze while the hangman behind me adjusted the noose and the minister beside me mumbled his prayers. A hush would descend, broken only by the wail of a child. I would not blink, or flinch. And Maria would nod in recognition.

"Let it be done!"

My soul would fly out to her . . .

Now that it was so close, however, the noose was no longer a prospect I cared to contemplate, even for Maria's acknowledging nod. Should I have to turn the pistol on myself, I would not be taken.

I knelt and offered it as a silent promise to the deaf stone (though if it had had ears to hear, a mouth to speak, the stone would have screamed its horror at what I was about), then seeing an elderly man and woman come in at the gate and feeling a little foolish to be found like that on my knees, I uprooted several of the larger dandelions from around the base. Two more words were thus revealed, "Also David": the measure of my brother's brief passage from womb to grave.

I tore at some strands of ground elder, but the roots, when I worked my finger under them and tugged, ran back across Jane Brigs and into the plot beyond. You could be all night about it once you had started. I decided just to let it lie.

The breeze had dropped. The gorse fires were becalmed halfway across Black Mountain, but the children were still chanting as I passed back down the Antrim Road and on to Donegall Street.

"A sailor went to sigh, sigh, sigh, to see what he could sigh, sigh, sigh, but all that he could sigh, sigh, sigh . . ."

There was a boiled fowl for dinner. A grey-looking thing hemmed in by greyer-looking potatoes. I ate it readily enough, when at last I was able to get at it. Nisbet sat with us, as had for some time now been his custom. As was also becoming customary, it was he who, on a nod from my grandfather, had led us this evening in the saying of Grace, in several instalments, without regard for the temperature of the food (rarely the warmest when it arrived with us anyway) or the actual nourishment of our bodies, as opposed to souls. Beyond that he spoke only when my grandfather directed a question to him – there were several pertaining to the function of the Hebrew alphabet in the Lamentations of Jeremiah – or very occasionally in an undertone to Hannah, who served as she might continue to serve for a few months yet without her secret being discovered: there was barely a pick on her. Afterwards my grandfather rose – Nisbet starting a fraction of a second after him nevertheless got out of his chair fast enough to help my grandfather from his – to carry on his enquiries into the Lamentations in his study. He turned in the doorway. "I will say 'good night' now, Gilbert, in case I do not see you again before the morrow." I did not know for certain that I would ever see him again. I rose myself and bowed.

"Good night, Grandfather," I said, "and thank you."

He shook his head. "Thank Molly. Thank Hannah. Thank him whose bounty fails us never." ("Praised be his name," Nisbet murmured.) "But do not, please, thank me."

So he left and I sat and ate two dates out of the basket that had constituted our communal dessert. I added the stones to the two already on my plate. I made of them a cross, a four-leaf clover, a rudimentary G and left them finally in a line, like a long trailing off into silence . . . .

I did not sleep. I did not try to. I did not even remove my shirt and trousers, but stretched out on the bed covers in all but my coat and boots, listening as the town wound down to its own slumber, a day-long symphony fragmenting into random notes and percussions: a whistle through fingers, a sash window falling, the last weary thuds of the Hope Hotel drummer, fewer and further between, and fewer and further, and further, and further . . .

At the stroke of two I slipped down off the bed and crouched to coax the bag out from behind the chest of drawers. I pushed back the neck to reveal the butt – I do not know what I had been expecting to find else – and checked for the eightieth or ninetieth time the powder and the wadding, the flints, the shot. All present and correct.

I tightened the neck again and finished dressing (I would say "as though for work", but that would signify nothing: all my adult life I have dressed as though for work) then closed the bedroom door behind me. The stairwells, the landings, the hallway, all the familiar coordinates of my life here, looked to have been draped in layer upon layer of black crêpe. My very feet were lost to me in the gloom, so that I seemed to float rather than walk, already half ghost.

I floated right through the door and on to the street. A lantern, even a closed lantern, would have been an invitation to scrutiny by whatever other ghosts were abroad. Besides, I had the connivance of a quarter moon, which once the White Linen Hall was behind me, and the houses were grown scanter, picked out a path for me, marked here and there by what, despite the season, looked very much like frost. I had quickly been reunited with my feet, my hands, my entire corporeal self. (Why had I not after all kept the coachman's coat as well as the contents of its pockets?) I began to stride, clapping my arms to get the circulation going, murmuring, "healthful body, healthful mind"; soon I was trotting, the murmur become a chant, through the rustling, swaying plenitude of the land about Malone, "healthful body, healthful mind, healthful body, healthful mind . . ."

The road suddenly dipped between trees into darkness as thick as silt. I had, almost without being aware of it, and far sooner than I had allowed for, arrived at the crest of the road running down to Shaw's Bridge. The Ring lay another quarter of a mile to the right, through woodland so dense that even a full moon would not have penetrated it. I turned circles on the road, circles in my mind. Then – ha! – It came to me. Of course! The day I passed this way with Millar, we had left the road to inspect the bridge's undersides. With a confidence bordering on the reckless I plunged ahead, swinging myself over the parapet and down the slope, going for the moment from black into blacker, holding on to the grass until I felt the ground level out again beneath my feet: towpath. Crouching then, I groped my way under the arch. I wedged my back in-to its curve – it might have been made for me – and drew my knees up to my chin.

Someone had been cooking meat of some description.

I could smell it quite distinctly above the smells of the river and its bank, concentrated though they were by the stone surrounding me. The earth, I discovered with a little more groping, had been disturbed, two or three feet to the left of where I sat, was warmer, too, then hot. Here, some two hands deep, was the pit or oven. I knelt and blew into it and got for my pains a faceful of sour ashes. I wiped my mouth and nose and blew again, more gently, and was rewarded this time with a faint glow, which grew from half an inch to an inch, from one inch, almost, to two. I scraped together whatever I could find in the way of dried grass and twigs and after a great deal more blowing was able to coax the embers back to life. With my hands cupped over them, I let the warmth spread along my arms, my shoulders, and finally into the cavity where I had used to think my heart resided.

At some point, perhaps half an hour after my arrival there, two men passed along the road. I heard their voices from a long way off, heard the clump of their boots, the creak, the nearer they drew to the bridge, of their lamp, and managed to fill in the pit with earth before the smoke gave me away. At the last moment it occurred to me that the meal whose remains I had smelt had been theirs – ogres walking off the last tasty morsel to have wandered all unwarily into their lair – but there was no discernible break in their stride, or in their chatter, which, as to its accent, although we were yet so close to the town, was as different from what I heard every day as chalk from cheese.

They had been drinking – were passing a bottle, or a jug, between them as they walked: slurps and sloshes added to the clumps and creaks – which might have accounted for some of my difficulty. And one of them, if I understood it correctly (I was getting about one word in three), was reporting an argument with a third man, whose wheedling voice he assumed from time to time, which might have accounted for some more.

As they crossed above my head – the Lord alone knows what actual ogres would have sounded like – the teller of the tale broke off to hawk up and spit over the far side of the parapet. The phlegm seemed to bend rather than break the surface of the water, because a few moments later I saw it quite clearly, passing in front of me, turning this way and that, at the start of its long, slow journey out to sea. The men carried on – their voices, and the voice of the absent acquaintance, growing fainter – until when I expected it least one of them let go a laugh of such force and brightness that I was sure it must have lit up the sky, like a firework. And when I uncoiled myself from the ball into which I had retreated, the darkness did indeed appear to have lost a little of its grip. I waited a quarter of an hour more, then brushed down my clothes and took to the road again, another trial endured.

I met no one on that last leg of the journey and before the first cock crew, sounding like the first cock ever to crow, I had already arrived at my destination, or my destination had announced itself to me. For as before, the rampart rose up in the end unexpectedly, as though just that moment conjured from the earth. On this occasion, though, I fought down the sense of awe; this was a place of wile this morning, not of wonder. I skirted around the base, choosing one of the less convenient breaches to enter by and coming at the *cromlech* from the rear, so as not to leave too clear a track in the dew for Lord Donegall to see. He must be kept at a disadvantage until the moment I stepped out in front of him, the answer to all the questions crowding his mind.

Even in that twilight, I had a clear view through the stones of the way he must come, although, just as in the painting I had imagined hanging in the gallery, mist was trapped still in the lower branches of the trees. One by one I removed the items from the bag and laid them, like a surgeon would his instruments, on the nearest thing to a flat surface that I could find: the stone that I had thought, last time I was here, would do Millar as a pillow. I went through then the procedures I had rehearsed and rehearsed in my room, until I felt I could do them with both eyes closed, although I scarcely dared now even to blink. I pulled the firing pin back to half-cock and poured a measure of powder into each barrel in turn before placing a square patch of wadding over the upper one only to take the ball. I pressed it in to the depth of my thumb's first joint then repeated the process with the lower barrel. Then I picked up the ramrod – this was its moment. One, two, three into the upper barrel, keep pressing, and pressing . . . *There*. One, two, three into the lower. The only way now to clear them was by firing, in preparation for which, finally, I tapped more powder into the frizzen pan, taking care as I closed it not to let the powder spill, and, when everything else had been returned to the bag, placed the gun on full-cock.

I kept tight hold of the butt to begin with, but when my palm began to sweat I transferred the gun to my coat pocket then almost at once removed it again – what if it were to become entangled at the vital moment? What if it were prematurely to go off?

I set it back on the ledge. Then I waited.

For a time the sun seemed to be in two minds about rising, hardly doing more than peek over the horizon: leaking light instead of shining. Slowly, though, it became more definite, presenting itself at last as an irrevocable fact to all who laboured and suffered under it: "The day is here and must be got through."

I was too far removed from the habit of prayer to believe that anything I might say now would be heeded, or even heard, but I recited some words anyway. Clemency, not outright forgiveness, was all that I asked. I was doing what had to be done. I felt the weight of the centuries, as though this, not the ancient pagan ceremonies, still less the latter-day horse races, was the reason that these massive stones had been hewn out and transported here – however they had been transported, wherever they had been transported from; the reason for all this impenetrable geometry.

I had been trying by my routines and repetitions to keep my emotions in check, but I think unquestionably by that stage I was a little delirious.

I am almost sure I nodded. St Peter appeared to me above the trees, reading aloud from a scroll that stretched out behind him, miles and miles and miles across the sky, which was at the same time the garden behind the house on the Flags: the names of those to whom no clemency was to be shown. At the sound of my own name I opened my eyes.

Hoof beats, coming towards me at speed from out of the mist. He had caught me out. I fumbled the gun off the ledge as the horse whinnied and the rider dismounted heavily. He would be armed, I was certain of it. I almost fell out from behind the stones, left arm holding up the right, which would otherwise have failed me. "Not one step further!" I yelled at the same moment as the voice of St Peter called again from my grandfather's mouth, "Gilbert!", and my finger, almost convulsively, squeezed the trigger.

I tried to let go or redirect my aim, but it was as though the pistol was moulded to my hand, my arms locked in position. The powder flared in the pan and the expression on my grandfather's face passed in a fraction of a second from horror to resignation. He was already halfway to God and Spencer Perceval. But there was no shot. No breath from either of us, only the fluting of a blackbird somewhere on the edge of that vast arena. Even the horse seemed frozen, its nostrils flaring, its eyes swollen to bursting as it watched with us the powder burn itself out and the smoke drift away.

I managed at last to shake the dreadful thing from my hand. My grandfather bounded forward (memory perhaps exaggerates the distance, but still: he bounded) and wrapped his arms around me, more seizure than embrace,

"What have I done!" I cried.

"You are fortunate you have done nothing that cannot be undone," he said, and eased me back against the stones. I slid to the ground, my chest heaving. Tears followed, great gales of them, and all the snot and slabber of a boy utterly broken. My grandfather beside me pulled a handkerchief from his pocket, but had not the energy to reach it to me. Only now that the danger was past did he look what he was, an old man and frail. I collected myself, scrambled to my feet.

"We must leave at once," I said. "Lord Donegall . . ."

"God grant, will not be coming," said my grandfather, handkerchief now to his brow, which was not, as I had expected to see it, red from exertion, but blae: pure, pure blae. "Nisbet rode out to Ormeau before first light to tell him there had been a great mistake."

Of course, if he had known to find me here he must have known too the reason for my coming. Still I could not account for it.

"Who told you?" I asked him.

"Mrs Barclay sent a man," he said, "knocked the entire household up. A young woman who lodges, or works, with her at the inn came to her last evening in great distress over a letter she had received." He was not looking at me, but I blushed nonetheless, face, neck, shoulders, back. "She feared that something dreadful was about to occur, she could not say for certain what, or even where, the letter was too cryptic, but she believed from certain references that it might concern the Ring here."

He took in his surroundings as though for the first time. There was respect in the regard, as for a worthy opponent: *so this is what I have been up against all these years?*

"Hannah told us she had heard someone leave by the front door shortly after two o'clock," he resumed, and dabbed again with the handkerchief. "We overturned your room completely, looking for anything else that could make sense of what you were about." He produced from another pocket a sheet of paper, which he handed to me. The creases told the story of its having been screwed into a ball before being smoothed flat and folded. "Dear Lord Donegall," I read. "You will forgive, I hope, my presumption in writing, but I crave a meeting with you on a matter . . ."

If I had not known otherwise I would have said it had been written by a chimpanzee in woollen mittens.

"It was under the bed. Molly had to lie flat to retrieve it with a brush, Hannah having requested that she be spared such an exertion."

My ears had continued to receive, but my mind was still some sentences back.

"Mrs Barclay?"

"I have lived a long time in this town," my grandfather said. "Enough, I sometimes feel, for two or even three lives. Mrs Barclay was a friend in one of them."

The colour had begun at last to return to his face. "If you could help me stand," he said, and motioned for me to take his arm. "I think we should walk."

"The horse," I said. The horse had removed itself to a distance safe from shouts and bawls and flashes in the pan and buried its nose in the dew-rich grass. I recognised it now as belonging to Dr McDonnell. What emergency, I wondered, could my grandfather have invented for his cousin in Gransha that necessitated the borrowing of a mount at half past three in the morning?

My grandfather got to his feet gingerly. He cast a sidelong look at the animal. "I think I would rather walk."

So we walked, out of the Ring and down the lanes, and my grandfather, for the first time in our lives together (though I am one to criticise), talked.

He had known them all, he told me. All the "Men of Ninety-Eight": Neilson, Russell, Hope, McCracken. There were scarcely twenty thousand souls then in the entire town: not many were complete strangers. But neither had his encounter with those particular souls been a matter of chance. He had gone several times to meetings of the "Muddlers' Club", for it was under that innocuous name that they first met, in the tavern in Sugarhouse Entry that Mrs Barclay and her husband had, the Dr Franklin. (Forget for a moment Peggy Barclay and Henry Joy McCracken: my grandfather in a tavern? Truly this was another life.) A veritable warren of a place where a room might always be found for friends and for Muddlers who did not wish their conversations to be overheard, but where equally, so numerous were the comings and goings, the corridors and the corners, anyone might observe you without your being aware of it.

Among the couple of dozen serving girls and potboys and cooks and waiters required to keep the establishment running was one young woman, Belle Martin, of whom my grandfather had heard some report from a connection in her native Portaferry. "Handsome and in manner easy-going," the connection said, "and utterly untrustworthy." What she fished for at one door she used as bait at the next, trying to set friend against friend, neighbour against neighbour. By the time she left to find work in Belfast there was not a house in the town where she was welcome.

My grandfather had tried on more than one occasion to broach these suspicions with James Barclay, to suggest to him that Belle Martin should perhaps be kept away from the room where the Muddlers' Club met. But that gentleman believed in taking people as he found them – who was to say but that spite at her advancement had set the Portaferry tongues wagging? And, besides, the Muddlers were particularly fond of the girl.

Half a dozen of them saw the inside of a Scottish prison as a result of their fondness. They were the lucky ones. She betrayed as well four members of the Monaghan Militia, then billeted in the town, who went to their deaths before a firing squad at Lisburn.

James Barclay was taken up along with his clients when the soldiers raided. It was six years before he returned home, by which time Belle was long, long gone from Belfast town.

"That", said my grandfather, "ought to have been a warning to the others. If they could not organise safely in a town of twenty thousand how could they hope to organise across a country of eight million? They were some of the best men living, and full of the noblest intentions, but they allowed their ambitions to get ahead of their ability to deliver on them."

He broke with them definitively a year and more before they rose up. Several of the United men – he never did discover which – had taken the decision to act against another suspected informer, a man named Small, who made the honest portion of his living selling brushes from door to door about the town. They invited him one night to a house where there was to be music and drinking and a swearing-in of volunteers. Small was exceedingly partial to the first two and for information on the third would be handsomely rewarded by his paymasters in the barracks, assuming those were his paymasters and not just heavier than normal users of yard brushes and scrubbing brushes, the half-dozen varieties of brush required to keep a horse well groomed.

Of course he accepted.

Towards the end of that week, Mrs Small appeared in the town with her children – the brush-makers – in tow, asking had anyone met with her husband or heard anything of his whereabouts. They were still walking the streets at nightfall, as pitiable a sight as could be imagined. Shortly after that, soldiers searched the houses of a number of people known to be sympathetic to the United men's cause, turning the furniture out of the windows and threatening pitch-cappings and half-hangings, the whole gamut of tolerated tortures (an extreme reaction admittedly to the disappearance of a favourite brush-seller), but not one word to the purpose did any of those so menaced utter.

Months later a man's naked body floated to the surface of the

Mill Dam. There was speculation, of course, but the body had been in the water much too long for anyone even to hazard a guess as to its identity; too long certainly for Mrs Small to be put through the further ordeal of making a judgement.

"Small," my grandfather repeated, as though that one word were the whole of the man. "I can see him as well, bowed down under the basket on his back. It was hard to know sometimes looking at him where his hair ended and the bristles began."

We were walking at no great pace, the horse even then dawdling behind us, all unperturbed by the course that its day was taking, the frantic gallop giving way to the indulgence of fresh grass, and now this leisurely retracing of its steps through the countryside, towards town. My grandfather's narration matched his gait, halting, easily deflected.

"I tried for several days to find someone with influence within the Society to whom I could speak, but those who were not off organising elsewhere were lying low. In the end and quite by chance I ran into McCracken, home in secret from a mission of his own to Armagh. I could not even wait, in my agitation, until we were some place private, but began asking him straight away, in the middle of the street, what he knew of the affair. And to his great credit – and at great risk, for it was no secret that the authorities wanted only the pretext to arrest him – he took the trouble to answer me. He swore to me that he would have no part in such a deed, or have dealings with any man who did, that he had heard from Jemmy Hope of a meeting at which the setting up of a committee for managing assassinations had been proposed, and that Hope had personally seen to it that it was thrown out the door.

"His right hand, as he said this, was flat against his heart.

And yet, I told him, somebody must have done something. I had seen the woman with my own eyes, turning circles outside the Market House, asking all and sundry, 'Please, can anybody tell me where these children's father is?'"

My grandfather said nothing further for a moment – for a moment, in fact, stood quite still on the road – then he let go the name a final time. "Small." He sighed. "I said my prayers on the night that that body was recovered from the Mill Dam, said them as I had never in my life till then said them, and when I unclasped my hands at daybreak I was as a new man."

He performed the clasping and unclasping of his hands as he spoke, the latter not without difficulty. It had been a long time since any bit of him was new.

The ointment on my ankle the day I was carried into the house after the tumble on Cave Hill . . . He had known at once that he had smelt it before, although it took until later that evening, by which time he had been driven almost to distraction, for the "what" and the "where" of it to fall back into place: a night more than three decades before when a party of drunken dragoons went on the rampage through the town. There had been an altercation earlier in the day involving a townsman whom some of the soldiers had accused of showing insufficient respect in refusing to doff his hat. Their officers had reined them in then, but now, under cover of darkness, they were out for revenge. They found their way at length to Sugarhouse Entry where they set about trying to remove Dr Franklin from his bracket above the door, cracking the head of any man foolish enough to protest. They cracked my grandfather's, who was doubly foolish, being the father of two small girls. "I was already walking a different path from the Muddlers and the Barclays and even Dr Franklin, but it was the principle of the thing," he told me that morning. "Our Lord himself would not have stood idly by. And the dragoons were most dreadfully drunk."

Peggy Barclay, when the storm had passed and my grandfather could be got into the tavern, had attended to his injuries in person: welts on his back as well as lumps on his head. And, yes, the ointment had smelt as rank then: rankness was written into the recipe; rankness, Dr McDonnell said, was half the good of it.

(I did not even stop him to ask where Dr McDonnell fitted into this. Years passed before I learned of his gift to Wolfe Tone of a medical kit to take with him into exile; of his failure, only a few years later, to respond to the summons by Miss McCracken to try to revive her brother after his body was taken down from the scaffold, although her brother was in any case quite dead.)

Peggy Barclay was one of those people, it was hard to put an age to her: old enough to command that large household, young enough to adapt to whatever life brought her way, early hours and late nights, informers among her serving girls, assaults by the military.

"Even after the Rising was put down and the prisoners released the soldiers would not let her be. I would hear whisperings now and then when I was out about my business of some new raid or other act of harassment. Then her husband died – this would have been 18 and 9, or 10, before you were born certainly. He was not too many years back from the Scotch prison. It must be asked whether his confinement there hastened his demise. She carried on for a few years more in Sugarhouse Entry before giving up the tavern to a man named Bambridge, and I heard no more about her. I had thought it likely that she was already dead. So many I knew then are."

Peggy Barclay, it seems, had thought that my grandfather must be dead too. When the "young woman" had mentioned my name, though, and where I lived, she at once made the connection. Rice was not at that time a common surname in the town, and she remembered having been told, some years past, of the unfortunate series of bereavements, ending with a son-in-law of that name, that had delivered me into my grandfather's care. She remembered, too, the assault by the dragoons on the Dr Franklin Tavern. It had been a long time in coming, but she was pleased at last to be able to do him a kindness in return.

We had paused for breath beneath a stand of beech trees near to where a lane joined the road on the eastern side running up from New Forge. The horse, standing apart from us, raised its tail and dropped four grassy balls of dung. Another day it might have been a source of awkwardness between us. My grandfather scarcely noticed it. The traffic, almost non-existent when we had emerged from the Giant's Ring, had grown now to a steady stream, all of it headed in the opposite direction to us: gigs, sociables, landaus, vis-à-vis (broughams belonged as yet to futurity), even hay carts and coal carts, taking the hopeful of Belfast – who would have guessed there were so many? – to Derby Day at the Maze. I did not see among them the car carrying my colleagues from the Ballast Board, although for the first time in weeks I found I could smile at the thought of the figure it would cut, Ferris and Bright hallooing from the windows.

"I do not presume to know what you were hoping to achieve," my grandfather said, apropos of nothing that had passed between us in the minutes immediately preceding. "As to the harbour, though, the Donegalls will back down, if not on this Bill then the next, or if not on that one then the one after that. It is the way that change most often comes about in this country, by brinkmanship and amendment. And, besides, Reform *is* coming. Not the variety that I would wish for, although I will keep toiling, as we should now keep walking."

A quarter of a mile further on we stopped again to breakfast at an inn that resembled more a dwelling house whose occupants had made a bit of room at their table. On the floor by my chair lay an infant in a cradle, being rocked by a sister who could not have been long out of the cradle herself. Various older children took turns in the chairs facing ours, applying themselves to a large loaf, whose eradication – and that of a saucer of butter – appeared to be their common goal. The man of the place, all the while, smoked his pipe and read an almanac, as naturally as if he had exhausted his conversation with us at a convivial dinner the night before. His wife served us porridge followed by boiled bacon with bread off the griddle, and tea as black as the great battered pot from which it was poured. I believe it may have been the best breakfast that I ever ate.

I was almost able to forget for the duration of it that I still had in my possession a loaded pistol. My grandfather had picked it up and handed it back to me as we prepared to leave the Giant's Ring. A gun had no place there and even if buried in the countryside round about, as I had suggested, would only be the cause of some mischief or mishap when at last it came to light, as come to light one day, not in my lifetime perhaps, certainly not in his, it inevitably would. The river, likewise, was too unreliable a repository. A furnace was the only fit place for it.

Back on the road again, the gun, like my shame, weighed heavier the closer we drew to the town and the more obvious was my grandfather's fatigue. It was three minutes past noon by the clock of the White Linen Hall when we came into Donegall Place. The street might have been evacuated overnight. The doors of the bank were closed. A notice hung from the knocker that I could not read and did not need to: *Gone to the Races*. Only Hercules Street, to gauge by the sounds reaching us from that quarter, was still going about its business unaffected by the distractions elsewhere. In the summer above all a town must re-provision itself daily.

Not one of those few neighbours and tradesmen around to bid us good day could have guessed what we had been about in the hours previous, any more, I realised now, than I could have guessed what they had been about in the years before I first trod the streets of the town. They had not all been killed or shipped out, presumably, the pitch-cappers and half-hangers, the spies, the volunteers and the assassins, the turners of blind eyes. There were different orders of silence. Maybe the soonest way to mend the wounds of that time was to say as close to nothing as possible. Maybe.

Nisbet met us in the hallway, his face a perfect mask of horror at the sight of my grandfather.

"Well?" my grandfather said, waving away his attempts at assistance.

"The groom had already brought the horses round to the front of the house when I arrived. Five minutes more and I would have been too late."

"But you were not," said my grandfather and sat – "Ooph!" – on the chair next to the hall table.

"His lordship was perplexed to know how I had been apprised of the contents of his mail, although he himself in his blustering and his expostulations supplied me with most of the detail . . . A racehorse," Nisbet said in an aside to my grandfather, who with all else that had passed between us on our walk had not thought to enquire how I had meant to entice the Marquis into our rendezvous. "It was to have been shown or offered for sale. Lord Donegall, I think, was half inclined to see my having gone there as an attempt to gull him out of an opportunity, but the groom persuaded him finally. His lordship appears to set great store by his opinion." He turned his eyes towards me then away. "There had been some injunction in the letter against bringing servants, but Lord Donegall meant to defy it. Not only the groom to look the animal over, but also a stable-lad with a cudgel in case an attempt was made to rob him."

Either I would have had to kill three men with two shots or, which was a thousand times more likely, I would never have made it away from the Giant's Ring with my own skull intact.

My grandfather's thoughts were evidently following a similar line, for, raising himself first out of his seat again, he insisted we pray where we stood in the hallway, kneeling being thought to draw attention to the sinner and not the sin, and kneeling in any case being far beyond him at that moment. His hand found out my shoulder.

"Oh, Lord, you have reminded us again this day of our all-too-human failings. We are all, Lord, as children without your guidance, prone to err. For your deliverance of us from greater error, for the promise made, in blood, at Calvary to forgive whosoever shall embrace you, Lord, we humbly thank thee."

Nisbet's "Amen" was loud enough for three, but mine was in there too, make no mistake.

A letter was lying, folded small, on a salver on the table. I recognised Millar's hand even before my own name. I picked it up at the same moment as my grandfather opened his eyes and instructed me to accompany him to the kitchen. "We will join you again presently," he said to Nisbet, who having already taken one step forward was now obliged to take it back. I passed the letter from palm to trouser pocket, and in the welter of that morning's events, put it almost instantly out of mind.

Hannah stood up from the kitchen table as we came in. A tousle-haired boy sat there, who, Molly explained, snatching up the plate from in front of him (there was still a slice of black pudding on it), was the lad who had earlier brought the horse from Dr McDonnell's, and whom she had found twenty minutes before in the corner by the dresser, dead to the world.

"It is little wonder you needed the sleep, the early start you had." My grandfather addressed the boy directly and at once Molly relaxed her guard, although not her hold on the plate, to the boy's obvious dismay. "Perhaps Hannah would help you pick some raspberries to take back with you to Dr McDonnell." Having just seen the last of his breakfast whisked away, as though he had been the one who had put it there, the boy looked bewildered at finding himself now hauled up, given a bowl to hold, and hustled towards the door. Hannah, doing the hustling, looked only too glad of the excuse to get out. Molly waited a moment more in the kitchen, glancing from me to my grandfather. "Perhaps", she said, and took down a colander from a hook by the window, "the doctor would like some peas too."

When we were safely alone, my grandfather handed me a poker and asked me to open the door in the wall below the oven and make a deep well in the coals. The heat, when I laid the fire bare, almost took my eyebrows off. "And now," said my grandfather, "let us be rid of the item once and for all."

I removed the gun with care from my pocket, though it was now neither cocked nor primed, then, abandoning caution, flung it into the well I had made and shut the door fast behind it. For a few seconds more, we stood as we had at the Giant's Ring, paralysed by anticipation and dread. Then, one after the other, the powder charges in the barrels ignited, though if the balls were discharged the firebrick and the cast iron absorbed the force of them and reduced the reports to beer-cork pops.

And that was that.

After another minute or two my grandfather suggested that I give the fire a rake. Already, when I opened the door the second time, the "item" had ceased to be a gun. Flames bloomed yellow and blue the length of the stock; the barrels glowed as though alchemised. How much better, I thought, if we too could be as quickly translated from one state to the next: no ground elder, no dandelions, no decay. I covered the remains with the fieriest coals and walked with my grandfather to the hallway again.

Nisbet had not moved an inch, but moved now, shadowing my grandfather as he began his ascent of the stairs, one hand light on the tiller of the old man's elbow. I stood for a few moments, before following behind, alone in the hallway, silently rejoicing in its ordinariness. Not an object in it but had been standing or hanging there on the day I was first brought, blinking, through the unlocked door.

My own room was another matter. You would have thought the dragoons of old had been let loose on it: chairs upset, clothing and papers tossed about. The end of the brush that Molly had used to retrieve the telltale letter was still sticking out from under the bed. Even the chest of drawers had been shoved aside. The bed-warmer lay sideways across the top, leaking water.

Later, I told myself. I would start to put it all back together later.

I cleared a space on the mattress and lay down, first on my left side then on my right then on my back then on my left side again, but each time I closed my eyes Maria's face came to me. *"In great distress," he had said.* I sat up. If only to let her know that I was safe, I had to see her again.

Nisbet was easing the study door closed when I arrived on the lower landing. My grandfather had just that minute fallen asleep in his armchair. "I would not advise disturbing him any more today," Nisbet said. "As it is, it is a miracle that he is not in the infirmary."

Whatever about God and my grandfather, I did not imagine that Nisbet would find it in his heart ever to forgive me.

I asked him, were my grandfather to rouse sooner than expected, to tell him he was not to worry himself on my account: I had some business to attend to. I would try not to be too long about it.

I was already past the middle stair before I heard him say, "You may be less time about it than you think." I turned, but saw only his back, receding down the landing. Even calling on him to explain himself would have meant wasting precious seconds. So too closing the door.

Half a minute only brought me on to Hercules Street. To enter the street on a warm afternoon was to pass through an invisible curtain. The air was thicker here, almost pulsing. Besides the butchers, there were fruit-sellers' and egg-sellers' barrows to negotiate, every stray dog in Belfast to avoid tripping over, but there were too, from the day's beginning to its end, horses and vehicles coming and going . . . I begged a lift with a carter, just leaving from the north end of the street, who told me he was happy to oblige if I did not mind a bit of company in the straw: two whole beef carcasses bound for the kitchens of Mr Simms at the Grove, which was not more than a quarter of a mile from my destination.

He talked as he drove, over his shoulder and through the pipe clenched in his nut-brown teeth, of the "extraordinary vision" he had had this morning on Donegall Street, like the destruction of King Solomon's Temple, "if I knew my Bible". I assured him I knew it very well, thank you, but between the pipe and the bumps and the need not to get too close to my straw bedfellows – "Boaz" and "Jachin", as my driver would have them – I could not altogether follow him.

I leapt down before we had come to a halt at the gates of Grove House, shouting my thanks, and pulling at my shirt as I ran to shake off the straw and the cloying smell of freshly slaughtered meat.

A haze lay over the surface of the road ahead, so that when at last it came into view the Mill for Grinding Old People Young seemed to hover uncertainly between this world and the world of my own imagining. A blink now and it might disappear irretrievably into the latter. As I drew nearer, though, it took root again on the corner of Buttermilk Loney, with its dozen front-facing windows, its hydrangeas, its double gateway, from out of which Dorothy strode, carrying a pail, whose contents she flung – grey water momentarily silver in the sun – across the road and into the Lough beyond. You would not have put it past her to have been filling the entire Lough in this way – in defiance of a belief only in people and dumb animals – since the days of Finn McCool. Seeing me, she drew herself up and rested a hand on her hip.

"She is gone," she said. Her tone was as harsh as ever I had heard it, but her eyes had more in them of pity than mockery. "I told you all along you were wasting your time."

I must have known deep down that Maria would not be there, for I felt now no sudden jolt of despair.

"When did she go?"

The pity vanished from Dorothy's eyes. She turned the pail upside down and hit it with the flat of her hand, dislodging something unsavoury. It flopped into the dust at her feet. "An hour and more since," she said. "Mistress herself took her into town for the Liverpool boat."

I looked over my shoulder at the Lough as she unleashed an invective against the preferment shown to Miss High and Mighty.

Not a funnel, or a mast of any size moved on the water.

The invective stopped. I glanced back. Dorothy shook her head. "Well, run then," she said. "You look to me as if you would be quick." She swung the pail from one hand to the other as she turned towards the inn. "Too quick."

I ran.

I never in my life again ran as hard.

The steamer *Hibernia* sailed from Donegall Quay on the high tide, Maze Races or no Maze Races. By the time I arrived at the quayside the engines were already being fired and the mass of people milling about had begun reluctantly to separate into those who meant to travel and those whose lot it was to tarry here. My head was turned this way and that, that way and this, by one woman after another who on second glance was as unlike Maria as it was possible for a woman to be.

She spotted me before I spotted her, trying to hold her ground, despite the buffeting on all sides, at a point almost midway between the shipping agent's office and the boat. Her right hand started up instinctively, only for the left to catch it before it opened into a wave, but that movement was all that was needed. I had eyes for nothing and no one else.

So desperate was I to reach her that I trod on the skirts of a woman – I will not pretend that I saw her face – whose husband without hesitation swung a fist – nor did I see that coming, but felt it only, glancing off my right ear – shouting after me that he would punch me good and proper if ever he got the hold of me . . . So desperate was I to reach her that I almost collided with Peggy Barclay, who had at that moment turned from saying her goodbyes and who with the barest of nods to me carried on into the throng. I ricocheted from her straight into Maria's luggage. I caught a hatbox, so light it must have been empty, and replaced it on the trunk on which it had balanced, unintentionally rebuilding the low wall between us. Maria, in the hat presumably that the box had contained, the only hat I had ever seen her wear, a little smudged at the trim even now, tilted her head, unable to meet my eye.

"You must not let them drive you away like this," I said.

"No one is driving me anywhere." It had been so long since I had heard her speak I had almost forgotten how marked was her accent, and how mesmeric.

"If it were not for you," I said, "someone would certainly have died this morning, either me, or . . ." – for all that the people around us were caught up in their own grief (Liverpool in those days might have been Labrador), we were still in public – ". . . you know who. It is thanks you deserve, not condemnation."

"I did not know either that anyone was condemning me."

The top of my ear throbbed where the irate husband's fist had connected, or had failed to connect as intended. I did not want to think what "good and proper" would feel like.

A porter skidded his barrow to a halt beside us. He wore a cap turned backwards to protect his neck from the sun; his brow as a consequence was scarlet. It was a lesson in something.

"These ones here, Missis?" he asked Maria, and shaped to lift the trunk with the box still on top.

"Wait!" I said, before Maria could speak.

From his crouched position, the porter looked at me and then at Maria. "A minute or two more," I said, to her as much as to him, and Maria nodded. The porter pulled himself up by the rope round the waist of his trousers, shook his head, before hauling his barrow on to the next tableau of despond: "These ones here?"

A cloud of starlings passed overhead. Maria's eyes followed their flight. The starlings banked and turned.

"I thought that you at least would have understood what I was trying to do," I said. "The Grand Gesture!"

Her gaze remained fixed on the starlings' display a moment more, then she looked at me for the first time full in the face, leaning in to reinforce her point. "And I thought you would have understood what I was trying to say. 'Murder' was not it."

I had known from the moment my grandfather caught me in his arms at the Giant's Ring that I had been foolish. Only now did I realise how far back my folly extended. I felt, more acutely than ever I had in her presence, how short a time was not-quite-eighteen years on this earth.

I had nothing else at my disposal. "Stay with me," I said. "I beg you. Stay."

Her expression changed, from resoluteness to helplessness. "I cannot. Matters are coming to a head at home."

"You have had your letter?"

She averted her gaze again. "Not that letter, no, but I know he will have gone to where the fighting is fiercest. The Russians are closing in now on Warsaw. I could not forgive myself if I remained any longer like this, hidden away. Mrs Barclay has lent me the money, which I will repay to the last farthing."

Her eyes, as she said this, flicked to the right, and looking round I thought I caught a glimpse of the familiar black tulle at a discreet remove, among the bonnets and the tall hats and the porters' caps.

"But anything might happen to you," I said. "And you must see it yourself, the cause is already lost."

She shrugged. "For now, maybe."

"So stay for now," I began to say, but our particular porter friend returned at that moment, the peak of his cap now determinedly to the fore. "Are you ready yet, Missis?" he asked, and Maria without further reference to me told him that she was.

I stood by while she directed the man, who was used no doubt to everyone knowing his job better than he did when it came to their own luggage. "Be sure not to lift that by the straps," and, "Take care, the lid of this one is loose."

"Right, I hear you. Right, right."

When he had gone there was only space between us. I took a step into it; took another.

"Please." She held up a hand. It was shaking. "Come no closer."

I did as she bid and stopped. Already, though, I was within an arm's length of her. I reached out and with my fingertips touched her cheek. Her eyes, almost despite her, closed. She rolled her head a little to the right, presenting me with the angle of her jaw, the softness behind her ear, the taut tendons of her neck. I poured all the love I possessed into those caresses. "Remember our walks, how we sat beneath that chestnut tree, the two of us," they said. "Remember that one night." If I could only keep her like this a while longer, my fingers curling now round the other side of her face, in underneath her bonnet, my thumb stroking the corner of her mouth, her lips . . .

She took my hand suddenly in hers. She smothered the thumb the fingers the knuckles the wrist with kisses. She pressed the palm flat against her face. Her eyelashes were wet. I felt as much as heard the words that her mouth formed.

"The world is too good that we will not meet again some-where in it."

And then almost before I was aware of what was happening she had let my hand fall and was pushing through the crowd towards the boat. I called her name – *guldered* it. Every head, it seemed, turned except hers. I caught sight of the back of her bonnet twice more as she ascended the gang-board. Only when she had reached the deck did she look round. She completed the wave that she had started when she had first seen me. I raised my own hand in response, mirrored the action of hers in touching my fingers to my lips then turning them out towards her. Then the wind gusted and the deck was obscured by smoke from the *Hibernia*'s funnels. When the smoke cleared a young mother had taken Maria's place at the rail and was holding up a baby to someone on the quay for whom that red face was the embodiment of love freely given. The baby squeezed its eyes shut and cried.

Above the howls, above the last shouted farewells, above the racket now of the engines, a bell was ringing. Deckhands drew up the board and wound in the mooring ropes loosed by their counterparts on the quayside. The smoke from the funnels grew denser, the waving, all around me, of handkerchiefs, more frantic, and these alone signalled the exact moment of departure. By the time the smoke had thinned out again the *Hibernia* was already abreast of Ritchie's Dock, its stern beginning the leftward drift in preparation for the first bend in the channel. One by one the handkerchiefs were returned to their pockets, some having been applied en route to noses in sudden need of blowing, and the handkerchief owners faced again towards the town – those, that is, who made it past the doors of the Donegall Quay Tavern. The dockhands and the porters, too, had turned their attention to other tasks. When all was said and done, it was just a boat. There would be another from Liverpool putting in the day after tomorrow, another sailing out at the same time two days after that, to say nothing of the boats coming and going in between from London, Dublin, Greenock, Glasgow: more beginnings and endings and stories picked up where they had been left off days or weeks or years before.

A hand gripped my shoulder, spinning me round: a man's face I could not recall ever having seen before, passing from angry to angrier by reason of my very blankness. In the next instant his fist had slammed into my left ear and his face disappeared again in the redness that flooded my vision. Through the roaring in my head I heard the voice snarl that that would teach me to shove a lady so, ripping her dress!

I staggered about the quay till the redness gradually bled away. The roar, though, got worse instead of better. It was a minute or two before I realised that it was not now all confined to my head. There was cheering coming from somewhere up the town, a great siphoning off in that direction of people who had lingered on the quays; even a few of those who had been making for the tavern checked back out. I caught several times the word "pillars" being shouted, as incongruous in that context as a pair of parakeets among the starlings that continued to clot and swirl overhead. And only then did I make sense of the meat-carter's vision: not a temple being dismantled, but a church being erected. I remembered the letter I had picked up from the hall table. I tried five pockets before I found it. The words danced on the page until I stared them down. "In haste, Old Friend, I called at your door this morning, but the household was in a confusion and no one could give me a sensible report of you. (Perhaps you are gone from town: you did not respond to my last.) I had hoped to give you more notice of the

Spectacle, but Boyd only laid the plan before me late last night
. . ." The streets being emptier than usual, that Derby Day, Millar's portico was on the move.

And I would have moved then myself to witness it, but there was another noise competing with the cheering to dislodge the roar from my head. I turned and took half a dozen shaky steps to the edge of the quay. The *Hibernia* was in position now to push on up the channel, or ought to have been. Something was wrong. The engines were straining themselves to a whine, but the steamer was not responding. I watched a minute more to make sure that this was not some further disturbance of the senses brought on by the blow to my head. A horn sounded: three long moans. A couple of dockhands hurried back to where I stood.

"She has run into the sandbank," said one.

"Is she in danger?" I asked, alarmed.

"No," said his companion, who had, I only now noticed, perched on his head a small black silk hat, "but I should say she is stuck fast."

I tried to run, but my legs went from under me. The bigger of the dockhands helped me to my feet. "Too much to drink at the races today?"

"Watch me," I said and took off the second time with more success, but little grace, lurching along the quay.

I was heart-scared of taking my eye off the boat and though I was forced to veer away from the riverside on to Corporation Street until I was around the first of the shipbuilding yards, I managed to keep sight of the funnels at least, which despite all their belching black smoke remained firmly fixed on the County Down skyline, like a premonition of the town to come.

The watchman at the graving docks beyond the yard was in the Ballast Board's employ. (I wrote his fifteen shillings' pay in the ledger every week and every week received his firm X in acknowledgement.) Far from challenging, he saluted me as I passed through the gate, shouting a greeting that did not reach me, but appeared to please him greatly. A three-master sat high and dry in the smaller of the graving docks, its keel half tarred. The other dock was empty. I came alongside the water again at the border of the Board's grounds and the next shipyard, the timber yard beyond.

The *Hibernia* was not more than a hundred and fifty yards distant. Passengers had come out on to the deck, or had not had the opportunity to quit it before the impact. They clustered together, in threes and fours, looking over the ship's rail. Below them, a number of small craft were already closing in, coming from the port, a Harbour Master's ensign prominent among them. (Shaw, the south-side master, had lost the coin toss in the end to Courtney of the north on the best of seven.) It was a race against time and – always and ever, always and ever – tide. The longer the *Hibernia* remained stuck the less water there would be in the channel to float it free. I scrutinised the groups at the rail as nearly as I could at that distance – the baby was there, less red in the face, in the arms of some gallant who had relieved the mother of her burden – but could see no one resembling Maria.

Minutes passed, became an hour . . . there was a renewed outbreak of cheers and whistles from the direction of the town: the last of the pillars arriving at their destination, perhaps (I wonder were Duff and Jackson abroad that day? I wonder did they stop to watch?), or the return from the Maze of the lucky few and the many more determined to try their luck again next year . . . an hour became two hours then three. Still the little boats flitted about the prow, still the *Hibernia*'s engines grumbled, and now and then growled; still the water level fell. As dusk gathered and the larger of the vessels that had been dancing attendance began tacking back towards the quays before they too became stranded, Maria appeared.

Although I have asked myself the question almost daily since, I cannot account for how she knew where to find me, but from the first moment she walked out on to the deck, a shawl now, deep red, about her shoulders, she was looking directly towards where I was standing. Unless, as someone else had once said, I was by wonderful accident exactly where I needed to be.

The engines at last fell silent, all hope of effective action abandoned for the night. We could have called out to one another, but did not. We would soon have exhausted ourselves, and what was there after all left to say? So we passed the whole of that night in silent communion, face to face across the water. I had no proof, of course, that she remained there without interruption: the lights of the town did not extend that far and thick drifts of cloud prevented Nature's own night-light from assisting much. At odd moments too I must have lapsed into sleep where I stood, or, eventually (for even without my brain being rearranged I was on my last legs), sat. At other moments, however, a gap appeared long enough for the moon to pick her out, shawl each time pulled a little tighter than the time before.

Between us – I am certain of it – we kept the vigil.

It was still night when the tide turned and the channel began to fill again and the *Hibernia*'s engines coughed themselves back to life. The smaller craft returned at daybreak and a short time later, heralded by more smoke and noise, a motorised tug appeared in the Lough on the seaward side. The rescue this time was quickly accomplished, the boat borne off like a leaf in the jaws of so many ants. The moon in surrendering the sky had dragged the clouds with it and the sun rising behind the *Hibernia* was from its first showing above the funnels almost impossible to look into, but I told myself that if she did not quit her post I would not close my eyes, would not, would not, whatever the cost, I lost her finally not to darkness but to dazzle, trying to keep the boat in sight, until I could not distinguish between the Lough, the Lagan, the tears brimming up inside me, filling my head to bursting.

III

Report to E. S. Finnigan Esq., City Coroner

The telephone rang at twenty minutes to nine on Saturday morning last, 25th December (Christmas Day). I was at first amused, on taking the receiver, to find myself addressed by Sir Gilbert Rice's housekeeper, Mrs Mawhinney, knowing how uncertain that lady was of the apparatus, but she only had to say Sir Gilbert's name for that amusement to turn to alarm. I understood from the torrent of words that poured from her that her employer had not responded when she had knocked on his door at half past seven, that she had thought to let him lie given the lateness of his going to bed the night before (although he had been in my company and left it at a reasonable hour), but that when she received no response at half past eight she had been sufficiently concerned to let herself into the room. Here she gave a cry so piercing – and so irrefutable in its import – that I almost dropped the telephone. I asked her, when she had recovered herself a little, if she had summoned a doctor and being assured that she had told her I would be with her presently.

My own household was running on a reduced staff, owing to the holiday, and it was some time before I could organise a carriage. On my arrival at the house – it was by now a little after a quarter to ten – I was met in the hallway by Mrs Mawhinney herself. I accompanied her directly to the master bedroom, situated on the front left of the property to look at it from the outside, the right when approached from the landing. The room was dark, the air heavy with oil fumes, the lamp on the table by the bed having been left to burn itself out in the course of the night. Sir Gilbert was lying on one hip, his back somewhat curved and turned to the door. His head, from where I stood, was not yet visible, appearing to have slipped forward off the pillow on to his chest. Any remaining hope I had had as I crossed town that the housekeeper had been mistaken was instantly dispelled. He was plainly dead.

The realisation seemed to hit Mrs Mawhinney with renewed force, for she sank all at once to the floor and it was with the utmost difficulty that I got her to her feet again, neither of us being in the first flush of youth and that lady, in her embarrassment at her display of emotion (the more understandable when you consider how long she had been in Sir Gilbert's employ), being half inclined to let the carpet swallow her completely.

Dr Gordon then arrived, with seasonal apologies for his lateness. He went straight to the bedside and took Sir Gilbert's wrist in his hand, more it appeared by rote than in hope. After only a matter of seconds he released the arm again and reached out with his first two fingers as though to lower the eyelids. He dropped to his knees, then went out of sight, I assume to examine the chamber pot, which evidently contained nothing that could aid in his assessment, for when he reappeared he asked Mrs Mawhinney to go over again the circumstances of her discovery. As she was rehearsing the knock on the door etc., Dr Gordon lifted from the bed a foolscap notebook, which Mrs Mawhinney, interrupting her account, identified as her employer's journal. It was, she said, his custom to attend to it last thing each night.

Dr Gordon brought the journal, folded open, round to where we stood and indicated a blot on the left-hand page. It appeared from the final entry that Sir Gilbert had awoken in some discomfort "a quarter of an hour past, at ten after two", and being unable to get back to sleep had attempted to write more. The blot, occurring some four lines later, would have been consistent with a sudden, perhaps fatal attack, giving a time of death of around half past two. (The doctor told me later that he had thought by this ingenious piece of detective work to obviate the need for taking a rectal temperature to determine *algor mortis*.) Mrs Mawhinney it was who – recovered from the shock of seeing her own name written into the narrative – drew our attention to the curious device on the page facing. I thought it at first a larger, less defined blot, caused by the pages somehow coming in contact with one another, but straight away discounted that, seeing evidence of intentional draughtsmanship in its twists and swirls. Mrs Mawhinney asked me if I thought it might be a plan of some description and explained to the doctor that although many years retired from business, Sir Gilbert had never truly ceased working.

I asked, in my turn, if I might be permitted a closer look, and having taken the journal from Dr Gordon rotated it through ninety degrees then through one hundred and eighty, rotations matched by the movements of our heads as the three of us tried to put a name to what we were looking at. There were people, I could see now, somewhat rudimentary, but clearly people, falling into . . . "A fiery pit," was Mrs Mawhinney's suggestion, and I worried that she would collapse again. Fighting back the tears, she declared that no man living had less to fear from fires in the next life than Sir Gilbert, a sentiment with which I could readily concur. When I arrived in Belfast in 1846 as a boy of fourteen I carried nothing but a change of clothes and a letter from Sir Gilbert (although he had not been "Sir" then) to my mother, promising me employment if ever she was unable to provide for me, which was the harsh reality of those Famine years, even in County Antrim.

I tried to reassure Mrs Mawhinney, although my own first impression – a volcano – had not been too many miles from hers, until I realised that the cone was inverted, with the widest section uppermost, like a funnel, or a hopper, perhaps.

I remembered then our meeting the night before, at the Reform Club, to hear an illustrated talk, by my nephew, on *The Time Machine* of Mr H. G. Wells, and wondered whether this was not in some manner connected.

Dr Gordon, however, having seen his original hypothesis thrown into doubt, now asked Mrs Mawhinney to withdraw to allow him to complete his examination. I elected to go with her to spare my friend the added indignity of my presence.

The doctor came out of the room again some twenty minutes later. His preliminary findings, which you will have received, were that the cause of death was most likely a cerebral stroke, or rather a pair of strokes, the first comparatively mild, corresponding to the blot in the journal, possibly inducing a state not far removed from trance, the second, and fatal, occurring, as best as he could estimate, at 4 a.m.

Mrs Mawhinney, the while, had draped the glass on the landing with black crêpe, produced with a housekeeper's genius from who knows where inside her apartments at the far end of the landing. She and I now returned together to the bedchamber where we found that Dr Gordon had drawn a sheet over the face of the deceased. I am conscious that this is the first occasion in the course of this report that I have referred to Sir Gilbert in this way: a function perhaps of the sheet. In any case, without forward planning or any communication that I can recall, Mrs Mawhinney and I each took a corner of the sheet and folded it back. We were greeted by an expression of infinite calm. Again without a word passing between us, we got down on our knees and prayed that his soul too might be granted such repose.

As I struggled afterwards to my feet I laid my hand again on the journal, which Dr Gordon had left at the bottom of the bed. I could make no sense finally of the drawing, but whatever it was intended to represent or convey it seemed to me worthy of preservation, for it had occupied the final minutes of Sir Gilbert Rice's life on this earth.

I handed over the book to Mrs Mawhinney for safe keeping, then descended to the hallway, from where I telephoned to Mr James McLorie, manager of Melville & Co., to initiate the funeral arrangements.

David Erskine, Esq.

Lark Ridge

Belmont Road

Belfast

IV

The death was announced in Belfast at the end of last week of Sir Gilbert Rice, manufacturer and philanthropist. The son of Mr William Rice, of Ballyfinaghy, and Laetitia née Semple, he was orphaned while still an infant and raised thereafter by his grandfather, Mr Samuel Dawe Semple, which remarkable gentleman was the subject of fulsome tributes in this and other newspapers on his own death in the cholera outbreak of 1832. (The posthumous publication of his idiosyncratic study of the poems of Keats was made possible by his grandson's diligence and painstaking.)

Having joined at sixteen the Corporation for Preserving and Improving the Port and Harbour of Belfast, or "Ballast Board", where he was to begin with, by his own account, "wholly unremarkable", Sir Gilbert then underwent something of a "sea-change" in his next decade, enjoying considerable advancement at a crucial juncture in the Board's activities, and indeed the town's development. In recognition of this he was invited by the 3rd Marquis of Donegall to join the platform party that welcomed the Queen, Prince Consort and Prince of Wales to Belfast in 1849, a month after the opening of the Victoria Channel, built after long delay on the plans of Mr James Walker. With a modesty that was characteristic of him, Sir Gilbert declined the invitation.

On leaving the Ballast Board a short time afterwards, he established an engineering firm on Dargan's (later Queen's)

Island, specialising in the design and production of the precision marine drawing instruments that made, and bore, his name. He was, according to those who worked for him, an enlightened employer, who thought nothing of taking off his coat and joining in a game of handball on the courts he had had built in the yard of his works. Guests on occasion were treated to a tour of the harbour improvements in a rowboat, with Sir Gilbert combining the roles of tour guide and oarsman.

Following the partial destruction of his premises in the party riots of 1857, at the hands of a mob incensed by his employment of Roman Catholics from the neighbouring Short Strand district of Ballymacarrett, he came in person to assist the bricklayers and masons engaged in the rebuilding.

He was raised to the Baronetcy in 1882, accepting the honour on behalf of all those who had been in his employ over the years, and granting his staff at that time two days' paid holiday as an expression of his gratitude. A year later, aged seventy, he withdrew from day-to-day management and although he remained on the board was unable to prevent the sale of the Rice Company to the London firm of Groves and Morgan in 1885, whereupon he tendered his resignation.

He saw out his remaining years at Myrtlefield Park in Malone.

A man of undemonstrative religious beliefs, he was nevertheless a lifelong benefactor of the Castlereagh Presbyterian Church, whose architect was his friend, Mr John Millar (d. Dunedin, New Zealand, 1876), and in particular paid for the upkeep of its "Bassae" Ionic columns, which, as he delighted in pointing out to visitors from England, had been employed in that rather remote location five years before their supposed first use in the more celebrated Ashmolean Museum.

Sir Gilbert passed the early hours of the evening before he died in the company of several old acquaintances at the Ulster Reform Club, enjoying dinner and a lively discussion on the subjects that had informed his entire professional life. He had several times been asked to publish as a monograph a memoir of his early days, but these invitations too he declined, or at least deferred, saying that perhaps if he lived to be a hundred he should consider it.

That so extreme an old age eluded him may, therefore, be considered by the people of Belfast a loss, but he nevertheless exceeded by an admirable distance the Biblical "three-score and ten". His passing will be greatly mourned by all who had the privilege of knowing him.

Sir Gilbert Rice never married and had no other family surviving. On instructions left with his housekeeper, however, his remains were conveyed to Liverpool as the nearest city where a cremation might be performed, and his ashes then scattered from the stern of the ship bringing them back up the Lough to Belfast, in hopes, as he had told that lady, that whatever the waters did not consume the winds would carry as far as those Polish lands, to the east of Warsaw, for which he had developed such a fondness and to which he returned on numerous occasions throughout his long life.

To speed them on their way, his executor, the noted industrialist, Mr David Erskine, read the closing lines of "L'île inconnue" by Théophile Gautier, best known from its setting by Berlioz: "Où voulez-vous aller? La brise va souffler!" *Where do you wish to go? The breeze begins to blow!*

The urn will stand atop the family plot in the "New" Burying Ground at Clifton Street, Belfast.

V

POSTERITY know ye that I a son of dust do cause this tablet to be here inserted that you may not attribute the design of this Building to others than myself which I designed in my Eighteenth year and third of my studentship 1829 During an absence from my native Belfast the superintendency was entrusted at its commencement to two quacks Duff and Jackson self-styled architects who so mutilated my designs as to make me almost disown them that portion of the dross you People of refined taste which I can foresee you must be can easily distinguish from the refined on my return I fostered my own child until it grew to what you now behold having begun and finished the Peripteral Portico under my own personal superintendence in the year 1831 JOHN MILLAR ARCHITECT

[Slate recovered from the ruins of Third Presbyterian Church, Rosemary Street, destroyed by German bombs on the night of 15–16 April 1941.]

Author's Note

This book owes a particular debt to "Belfast Sixty Years Ago: Recollections of a Septuagenarian", by Rev. Narcissus G. Batt (*Ulster Journal of Archaeology*, second series, Vol. II, no. 2, January 1896); to "Belfast Fifty Years Ago", a lecture by Thomas Gaffikin, delivered at the Working Men's Institute, Belfast, on Thursday, 8 April 1875, and published by James Cleeland's Bible Warehouse, Arthur Street, in 1894; to *The World Turned Upside Down; or, No News, and Strange News*, printed in York by J. Kendrew, *c.* 1815; and to *The Time Machine* of Mr H. G. Wells (London, 1895).

Other books that have proved valuable include:

Belfast: An Illustrated History, Jonathan Bardon (Belfast, 1982)

Belfast: the Making of a City, J. C. Beckett *et al.* (Belfast, 1983)

A History of the Town of Belfast, George Benn (Vol. I, 1823; Vol. II, 1880)

The Memoirs of Hector Berlioz, translated and edited by David Cairns (London, 1969)

Buildings of Belfast: 1700–1914, C. E. B. Brett (London, 1967)

Georgian Belfast 1750–1850, C. E. B. Brett, with Raymond Gillespie and W. A. Maguire (Dublin, 2004)

Studies in Hysteria, Josef Breuer and Sigmund Freud (Vienna, 1895)

The Man from God Knows Where: Thomas Russell, 1767–1803, Denis Carroll (Dublin, 1995)

Heart of Europe: The Past in Poland's Present, Norman Davies (Oxford, 1984)

At Day's Close: A History of Nighttime, A. Roger Ekirch (London, 2005)

"The Sports of Easter Monday", John Gray, *Irish Pages*, Vol. V, no. 1

Twenty-one Views in Belfast and its Neighbourhood, ed. Philip Dixon Hardy (Dublin, 1837; reprinted with notes and introduction by C. E. B. Brett, Belfast, 2005)

Religion, Politics and Violence in Nineteenth-Century Belfast, Catherine Hirst (Dublin, 2002)

A Social Geography of Belfast, Emrys Jones (London, 1960)

County Antrim: A Topographical Dictionary, Samuel Lewis (London, 1837; Belfast, 2002)

The Story of Belfast and its Surroundings, Mary Lowry (London, no date)

McComb's Guide to Belfast, the Giant's Causeway, and Adjoining Districts of the Counties of Antrim and Down, with an Account of the Battle of Ballynahinch, and the Celebrated Mineral Waters of that Neighbourhood, William McComb (Belfast, 1861)

The Life and Times of Mary Ann McCracken, 1770–1866: A Belfast Panorama, Mary McNeill (Dublin, 1960)

Living Like a Lord: The Second Marquis of Donegall, 1769–1844, W. A. Maguire (Belfast, 1984)

Keats, Andrew Motion (London, 1997)

As I Roved Out, Cathal O'Byrne (Belfast, 1946)

"From Perikles to Presbyterian 'Temples'", Suzanne O'Neill, in

A Further Shore: Essays in Irish and Scottish Studies (Eastbourne, 2008)

History of Belfast, D. J. Owen (Belfast, 1921)

A Short History of the Port of Belfast, D. J. Owen (Belfast, 1917)

Central Belfast: *A Historical Gazetteer*, Marcus Patton (Belfast, 1993)

Tavern Singing in Early Victorian London: the Diaries of Charles Rice for 1840 and 1850, ed. Laurence Senelick (London, 1997)

Port of Belfast: 1785–1985, An Historical Review, Robin Sweetman and Cecil Nimmons (Belfast, 1985)

In Belfast Town: Early Photographs from the Lawrence Collection, 1864–1880, Brian M. Walker and Hugh Dixon (Belfast, 1984)

Decency and Disorder: The Age of Cant, 1789–1837, Ben Wilson (London, 2007)

Historical Notices of Old Belfast and its Vicinity, Robert M. Young (Belfast, 1896)

Of websites consulted none was more eclectic or consistently informative than Joe Graham's "Rushlight". (http://joegraham.rushlightmagazine.com)

Acknowledgements

I am grateful to the Lannan Foundation for the award of a Literary Fellowship, without which this book could not have been written.

A version of Part I appeared in *Five Points*, the journal of Georgia State University (Vol. XIII, no. 2, "Belfast Imagined"). The Easter Monday passage appeared (as "Cave Hill") in *Edinburgh Review* 133 (winter 2012).